THEY CAME TO MESA VERDE

QUINT BURGESS—He had driven the stage out of Durango, but now as husband to a mixed-blood woman, he faces the greedy whites out to steal Indian lands.

LAUREL FOX—Trained in the white man's medicine, she will challenge her own people's ways in order to save them.

PAINTED WIND—He must choose between ambition and the desperate needs of his tribe.

KATE McEWAN—A news correspondent, she is put to the test in a harsh land among violent, unforgiving people.

WADE STRIKER—His gun is for sale, and he doesn't much care whom he kills if the corpse can be exchanged for cash.

The Stagecoach Series
Ask your bookseller for the books you have missed

STATION 1: DODGE CITY
STATION 2: LAREDO
STATION 3: CHEYENNE
STATION 4: TOMBSTONE
STATION 5: VIRGINIA CITY
STATION 6: SANTA FE
STATION 7: SEATTLE
STATION 8: FORT YUMA
STATION 9: SONORA
STATION 10: ABILENE
STATION 11: DEADWOOD
STATION 12: TUCSON
STATION 13: CARSON CITY
STATION 14: CIMARRON
STATION 15: WICHITA
STATION 16: MOJAVE
STATION 17: DURANGO
STATION 18: CASA GRANDE
STATION 19: LAST CHANCE
STATION 20: LEADVILLE
STATION 21: FARGO
STATION 22: DEVIL'S CANYON
STATION 23: EL PASO
STATION 24: MESA VERDE

STAGECOACH STATION 24:
MESA VERDE

Hank Mitchum

Created by the producers of
Wagons West, White Indian,
and Saga of the Southwest.

Chairman of the Board: Lyle Kenyon Engel

BANTAM BOOKS
TORONTO • NEW YORK • LONDON • SYDNEY • AUCKLAND

STAGECOACH STATION 24: MESA VERDE

*A Bantam Book / published by arrangement with
Book Creations, Inc.*

Bantam edition/July 1986

*Produced by Book Creations, Inc.
Chairman of the Board: Lyle Kenyon Engel*

ISBN 0-553-25808-7

Published simultaneously in the United States and Canada

PRINTED IN THE UNITED STATES OF AMERICA

KR   0 9 8 7 6 5 4 3 2 1

AUTHOR'S NOTE

While this book is a work of fiction, some events, such as the Ute marriage ceremony, are based on accounts reported by travelers in the late nineteenth century. Some of the Ute songs are adapted from traditional songs of several Plains and Southwestern Indian tribes.

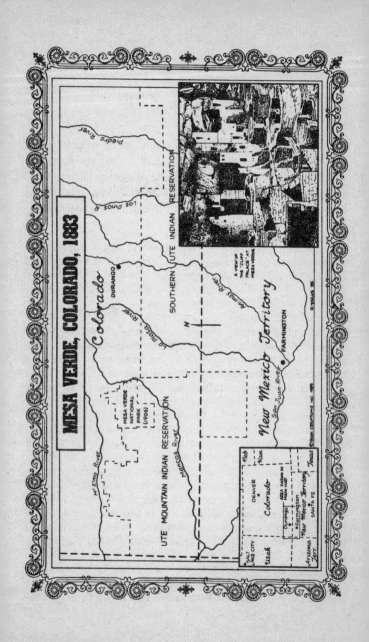

MESA VERDE, COLORADO, 1883

Colorado

Piedra River

Los Pinos R.

Durango

La Plata River

SOUTHERN UTE INDIAN RESERVATION

Animas River

A VIEW OF THE "CLIFF PALACE" AT MESA VERDE

New Mexico Territory

FARMINGTON

San Juan River

N

R. ZERBS '85

MESA VERDE NATIONAL PARK (1906)

McElmo River

Mancos River

UTE MOUNTAIN INDIAN RESERVATION

© GENRE CREATIONS INC. 1975

SALT LAKE CITY

Utah

DENVER

Colorado

Durango

Farmington

New Mexico Territory

SANTA FE

Arizona Terr.

Neb.

Kan.

Texas

AREA SHOWN IN MAP

June 1883

The old Indian was as weathered as the circular sandstone chamber in which he sat. Seventy summers had drained his skin until it cracked like the baked-clay floor of a dry lake. His braided white hair was as brittle as straw. His outstretched hands, palms upraised, seemed little more than aged, paper-thin leather stretched across bone. Even his dark-gray eyes showed the ravages of time, the pupils flecked with streaks of silver that increasingly obscured his vision. A physician would shake his head sadly and call it cataracts. To Surnia, the last in a line of Ute medicine men that stretched unbroken for six hundred years, it was the Gift of Second Sight, a silver mist that opened his eyes to the world beyond the one in which he lived.

It was dawn as Surnia sat cross-legged in the center of a circular, underground chamber in the largest of the cliff dwellings of Mesa Verde. This chamber was one of twenty-three ceremonial *kivas* of Cliff House, a huge stone structure of two hundred rooms constructed in a natural alcove high on the face of a remote canyon in southwestern Colorado. It had been built by the Anasazi Indians—known to the Ute as the Ancients—who created six hundred such dwellings between A.D. 1100 and 1300, then mysteriously vanished.

For six hundred years, no one inhabited these cliff dwellings. They were both feared and revered by the tribes of the Southwest, who saw them as places of power—

ful *po-o-kan-te* (poh-oh-KAHN-tay), or magic. Cliff House, the largest of the cliff structures, held the most powerful *po-o-kan-te*, and to visit there was to invite death at the hands of the spirits said to inhabit their former homes.

Two years earlier, following a vision, Surnia felt called to leave his Ute village thirty miles to the east and come to Mesa Verde. Saying that he was making a final spirit quest, he headed west on foot and took up residence at Cliff House, where he continued to perform the ceremonies of his ancestors as he awaited his own passing beyond the Fifth World—the world at the Earth's surface—to the Spirit World. From that day on, the old, revered *pwu-au-gut* (pwoo-aw-GOOT), or medicine man, was considered dead by his people.

Every evening at dusk for the past two years, Surnia descended a ladder through a circular opening in the stone roof of the *kiva* and remained inside until the rising of the sun. He spent the early hours before dawn seated in front of the *sipapu*, a small hole in the floor that was a spirit entrance to the Four Worlds below, from which the Ancients originally came to the Fifth World on the Earth. It was here that Surnia communed with the spirits of his ancestors. It was here that the silver mist clouded his vision and revealed the Great Spirit that is within all things.

The sun rose over the opposing rim of the canyon and spilled through the small round opening in the roof of the *kiva*, striking the stone wall facing the old man. He did not see the striped shadow created by the ladder rungs that protruded above the opening, but saw only the silver mist. The low, barely discernible hum that filled the chamber merged with Surnia's own inner vibration, and he felt himself riding the swells of a gently rolling sea.

Floating upon that silver mist, he heard the rising chant of a thousand voices reverberating through the walls and chambers of Cliff House and flowing into the *kiva*:

"*He'e'e' Ahi'ni'yo'*," the voices intoned.

"*He'e'e' Ahi'ni'yo'*," Surnia repeated, and then in the white man's tongue, "Walk with the Spirit."

As the *pwu-au-gut* completed the invocation, the whirling

silver mist spun ever more swiftly around him. The thousand voices, still chanting *"He'e'e' Ahi'ni'yo',"* seemed to be caught in the growing whirlwind. Surnia looked down and saw the small *sipapu* hole widen. The mist began to pour through the opening, spinning faster and faster until the whirlwind became a whirlpool carrying the voices of the trapped spirits of Mesa Verde to the Four Worlds below.

With a final sigh, the silver mist disappeared through the *sipapu*, which narrowed to its normal size. Glancing down at his lap, Surnia realized that he, too, was in his original position, and around him the *kiva* looked as unchanged as it had for the past six hundred years.

Surnia rose, his thin legs bowed and brittle, and slowly climbed the wooden ladder. When his head emerged through the round opening in the roof of the subterranean *kiva*, he had to close his eyes against the blast of early morning sunlight. As he stepped up and away from the doorway, he shielded his face and glanced around.

The *kiva* was in a courtyard slightly raised from the thirty-foot-wide rim of the alcove, at the edge of which was a drop of several hundred feet to the floor of the canyon beyond. Nestled within the alcove above and behind the courtyard was the network of interlocking sandstone rooms and towers that made up Cliff House. Staring up at the structure, Surnia felt a sudden rush of sadness as he realized that white men would soon invade and usurp these sacred cliff cities of Mesa Verde if he could not strengthen and sustain the protective energy of his Anasazi ancestors.

Surnia walked forward, heading toward the steps that led up to the buildings of Cliff House. Suddenly he stopped as he heard a man's voice singing slightly off key:

> "Gin a body meet a body,
>   Comin' thro' the rye;
> Gin a body kiss a body,
>   Need a body cry?
> Ev'ry laddie has his lassie,
>   Nane, they say, hae I!
> Yet a' the lassies smile at me,
>   When comin' thro' the rye."

The old man stood in place with his head cocked to one side. For a moment he thought he was hearing some new chant of the spirits of Mesa Verde, but this voice was strange and noticeably different—even different from the voices of white men he had come to know. And though some words were distinctly English and understandable, others had a peculiar foreign lilt, which Surnia could not identify:

> "Amang the train there is a dame
>   I dearly lo'e mysel';
> But whaur her hame, or what her name,
>   I dinna care to tell."

As the singer began to hum the same melody, Surnia cautiously walked up the steps. Coming over the top, he saw a man standing with his back to the cliff—a white man dressed in blue work pants and shirt and wearing a battered white-felt hat. Waves of blond hair cascaded from under the brim and curled up around his collar, reminding Surnia of sketches he had seen of the great white *pwu-au-gut* in the sacred medicine book of the Black Robes—the Christian missionaries who periodically came to preach to the Ute.

Mounted on a wooden tripod in front of this strange man was some sort of device, reminiscent of the Spirit Catcher picture machines he had seen. After every few strains of his song, the man leaned forward and glanced through the device, then scribbled in a notepad he was carrying.

Though Surnia did not speak or even make a sound, the white man apparently sensed that someone was staring at him, and he stood up from the tripod and turned around. There seemed no surprise in his expression as he looked at Surnia, and for a moment the old Indian felt as if the man were looking through him. The stranger's features were smooth and youthful; Surnia guessed that he had not yet seen his thirtieth summer. His skin was somewhat ruddy with sunburn, but seemed pale in contrast to the black wire-rim glasses that framed his light-blue eyes. Those pale eyes continued to look through or past Surnia, and so the old Ute took a few cautious steps forward.

Just then the stranger broke into a broad grin and exuberantly began to wave in Surnia's direction. As Surnia hesitantly raised his arm in reply, the younger man shouted, "Lucas! Over here! It's Paige . . . Wellington Paige!"

Surnia realized the stranger was waving beyond him, and he was about to turn around when suddenly a young boy, perhaps twelve years old, came rushing by. Like the man, the boy paid no attention to the old Ute Indian.

"The most amazing discovery of the century," the man named Paige told the boy as he waved his arm to embrace all of Cliff House. The boy named Lucas returned Paige's smile and nodded eagerly as his eyes scanned the stone ruins. "This whole area will become famous," the man continued. "It will bring great prosperity to your mother's people."

Surnia stood no more than twenty feet from the two white strangers, and yet they paid him no attention at all. It was as if the medicine man had died in the *kiva* that morning, and only his spirit had emerged.

Am I too late? Surnia asked himself. *Have I passed to the Spirit World on the very day that the whites have found Mesa Verde?*

"You are not dead," a voice spoke in reply. It was a familiar voice, and Surnia spun around to see a white-haired man approaching. It was Josiah Fox, the Quaker physician who had married Surnia's now-deceased daughter and had given him a granddaughter, Mountain Laurel. Around Josiah's neck was a beaded amulet—a turquoise sky framing a bright yellow sunburst with twelve distinct rays—and he was dressed in the same gray suit that he had worn when leaving the Ute village two years earlier with Mountain Laurel. But Surnia had heard, shortly before coming to Mesa Verde, that Josiah had died during that journey east and that Mountain Laurel had continued on alone in order to fulfill his dream of seeing her trained as a physician.

For a long moment, Surnia stared openmouthed at the seeming apparition, then stammered, "But . . . you . . ."

"Yes, my friend, it is just as you heard—I died two years ago."

Confused, Surnia turned from the vision of Josiah Fox to glance back at the two white strangers, who were busy viewing the area through the tripod device and taking notes.

"You aren't dead," Josiah explained. "But they can't see you. Don't be troubled. In time you'll understand."

"Then it is too late?" Surnia asked. "I was unable to protect Mesa Verde. The whites have come."

"It is not for you to protect these sacred canyons," Josiah replied. "It is not for you to change what must be."

"Have I wasted two years? Why am I here?"

"That, too, will be clear in time. But know that you are part of a changing energy. You aren't here to stem the coming tide, but to prepare the land to receive it."

"And what of them?" Surnia asked, indicating with a nod of his head the white strangers. "What do I do about them?"

Josiah Fox turned and descended the steps. "Let your heart guide you," he said as he walked out across the floor of the alcove. He stopped at the very edge of the cliff and turned back around. He spoke again, but in a whisper. Yet the words were as loud and distinct as if he were standing beside Surnia. "Walk with the Spirit, my old friend."

"*He'e'e' Ahi'ni'yo'*," Surnia repeated.

The amulet upon Josiah's neck began to fill with light, until the yellow sunburst became a brilliant white aura that embraced and at last replaced the image of the old physician. The radiant aura lifted from the edge of the cliff and floated over the abyss, rising higher and higher above the canyon until it was indeed a sunburst in the turquoise sky . . . until, like the fiery arc of a comet, it receded into the heavens and merged with the rising summer sun.

For a moment Surnia stood gazing along the track of the departed spirit. At last he turned to face the two white strangers. The blond-haired man continued to survey Cliff House with his tripod device. The boy, however, had walked off by himself and stood motionless with his head cocked to one side, as if listening to something. He seemed locked in some sort of union with the sun, which had tripled in intensity since merging with the spirit of Josiah Fox. The boy's lips parted—he struggled to speak—but no sound came. Surnia thought he saw his lips fashion the word, "Grandfather," then they relaxed into a smile.

With the brilliance of a flash of lightning, a thin white beam shot forth from the sun and struck the boy's chest, filling him with the same aura of light that had encompassed Josiah. In a soft yet distinct whisper, Josiah's voice intoned the words, "My grandson." Then the beam faded and disappeared, and the light around the boy compressed into a glowing sphere that was suspended in front of his neck. Slowly, that orb of light also faded, until it transformed into a yellow sunburst in a turquoise sky—the same beaded amulet that had been worn by Josiah Fox.

The boy reached up and lifted the amulet, then let it fall against his neck. Looking back up, his eyes locked on Surnia's, and he smiled at the old Indian.

Surnia found himself walking with hand outstretched toward the boy, who nodded and lifted the amulet toward him. As Surnia reached out and took it in his hand, he felt a powerful surge of energy flow through him—a rhythmic pulse that could be seen and heard as well as touched. It overcame him like the waves of a vast ocean, a great flood that carried away the young boy, the stone buildings, the cliff, the canyons of Mesa Verde—even Surnia himself— and left only the brilliant sunburst in the turquoise sky.

Surnia could no longer see or even feel his own body. All that existed was the sun, and from it poured a deep, hypnotic chant:

> the wind stirs in the willows
> the wind stirs the grasses
> the rocks are ringing
> they are ringing in the mountains
> a slender antelope
> he is looking to the mountain
> the whirlwind comes gliding
> the whirlwind comes gliding
> there is dust from the whirlwind

the whirlwind on the mountain
the wind shakes our tipi
and sings a song for us
the wind enters our kiva
and sings a song for us
in our kiva a spirit is born
the cry of the wind is heard
in the wind a child is born
comes dancing down the mountain
the child bringing the whirlwind
dancing from the mountain
in the whirlwind a child is born
that we may know one another
that we may know one another

The music and the sun began to fade, and Surnia realized it was his own voice that was chanting the Song of
Life Returning. And as he again became aware of his body
and his surroundings, there was no longer a young boy in
front of him. He wasn't even standing among the buildings
of Cliff House. He was back inside the *kiva* seated cross-
legged in front of the *sipapu*, and the sunburst that floated
in front of him was formed by the light that poured through
the circular opening in the roof and struck the opposing
wall.

Surnia smiled peacefully as he realized he had never left
the *kiva* and had not really seen the man and boy among
the ruins of Cliff House. Yet he knew that the vision was
as real as anything his outer eyes might have seen. Indeed
the whites were coming, and somehow Surnia must prepare Mesa Verde for their arrival.

But what of the man and the boy? Surnia could not be
certain, but he was convinced that they, too, were real
and that his path and theirs would cross within this life.

"Josiah's grandson," Surnia whispered, remembering the
words spoken by the spirit of Josiah Fox—the husband of
Surnia's daughter. "My great-grandson," he added, knowing that somehow his granddaughter, Mountain Laurel
Fox, now had a son—a white boy named Lucas who now
wore Josiah's amulet.

The old medicine man stood, crossed to the wooden ladder, and climbed out of the *kiva*. He paused for a moment with his eyes closed, feeling refreshed by the warming rays of the morning sun. Then he headed toward the steps that led up to the main buildings of Cliff House, confident that he was alone and that the whites had not yet come.

Surnia mounted the steps and walked over to where he had seen the young boy named Lucas. Standing where the boy had stood, he turned and gazed a final time at the sun. Perhaps it was a trick of the light or a reflection caused by what remained of the morning mist, but the sun had twelve distinct rays, and it glowed in a beaded turquoise sky.

Surnia raised his head and looked above the sun, and he could almost make out the image of a face, with eyes that smiled back at his own. The vision lasted less than a second, and the medicine man could not be sure if it was the face of an old man or young boy. And then it passed, leaving him with a renewed sense of tranquillity.

"*He'e'e' Ahi'ni'yo'*," the old *pwu-au-gut* intoned, raising his arms to the sun. "*He'e'e' Ahi'ni'yo'*"

Chapter One

Fifty miles east of Mesa Verde, twelve-year-old Lucas Burgess sat atop his father's buckboard wagon, alone except for his large black dog, a mountain of an animal appropriately named Little Bear. Lucas twisted around on the seat and glanced up and down the main street of Durango, Colorado, as if expecting someone. Not finding what he was looking for, he shrugged slightly and settled back in place.

Lucas slipped the brown slouch hat from his head and dropped it into his lap, then tousled his thick, sandy-blond hair. Though it was still early morning and the night had been frigid, the air was already heating up on this June day in 1883, and soon he might be allowed to remove the leather jacket his father had insisted he wear. For now, he contented himself with unbuttoning and spreading apart the flaps. In so doing, his hand brushed against the heavy, round object that hung around his neck from a leather thong. Closing his soft gray eyes, he reached up and grasped the amulet. As his fingers traced the intricate beadwork, his mind's eye envisioned the bright yellow sunburst on a field of turquoise.

Beside him, Little Bear fidgeted excitedly on the seat, totally captivated by the myriad smells, sights, and sounds that filled the street. Lucas, on the other hand, kept his eyes shut to the passing carriages and horses and no longer took interest in the intoxicating mixture of early morning scents: fried potatoes and bacon, wood and coal smoke, the sweet undried pine of buildings under construction. And the high-pitched screech of steam brakes as a passenger train entered the nearby station was as lost to the youngster as the cantankerous cursing of an old hostler fighting a team of four into the harness of the Durango Overland stagecoach across the street.

Though the boy had to shut his eyes to close out the images of the world around him, there was no need for him to cover his ears to block the sounds of a railroad boomtown awakening to a new day. Lucas Burgess was deaf.

Despite being functionally deaf, Lucas was not entirely without sound. Indeed, his head was usually filled with noise, but it was little more than a cacophony in which individual sounds were lost, making it all but impossible to understand speech. At times when the overlayering of noise was faint, he might distinguish a particular sound above the rest. This ability, combined with his skill at lip reading, had done much to help him perfect his growing ability to speak, thanks to the patient guidance of the teachers who had worked with him back east for the past two years.

Lucas did not hear Little Bear's eager bark, but he felt the sway of the seat as the dog stood up and furiously wagged his tail. Lucas opened his eyes and saw his father standing beside the buckboard speaking to him, a fifty-pound sack of flour over one shoulder.

"Thinking of Laurel?" Quint Burgess repeated as his son watched his lips. Quint pointed at the amulet still cradled in Lucas's hand—the beaded necklace given him by his stepmother, Laurel, not long after the death of her father, Josiah Fox.

Lucas replied with a smile, which Quint returned as he dropped the flour sack onto the bed of the buckboard. He was a tall man of thirty-five, with steel-blue eyes, thick brown hair, and a drooping mustache. He wore a gray-felt plainsman's hat and knee-length bearskin coat, which gave him a massive appearance. But now he removed the coat and placed it in the back of the wagon, revealing a lean, muscular body.

Seeing his son's questioning expression, Quint nodded and said, "Go ahead. It's warming up." Immediately Lucas slipped his jacket off and tossed it in back.

Quint walked over beside the driver's seat and roughly patted Little Bear's head, receiving an affectionate lick of his palm in return. As he looked up, Lucas pointed to the building behind him, and Quint turned to see that the storekeeper and his young assistant had begun to carry out the supplies he had purchased. They piled the assorted boxes and sacks at the edge of the porch.

"I must have bought everything in the store," he said to his son, speaking slowly and distinctly so that Lucas would understand. As he pronounced the word *bought*, he awkwardly signed the letters with his right hand—a skill quickly learned by Lucas and Laurel, but which he was having a hard time mastering.

Suddenly Lucas burst into laughter, and Little Bear began to bark playfully.

"What is it?" Quint asked in surprise, spinning around to see if something funny was going on behind him.

"No," Lucas said, his tone marked with a slight slur. He pointed at his father to indicate that he was the source of the amusement.

"Me?" Quint asked. "What did I do?"

In reply, Lucas signed the word his father had used.

"Yes," Quint responded. "I said I must have bought everything in the store." As he repeated the comment, he again signed the word *bought*.

Lucas tried to restrain his laughter as he shook his head and grasped his father's hand. Carefully, he placed his father's fingers in the shape of the first letter he had signed: the forefinger folded behind the thumb, the other three fingers raised straight up. "No," he declared, shaking his father's hand. Then he repositioned the fingers, bending the thumb in front of the palm and raising the rest of the fingers. "*B*," Lucas said. "Bought."

"Bought," Quint repeated, pulling his hand from his son's and studying the sign. He reformed the sign he mistakenly had used and examined it for a moment. Then he grinned, at last understanding the joke. *"F,"* he muttered. "Fought. I *fought* everything in the store!" He broke into a hearty laugh, punctuated by Little Bear's eager bark. As Lucas joined in the laughter, Quint playfully mussed his son's hair and said, "Well, I can still *fight* you!" They briefly sparred with each other, and then Quint pulled Lucas to him and hugged him tight. "C'mon," he said, holding the boy slightly away so that he could read Quint's lips. "Let's get those supplies loaded."

Lucas jumped from the seat and hurried up the porch steps. He went straight to the largest sack and began pulling it toward the wagon.

"Here, let me help," Quint offered, reaching out.

"No!" Lucas replied sharply. He looked up at his father and smiled. Carefully shaping his lips and tongue and concentrating on the vibration in his throat, he added, "Me . . . I can do it."

Quint backed away and watched with pride as his son hoisted the large sack in his arms and staggered toward the back of the buckboard. "Yes, Lucas Burgess, I do believe you can."

Kate McEwan sighed with relief as the Denver and Rio Grande train pulled to a halt in front of the Durango station, the end of the picturesque narrow-gauge run from Denver through Toltec Gorge to the rich mining regions of southwestern Colorado. It had been a tiring journey from Boston, where her editor at *New England Monthly* had assigned her a series of feature articles on the return of the half-breed physician Laurel Fox Burgess to the Southern Ute Reservation.

Kate remained seated while the rest of the passengers gathered their bags and disembarked from the single passenger car. Taking a deep breath, she shook off the effects of the journey and smiled in anticipation of the assignment she was about to undertake. Never having traveled farther west than Chicago, this would be a unique experience for her, and she relished the thought of encountering a new culture at the reservation. Already her mind was fashion-

ing the questions she would have for Laurel—Mountain
Laurel to her mother's people, Dr. Laurel Fox Burgess to
her father's.

Kate stood up in the empty aisle and fluffed the ruffled
lace at the neck of her white blouse, then smoothed the
lapels of her russet-colored jacket. As she reached into the
pocket of her matching trousers and pulled out a small
notepad and pencil, she wondered what reaction her outfit
would elicit in this frontier mining town. Such fashions
still caused a scandal in the East, but so far she had
noticed little more than an occasional upturned eyebrow
during her journey west. Out here people seemed more
accepting of functional clothing, with far more attention
being paid to her large, sultry brown eyes and striking
auburn hair.

As she jotted the date and time of arrival in her notepad
and returned it to her pocket, Kate reflected on her looks,
which she saw as both an annoyance and a gift. Though
she accepted that she was more than usually attractive, it
was of little importance to her. Indeed, she would have
preferred to cut her long hair into a more manageable
bob, but she kept it full out of respect for her mother,
Lydia, who had long since given up hope of seeing her
daughter in more *respectable* attire but who declared that
"my heart will break if you ever chop off those lustrous
locks—the kind every mother dreams her daughter will
have." Instead, Kate wore her hair pulled up in a swirl
and pinned at the top.

"Damned nuisance," she muttered about her hair as she
reached up and patted a few stray strands into place,
unwilling to admit that she, too, was proud of her hair and
her looks. "What's the point?"

Her mother would have scolded her, insisting that the
whole point was to attract the right sort of man—someone
who could take care of her so that she wouldn't have to
spend day and night struggling to make her own living. It
was true that Lydia McEwan was deeply proud of her
daughter's literary success, but at heart she felt it was
little more than a hobby, useful to buy the bread until a
more secure, long-term solution was arranged: matrimony.

The same narrow-minded thinking characterized the many otherwise eligible men who over the years had courted the twenty-six-year-old Scottish-American beauty. And while Kate could not deny that she would like to share her life with someone, she had long since given up hope of finding the right man—if, indeed, he even existed.

"Well, that's eno' self-pity for today, lassie," she told herself, exaggerating her usually delicate brogue. She reached under the seat, pulled out a large traveling bag, and headed down the aisle.

Once outside, she glanced around at the clapboard station and the other buildings that made up Durango. There seemed to be no plan to the town, with flimsy one-room shacks crowded cheek by jowl against more substantial two-story structures, as though the whole conglomeration had been tossed helter-skelter into place from the surrounding peaks of the Rockies.

Kate turned from the scene and headed along the nearly deserted railroad platform to where the baggage car was being unloaded. Within moments she spied her large carpetbag and a second item: a three-foot-long object in a canvas cover, one end square and bulky and the other straight and thin. Holding the traveling bag in her right hand, she tucked the long package under her right arm and then picked up the carpetbag in her left. Thus encumbered, she made her way down the platform and entered through the open door of the station.

The waiting room held little more than a few rows of backless benches. The left-hand wall held a chalkboard displaying the schedules of both the train and the connecting stagecoach runs. Along the right-hand wall was a closed door leading to the back office, with a barred ticket-agent's window beside it. On the far wall, a pair of open doors led out to the main street of Durango.

Kate watched the last few passengers file out through the far doors to the street beyond, then she turned and crossed to the ticket-agent's window. After leaning her bags against the wall, she reached through the ticket cage and rang the service bell.

"Coming! Coming!" a high-pitched voice sang out, and

almost immediately a portly old man came out from behind a set of file cabinets and fairly danced over to the window. The man looked almost comical in his natty, overly starched blue uniform with yellow piping. His head was nearly bald, but he compensated with thick muttonchop whiskers that connected to his gray walrus mustache. "Going? Going?" the man asked, reversing his earlier comment.

Suppressing a giggle, Kate mumbled, "Excuse me?"

"On the train," the man explained. "If you're going on the train, you'll have to wait until two. But not to worry. There's a delightful eatery just down the street—and I'd say the same even if my sister Gussie *wasn't* proprietress!"

"No, I'm not leaving on the train."

"Ah, then it's the stagecoach you'll be wanting. Yes, we handle the tickets right here. North to Silverton or south to Farmington? If it's Silverton you'll have to hurry. The coach is already boarding and leaves in twenty minutes—but of course Gussie can provide a basket lunch."

"Well, I'm going south, but—"

"Then it's an overnight stay for you. The coach pulls out at eight tomorrow morning. Gussie has rooms, as well, you know. The cleanest to be found in Durango!"

"I'm sorry, but I'm not looking for tickets or a room. I was hoping for some information."

"Information?" the man said, his eyes beaming now. "Then you've come to the right place. Nothing happens in Durango that doesn't pass before the eyes or ears of Silas Orcutt. This window doesn't merely look out on a waiting room; it views the everchanging spectacle of life." Hooking his thumbs in his lapels, the man added, "Pretty poetic for an old ticket codger like me, wouldn't you say?"

"Yes, very lovely, Mr. Orcutt."

"Silas, Silas, Silas," he insisted. "That's what all the beautiful young ladies call me. And as far as beauty goes, you more than qualify." He looked her up and down for a moment, but there was nothing disrespectful in his examination. "Let's see how these old eyes can do. I'd say you were five foot five and a trim one hundred ten pounds." He looked up expectantly at her.

"Five foot four," Kate corrected him.

"Close enough. You see—nothing misses the eye of Silas Orcutt. Now, how can I be of assistance to you, my child?"

"My name is Kate McEwan, and—"

"Kathleen . . . 'tis a lovely name for a lovely lass. I take it, from the sweet lilt of your voice, that your people are descendents of the great Mary, Queen of Scots?"

"Well, we *are* Scottish."

"Ah, I thought as much. My people are English, I'm afraid, but we come from the north, so we're kind of kindred spirits. Now, as to this information you are seeking?"

Kate took a deep breath and attempted to plunge in. "I am a correspondent for *New England Monthly*, and I've been sent out here—"

"A journalist?" the old man cut in. "And not just any journalist, but *the* Kate McEwan of the *Monthly*? We may be at the edge of the earth out here, but we've heard of the *Monthly*, and we've heard of you." Silas paused, leaning forward and looking around the waiting room as if to verify it was empty, then whispered conspiratorially, "At least *I* have . . . and, of course, Gussie."

"That's most kind of you."

"And what brings you to Durango?"

"My magazine has assigned me to do a series of articles on the return of Dr. Laurel Fox Burgess to the Ute reservation. That is why—"

"Of course, that explains why you are going south. And you're only two days behind her. Laurel arrived on the midweek train and left almost immediately on the stage." Silas rocked back on his heels and sucked in his breath in a vain attempt to puff himself up with pride. "We're on a first-name basis, you know—that is, Laurel and me. And of course you, too, Kate, if you have no objections."

Masking her smile, Kate nodded her approval.

"Fine, Kate. Now, about Laurel . . . she's married now, you know. Fell in love with one of the stage drivers when she was heading back east to study medicine. A fine gentleman named Quint—but of course you know all that; it was in all the papers. He took his son east with her hoping to find a cure for the boy. A sad story, that is. Lucas is a fine lad, but hopelessly deaf. There was nothing those eastern doctors could do for him except teach him how best to cope. And he does real well. He reads and writes, can talk with his hands—not that many folks can understand him, mind you—and even speaks a little."

"You say Laurel left two days ago for—"

"I'm just coming to that. It seems that she and Quint courted each other for two years while back east and recently tied the knot. But that doesn't mean anything to those Ute folks. They have a whole other way of doing things—they don't think like us civilized folks. So Laurel went on ahead to the reservation to sort of clear the way. Quint and Lucas will be following shortly."

"Then they're still here—in Durango?"

"For a few more minutes, at least. Last I noticed, they were down the street at the general store loading up a wagon. Looks like they're heading off today."

"Really?" Kate quickly gathered up her belongings. "Thank you so much."

Silas looked a bit confused as he saw the woman about to race off. "B-but, wasn't there some information you were seeking?"

With a bright smile, Kate turned back to the window and said, "Silas, I love you!" With that she stood on tiptoe, leaned through the bars, and gave the old man a gentle kiss on the nose. Then she hurried toward the street exit.

Beet red and totally flustered, Silas raised his arm and called out, "B-b-but, b-but . . ."

Kate glanced back briefly and smiled as she passed through the open doorway.

At a loss for what to say, the old man blurted out, "Don't forget Gussie's!" As she disappeared down the boardwalk, he shrugged and touched his forefinger to his nose, then broke into a broad grin. Adopting a crude, wavering brogue, he softly began to sing:

"Canst thou leave me thus, my Katie?
Canst thou leave me thus, my Katie?
Well thou know'st my aching heart—
And canst thou leave me thus for pity?"

Then Silas Orcutt turned and walked in a sprightly manner to his desk. Dropping into the cushioned seat, he propped his feet on the desktop, laced his fingers behind his head, and leaned back precariously as even more precariously he continued to sing the popular Scottish ballad.

Quint Burgess loaded the last package in the back of the buckboard and climbed up onto the wagon seat beside his son. As he released the hand brake and lifted the reins, the two horses raised their ears and fidgeted expectantly.

"Are you ready?" Quint asked, turning to his son.

Protectively wrapping his arm around Little Bear, Lucas nodded.

"Then let's get going!"

As Quint was about to slap the reins on the horses' backs, a frantic voice called out, "Mr. Burgess! Mr. Burgess! Wait!"

Quint pulled back on the brake and spun around in his seat. A woman was running down the boardwalk, her arms loaded down with traveling bags. The long package under her right arm was slipping from her grasp, and she had to slow down a moment to get a better grip. Then she came hurrying along. When she came up alongside the wagon, she dropped the bags and struggled to catch her breath.

As Quint waited, he gave the woman a quick appraisal. Besides noting her obvious beauty, he gauged her to be in her midtwenties. Her stylish clothing bespoke an easterner, and the bold fashion of wearing a pantsuit indicated an independent one, at that.

"You *are* Quint Burgess, are you not?" the woman managed to ask between breaths.

"Yes, and this is my son, Lucas." He glanced at his son, who nodded politely at the unfamiliar woman. "Can I help you in some way?"

"My name is Kate McEwan—a correspondent for *New England Monthly*."

Quint's smile dimmed slightly; before leaving New York, he had had his fill of journalists interviewing Laurel.

Kate seemed to read his mood and added, "We're not *all* scavengers, Mr. Burgess." She laughed lightly. "Some of us are merely parasites."

Quint shared her laughter, and Lucas joined in as well, though he did not understand some of the words her lips had fashioned.

"Well, Miss McEwan, I've been called a buzzard and worse, so you're in friendly company. How can I help you?"

"I want to visit the Ute reservation. I'd like to document what it's like for the first Indian woman physician to set up practice among her people."

"You will have to discuss that with Laurel," Quint replied.

"But she *is* your wife. I was hoping to elicit your support. I'm not interested in writing a mere news story, but a look from the inside." Kate paused and stared directly into Quint's steel-blue eyes; she had learned long ago that maintaining eye contact was one of the surest ways of disarming an opponent. "Will you help me?" she finally said.

"Laurel is her own woman," Quint explained. "But I have the feeling her hands will be full enough just trying to gain the trust of her people. The Ute have their own way of doing things—a long and proud tradition. I don't see how she'd have time for a series of interviews."

"It needn't take any of her time. I don't want to interview her as much as observe and report on her experiences. And I'm certain such an in-depth series of articles would go a long way toward improving our understanding of the Indian."

"That may be so, but you'll have to take it up with Laurel." Under the gentle scrutiny of Kate's large brown eyes, Quint added, "But I'll put in a good word for you."

"Fine," Kate said with a smile. "Then I suppose I'd best ride down to the reservation with you and ask her myself—if you don't mind. That will give me plenty of time to record your own impressions of your wife's work."

"But—but that's impossible. It's a two-day ride, and the wagon is already overloa—"

"But I take up no room at all," she cheerfully cut in. "I'll just perch myself on top of one of those boxes back there. And my magazine will be glad to pay you the full stagecoach fare for your efforts—which I'm sure you and your wife can put to good use."

"You have every right to visit the reservation, Miss McEwan, but—"

"Kate—please call me Kate," she insisted in a further effort to disarm him.

"You have every right, *Miss McEwan*, but don't you think you would be more comfortable on the stage?"

"I'm a journalist, *Mr. Burgess*, and discomfort comes with the territory. Besides, there's no stage until tomorrow, and for all I know, there could be several other journalists on board with the very same idea as mine. I intend to be first." She flashed another smile and then added, "But of course you are right. It was wrong for me to impose on you and your son. I'll just have to rent a horse and ride down on my own. After all, I've heard they're very simple animals to handle—once you get the hang of it. Isn't that true?" She stood with her head cocked to one side, a carefully crafted look of innocence on her face. Not waiting for a reply, she concluded, "Good day, Mr. Burgess." Then with a friendly nod to Lucas, she awkwardly picked up her bags and started back down the boardwalk.

For a long while, Quint watched her staggering away under the weight of the load, sure that her clumsy gait was designed for effect; she certainly had made good time racing to catch up with the wagon. He sighed, and though he wasn't for a moment taken in by her performance, he found himself chuckling.

"Miss McEwan!" he called out. "Kate!" As she turned and looked at him expectantly, he beckoned with his arm and shouted, "C'mon. We haven't got all day!"

With a wide smile, Kate came running back along the

boardwalk. Sure enough, her step was now as graceful as an athlete's, and the bags seemed to float beside her of their own accord.

Fifteen minutes later, after Kate had purchased some supplies for the journey, the buckboard rode south out of Durango. And though she had been sincere in her offer to sit among the baggage, Lucas and Little Bear would not be denied that pleasure, and so she gratefully found herself sharing the front seat with Quint. In return for their kindness, she saw to it that each of them carried one of Gussie Orcutt's special basket lunches for the ride.

Chapter Two

"**T**hree Eyes! Will you give me a hand over here?"

The Indian youth looked up from the cottonwood pole he was stripping to where Mountain Laurel was bent over, trying to lift another of the tipi poles. He quickly put down his hatchet and sprinted over to help her. Nodding slightly as he came up beside her, Three Eyes took hold of the smooth twelve-foot pole. Together they began to drag it through the forested glen to her pony, a distinctive white Appaloosa with a mottling of gray and black spots at the rear.

As they worked, the Ute boy stole an occasional glance at the woman known as Mountain Laurel, but who had taken the name Laurel Fox Burgess. She had left the village two years before, when Three Eyes was twelve, and he had remembered her only as the daughter of Silver Fox, the physician whose white name was Josiah. Though Three Eyes, and indeed all the Ute, had gotten along well with this half-breed woman, she had kept mostly to herself, either working with her father or taking long journeys beyond the village—where rumor had it she was being trained in the sacred way of the *pwu-au-gut* by her grandfather, the legendary Surnia.

Now Three Eyes saw Mountain Laurel with the eyes of a fourteen-year-old youth on the verge of manhood. Though the boy was tall for his age, Laurel was even taller—and far taller than any Ute woman. Her features were an attractive blend of her Indian and white heritage, with high cheekbones framing a narrow face and nose, made all the more striking by her hazel eyes and silver-streaked brown hair—the legacy of her father, called Silver Fox for his own prematurely gray hair. At twenty-four, an age when most Ute women were married and already had several children, Laurel had only recently chosen her husband, a white man who used to drive the stagecoach through Ute land, and Three Eyes had heard talk that there was also a son close to his own age.

Three Eyes helped Laurel lash the cottonwood pole to the others they had gathered. The narrow ends of the poles were tied to a harness on the back of the Appaloosa, five on each side, with the far ends dragging behind on the ground. Only two more poles were needed for the ceremonial tipi in which Laurel's Ute marriage would take place.

As Laurel and Three Eyes walked over to retrieve the pole he had been readying, his mother joined them. Singing Water was somewhat portly, but with gentle, pleasing features. Her husband—Three Eyes' father—had died four years before of scarlet fever. Since then, the thirty-year-old widow had been courted by several men, but Three Eyes knew she cared for only one man, her husband's brother, Painted Wind, who seemed unaware of her interest.

"The last pole is ready," Singing Water said, pointing toward where she had been working.

"I will take them to the horse," Three Eyes said. Laurel moved to assist him, but the boy had already hoisted the first pole onto his shoulder and waved her away.

As Three Eyes carried it away, Laurel turned to Singing Water. "You have a fine, hardworking son, my friend."

"Yes," Singing Water agreed. "He is the pride of his uncle."

"How *is* Painted Wind?" Laurel inquired. "I haven't seen him these past three days I've been back."

"He has journeyed west to visit the new home of our brother Ute."

Laurel knew she was referring to Utah, where the United

States government had relocated thousands of Ute from the northern part of Colorado. Only the Southern Ute remained on their ancestral land, though moves were already being made to dispossess them, as well.

"And he is well?" Laurel asked.

"He is . . . not at peace," Singing Water hesitantly replied. "He is a leader among our people, but he wants to be more."

"A *pwu-au-gut*," Laurel concluded.

"Yes. Ever since Surnia took his final journey, we have been without a medicine man. Painted Wind fears our power has left us. He dreams of returning the *po-o-kan-te* to our tribe."

"Is that why he has gone to Utah?"

"We have been offered a new home in the west. My husband's brother has gone there to see if that is where our *po-o-kan-te* lies."

"Has he had a vision?" Laurel asked.

Singing Water sighed. "Painted Wind has many visions."

Laurel was quite familiar with Painted Wind and his visions. Though Laurel was only an infant when, at fifteen, Painted Wind received his name through a vision, she had heard the story often. Returning from a spirit quest, he had told of how a rainbow-colored wind had swept down from the north and poured through him, filling him with the healing power of the Great Spirit. The wind had told him that it would show itself to the people that night as a sign that he had thus been blessed. At midnight, all the Ute gathered at the center of the village and looked to the north. The clouds cleared, and just as Painted Wind had promised, the sky was lit with a brilliant aurora borealis.

Afterward, Surnia had agreed to teach Painted Wind the way of the *pwu-au-gut*, though many years later he confided to Laurel that he had never placed great stock in Painted Wind's vision. Surnia lived in a cavern to the north of the village, and he had been aware of the northern lights for several nights before Painted Wind's vision. He knew that it was the clearing weather that allowed the villagers in the valley to see the phenomenon that Painted

Wind and Surnia had each seen the previous night in the clear sky of the mountains to the north.

Still, Painted Wind had such a fierce desire to learn the sacred arts that Surnia had accepted him as a student. The apprenticeship lasted three years, at which time a rift developed between the two, and Surnia sent him back to the village. Neither of the men ever spoke of the incident. But Painted Wind made no secret of his resentment when Surnia began to teach Laurel—a woman, and a half-breed at that—the path of the *pwu-au-gut* that rightfully was his.

Laurel watched as Three Eyes headed over to the final pole and carried it away. Then she turned back to Singing Water. "Painted Wind will not be pleased at my return."

"No, he will not," Singing Water admitted. Then she turned and laid a hand on Laurel's forearm. "But he does not hate you, Mountain Laurel. He admires all that you are. But he believes you walk the path of the whites, and he does not want our people to follow you. Since you and Surnia have been gone, he believes he has rediscovered his *po-o-kan-te*. I fear he will see your coming as a threat."

"I do not wish to challenge his power. But I have my own gift, and I must share it with my people."

"I know that, Mountain Laurel. And perhaps in time my husband's brother will accept your gift, as well."

Three Eyes came running over to the women. "The poles are ready," he called out.

"Then let us return to the village," Laurel suggested. "I must finish my tipi before dark, and I still have the flowers to gather."

Singing Water put her arm around her son's shoulder; he was already an inch taller than she. "Go bring our horses," she told him. As soon as he was gone, she turned to Laurel. "Let me gather the flowers, Mountain Laurel. I will bring them this evening, and we can decorate your tipi together."

"That is kind of you, but I wouldn't want—"

"I *want* to do this for you—and myself. Painted Wind will soon return. Perhaps if I decorate my own tipi . . ."

"Yes," Laurel eagerly agreed. "That is a lovely idea."

"Go with Three Eyes," Singing Water told her. "He will help you raise the tipi poles."

The two women embraced, and then Laurel walked to where Three Eyes was standing with the horses. As she and the boy mounted up and started through the trees, Singing Water called out, "That white brave of yours will find much warmth in your tipi, Mountain Laurel. *He'e'e' Ahi'ni'yo'.*"

As Laurel looked back at her and waved, she wondered if Painted Wind would understand the significance of Singing Water decorating her tipi like Laurel's marriage tipi.

"*He'e'e' Ahi'ni'yo',* my friend," she called in reply.

The sun rose in the sky as Singing Water led her horse through the knee-high grass of a forest clearing, gathering wildflowers and placing them in two large baskets that were slung over the horse's back. As she worked, she sang:

> "Hummingbird, wake to the dawn,
> That the flowers may bloom,
> That the flowers may grow.

> "Hummingbird, fly to my love,
> That the flowers may grow,
> That the flowers may bloom.

> "Hummingbird, sing him my song,
> That the flowers may grow,
> That the flowers may bloom.

> "Hummingbird, bring home my love,
> That the flowers may bloom,
> That the flowers may grow."

As she placed each flower in a basket, Singing Water visualized the strong, comforting image of Painted Wind. He had taken her tipi and set it beside his own when his brother died, and he had raised Three Eyes like a son. She had always dreamed that one day he would take her within his own tipi, like many another brave did for his brother's widow. But she would never ask, and for now she was content to cook and care for him as a sister.

Singing Water picked up a large daisy and laughed as she remembered the game Mountain Laurel once taught her. Singing Water had been fourteen and hopelessly in love with a brave she no longer could remember. Mountain Laurel was no more than eight at the time, but she was wise beyond her years and claimed she knew the white man's way to determine if Singing Water's love would be returned. She took her Ute friend to a meadow much like this and swore her to secrecy before imparting the great wisdom she had learned from her white father.

Singing Water laughed again as she reenacted the foolish ceremony of her youth, this time focusing on the image of Painted Wind. "He loves me," she solemnly intoned as she plucked one of the petals from the daisy. "He loves me not," she continued as she plucked another. "He loves me. . . . He loves me not. . . . He loves me. . . ."

A stirring of branches caused Singing Water to halt her game and look up. All was silent, but her horse appeared to sense something as well and stamped nervously. There was a sharp snap of a twig, and she spun around to see a rider appear from the thick brush at the edge of the woods. It was a white man—gaunt and shabbily dressed, with narrow-set eyes, greasy black hair, and a stringy beard. Singing Water turned to grab her horse's bridle, only to find herself staring at three other riders who had emerged from the woods at the far side of the clearing.

As her skittish horse turned in place, the Indian woman weighed her chances of getting away. She could see that these men were heavily armed, and she was certain they were far from friendly. But even as she stood there, they fanned out in a circle and rode in, effectively closing off any chance of escape.

"You speak English?" the gaunt one demanded. Though Singing Water understood what he said, she remained silent, patting her horse's head to calm it.

"I said, you speak English?"

"Hell, it's just a squaw, Striker," one of the others said. "They don't speak. Only grunt."

"Yeah, and moan," a third man offered, chuckling lewdly. "And they sure know how to buck when you ride 'em."

"This one's not half bad," the second one added. "Reminds me of that Cherokee whore we shared in Manitou, Striker."

"Shut up," the man named Striker ordered. He dismounted and walked up to Singing Water. Fingering the collar of her buckskin dress, he said, "You sure you don't speak English, pretty squaw?"

Again Singing Water remained silent, determined to show no fear, her mouth set in a grim line.

"Well, just in case you do, remember this: When you get back home, you tell your people they better move off this land. Move . . . or be buried on it. Understand?"

This time, when she did not respond, the man grabbed her blouse with both hands and yanked down, ripping it open and exposing her breasts. "Maybe you'll understand this language better!" he declared, striking her across the face.

Singing Water lashed out, raking her nails across the gaunt man's face and drawing blood. Suddenly, she found herself surrounded by the other three men, who tore away her clothes and forced her to the ground. She fought back her tears as the three men spread wide her arms and legs and their leader began to unbutton his pants.

Singing Water knew there was no escape. As the dirty, unshaven man climbed on top of her, she closed her eyes and began to turn her thoughts inward, until they carried her away from the defilement being inflicted upon her body. She was a woman, and she understood that men can ravage a woman's body—but she had no intention of allowing them to ravage her spirit.

Singing Water went into her spirit and knew that no matter what they did to her or how many times they abused her, she would live. She would live for her son. She would live for Painted Wind. She would live for her people. And she was certain that in time the Great Spirit would exact payment for everything these white men had done.

Several miles to the east, a buckboard wagon was riding south along the edge of the Ute reservation. On board, Kate McEwan took in the surroundings. The previous day, they had crossed the Animas River and headed into the lush, wooded high country. After spending the night before at a way station, they had come down into the flat, semiarid land that made up much of the reservation.

"I don't see where you're going to find a deer around here," Kate commented, picking up a conversation she and Quint had begun earlier that morning.

"You'd be surprised at the number of deer in this area," Quint replied. "But if I had to, I'd backtrack all the way to New York to get one."

"This ceremony is that important to you?"

"Yes, it is. Laurel and I were married at Geneva Medical College right after she received her degree, but a New York wedding means nothing to Laurel's people. They have a different idea about marriage than we do."

"Which is. . . ?"

"It's really very simple. Two people love each other and choose to spend their lives together—for as long as they are in love. All that is left is for them to declare their love to each other, to their village, and to the Great Spirit. So it doesn't matter if we are married in the eyes of the church and the United States government," Quint explained. "If we don't dedicate our love in the Ute tradition, we are not married in their eyes."

"And that's where the deer comes in?" Kate asked as she pulled out her notebook and pencil and began to take notes.

"It's really a very beautiful ceremony. Basically, the brave hunts a deer and brings it to the tipi of his beloved while she is seated outside doing her weaving. He leaves the deer slung over his horse and enters the tipi without acknowledging her. If she continues weaving and pays no attention to the deer, she rejects his pledge of love. If she removes the deer and dresses it, then she accepts."

"Is that all there is to it?"

"Not quite," Quint replied. "After dressing the deer, she cooks some of the meat and brings it into the tipi. There the two of them declare their love and partake a portion of the meat. The rest is offered to the tribe, so that they, too, can share in the dedication."

Kate put down her notebook. "It sounds very beautiful. But I think I'd miss the church organ."

Quint laughed lightly. "Oh, there'll be plenty of music— flutes and drums and maybe even a stolen army bugle or two. That comes at night, when the new couple is bedded down in their marriage tipi. The rest of the tribe gets to singing and dancing and partying, all night long—sort of like a shivaree. I guess they figure if a couple can survive that first night, they have a good chance of staying together for the rest of their lives."

"I'm not sure if that would add to any first-night jitters, but at least it would give them a face-saving excuse if they had any," Kate declared.

"Precisely," Quint agreed, joining in her laugh.

"Well, you and Laurel won't have to worry about that," Kate commented, then suddenly looked embarrassed. "I'm sorry. I just meant—you two being married already."

Quint was thoughtful for a moment and then glanced at the notebook in Kate's lap. "This is not for publication, but when I said this ceremony is important to us, I meant more than just as a symbol for Laurel's people. We come from two cultures, and we do not consider ourselves married until we have completed both ceremonies."

"You mean . . . ?"

"Yes," Quint said. "We are already married in the eyes of the church. But we will not be man and wife until we also are married in the eyes of the Ute."

"I see," Kate replied, then fell silent. She did not know if she would have the willpower to wait, as Quint and Laurel were doing. But perhaps with the right man . . .

Suddenly her thoughts were interrupted as Lucas, seated in back, leaned forward between Kate and Quint and pointed eagerly into the distance. Beside him, Little Bear sensed his master's excitement and began to bark playfully.

"There's the trading post up ahead," Quint said, pointing in the same direction.

Kate squinted into the sun and saw the distant cluster of buildings that made up Halloran's Trading Post, the only white-owned establishment allowed by the Ute within their reservation. Five miles east of the main Ute village, Halloran's served as a supply link with the Indians and provided a meal stop for the stagecoach between Durango to the north and Farmington, New Mexico, to the south.

Soon Kate could make out a large, central adobe building with a wooden barn and several small wooden outbuildings around it. A corral beside the barn held half a dozen horses. Another four were saddled and lined up at the hitch rail in front of the adobe building.

As the approached, Kate saw a group of four men emerge from the main building. They stood for a few moments, and then four of them stepped off the porch and mounted the horses at the hitch rail. The riders turned their horses and put them to a gallop, leaving the compound in a swirl of dust that temporarily obscured the man on the porch.

The four riders headed toward the buckboard wagon. It took less than a minute for them to pass it, three on one side and one to the right. Kate caught a fleeting glimpse of that lone rider in the seconds before he passed from view, and what stood out most was his stern impassivity, heightened by his gaunt, coarse features, narrow-set eyes, and stringy black beard. She couldn't be certain, but she thought his face was scarred or scratched.

As the riders thundered by and continued north, a swirl of dust enveloped the wagon and set Kate coughing.

"Good-mannered gents," Quint muttered, waving away the dust cloud.

Through the handkerchief she had raised to her face, Kate replied, "I'm just glad they're headed the other way."

The dust was settling as the wagon entered the trading-post yard. Quint steered toward the adobe building, where a short, stocky man with a gray beard stood on the porch.

"Isaac!" Quint called out. "It's me—Quint Burgess!"

"Well, I'll be damned!" the man shouted as he hurried down the porch steps and ran over to the wagon. "I knew you were coming, but I guess I didn't believe it till just now!"

Quint pulled the horses to a halt and climbed down from the seat. As he pumped the older man's hand, he turned to introduce his passengers. "This is Isaac Halloran," he said. "Isaac, you know Lucas and Little Bear, and this is Kate McEwan, a correspondent for *New England Monthly*."

"Pleased to meet you," Halloran said politely as Quint helped Kate down from her seat. Then Halloran reached up over the side of the buckboard, grabbed Lucas, and swung him to the ground. "I do declare, boy, you've grown a foot!"

Lucas grinned as his old friend tousled his hair. Hesitantly, the boy said, "G-good day to you, Isaac."

For a moment Halloran stared at the boy in surprise. "Well, I'll be good goddamned! They taught you to talk!"

"And if you speak slowly and quit cursing," Quint said, "he can read your lips—that is, if you have any lips behind that scrub brush!"

Halloran stroked his bushy gray beard and feigned a look of wounded pride. "I told you a thousand times this is no scrub brush. It's my scalp." He reached up and patted his completely bald head, then turned to Kate. "I lost it to a scalping party in the Sioux wars of sixty-five. But I chased them down, killed every last one of them, and brought it back. But the army surgeon was so drunk on rotgut that he plumb put it back on in the wrong place!"

Quint burst out laughing, and Kate politely smiled, though she wasn't so sure she appreciated frontier humor.

"Those fellows were moving pretty fast when they passed us," Quint commented. "Who were they?"

Halloran scowled and spat into the dirt. "Drifters. Their leader is a slippery little dude—all mouth." He started to chuckle. "Said he wanted to buy me out!"

"The trading post?" Quint asked.

"Can you imagine that? But he's just like every other drifter—big talk and big plans, but no brains or backbone to carry it off. Hell, he didn't look like he could afford his next meal, let alone my trading post. And even if he has a rich aunt willing to bankroll him, this place isn't for sale—and it never will be. I'm just too old to start over. When the time comes, they're gonna bury me out back!"

"Glad to hear it," Quint declared.

Halloran looked at him suspiciously and said, "To hear what? About me not selling out, or about burying me?" When Quint merely smiled in reply, Halloran began to laugh and clapped him on the back. "I saw Laurel when she arrived on the stage," he continued. "You're a mighty lucky man, Quint. She said you and Lucas will be needing a place to stay until things are ready at the village. Well, you're staying here! I've made all the plans, and Alice is plumb thrilled to be having company."

"Alice?"

"My wife," Halloran explained as he steered Quint toward the porch. "She'll be out to meet you just as soon as she finishes putting our baby daughter to sleep."

Quint pulled up short and looked down at the stocky older man. "Alice? A baby? When did you get married?"

"Soon after you left. Got me a mail-order housekeeper and, well, you know how charming I am to the ladies! She finally convinced me to make it legal and save on the pay!"

"Well, I'm looking forward to meeting a woman who can stand living with the likes of you!" Quint declared, patting his friend on the shoulder.

As the two men started toward the porch, Kate called after them, "Quint, could I speak to you a moment?"

Quint turned and walked over to her. "What is it?"

"I'd like to continue to the Ute village at once. The Durango stage is due in a few hours, and in case anyone's on board, I want to be sure I'm the first to talk with Laurel."

"But I can't go to the village until I have the deer," Quint explained.

"That's all right. You said it's only a few miles. Perhaps Mr. Halloran has a buggy I can rent."

"Sure do, ma'am," Halloran replied with a grin. "A pretty little one-horse cabriolet. Shall I bring it out?"

"I would appreciate that," Kate replied.

As Halloran hurried over to the carriage shed, Quint turned to Kate and said, "I don't think this is a very good idea. It takes quite a bit of skill to handle a buggy, even for someone who has been around horses."

"Quint, I assure you, I can handle a cabriolet."

"But I thought you didn't know anything about horses."

"Did I give that impression, Quint?" Kate replied with a mischievous grin. "Didn't I mention that I was raised on a horse farm in the Hudson Valley?"

Quint stared at her in surprise, but seeing the genuine warmth of her smile, he broke into a grin. "When you see Laurel, tell her I said she might as well cooperate on those magazine articles. Something tells me you'd get them written with or without her help!"

"Why, thank you, Quint," Kate said with a small curtsy. "That *was* a compliment, wasn't it?"

"Did I give that impression, Kate?" Quint responded with a look of mock surprise as he reached into the back of the wagon and began to remove her baggage.

A few minutes later, Halloran pulled up in the buggy, and Quint loaded the bags under the seat. After Halloran pointed out the road that led to the Ute village, Kate said her good-byes and gave Lucas a hug. Then she climbed into the buggy, took hold of the reins, and snapped them smartly against the horse's back. In a moment she was off at a gentle walk, to keep the dust from rising. But as soon as she was beyond the compound, she urged the horse to a trot and quickly disappeared over the hills to the west.

Halfway between the trading post and the Ute village, the wagon road passed near a stream that meandered through cottonwood groves. As the cabriolet drew closer, Kate saw a black horse grazing at the grass along the bank. Beside the animal, an Indian woman was kneeling at the water's edge, washing her arms and face.

Hearing the buggy approach, the woman jumped up, pulling tight what seemed to be a torn buckskin dress. The woman looked clearly afraid as Kate reined the cabriolet to a halt about twenty feet away.

"Are you all right?" Kate called out to the woman, who began to back away along the stream, shaking her head as if disoriented. "Is there something I can do?"

The woman bumped into her horse and froze as Kate climbed down from the buggy and cautiously approached. The woman continued to shake her head slowly from left to right, her lips quivering as if she was trying to speak.

"It's all right," Kate said, walking closer. She could see that the woman's dress was dreadfully torn, and she had numerous cuts and bruises all over her face and chest.

"Everything's all right," Kate repeated as she stepped up to the woman, who closed her eyes and began to shiver, until her body shook with emotion. Suddenly the woman dropped to her knees and screamed. Her hands clenched into fists, and she covered her face and began to sob.

Kate kneeled and took the woman in her arms. Rocking her gently, she whispered over and over again, "It's all right. Everything's all right."

As Kate McEwan drove into the Ute village, the Indian woman beside her pointed in the direction of her tipi. Kate knew little more than that the woman was named Singing Water and that her injuries, she had insisted in halting English after she had calmed down, came from a fall off her horse. She had refused Kate's offer to loan her a dress but had accepted a blanket Kate had found under the buggy seat. She was wrapped in that blanket now, and every few seconds she glanced back to reassure herself that her horse was tied to the back of the buggy.

As Kate pulled up beside Singing Water's tipi near the edge of the settlement, many Ute came out of their homes and approached cautiously.

Kate turned to Singing Water. "I am looking for Laurel Fox. Do you know where she is?"

The woman waved toward the far end of the village and whispered, "She is building her tipi."

Seeing the villagers approaching, Singing Water grew frightened again. She looked quickly at Kate, and in her eyes, Kate read the unspoken thanks. Kate smiled at

Singing Water, who quickly climbed down from the buggy.
Pulling the blanket tighter around her, she hurried around
the buggy and untied her horse. With a final grateful look
at the white woman who had helped her, Singing Water
led her horse over to the tipi, tied it to a stake, and
disappeared inside.

A crowd was quickly gathering as Kate's buggy continued through the village, which was arranged in a huge
circle, its center an open courtyard. As Kate drove into
the clearing, the crowd surrounded the buggy, until she
found it impossible to move.

Young children pawed at the carriage, while the adults
pointed at Kate's unusual clothes. The bolder women
reached right into the buggy and touched the fabric. For a
moment Kate sat transfixed, not sure whether or not to be
worried, but somehow sensing that she was in no danger.
Then she remembered the long package stowed beneath
the seat.

Bending down, she lifted out the cloth-covered object,
placed it on her lap, and removed the covering. Cradling
it in her arms, she stepped down into the crowd and held
aloft the tripod camera—one of the newly developed box
cameras that used dry plates, which could be shipped to a
laboratory for developing, rather than wet plates, which
had to be processed on location. Seeing this strange-looking
machine, the Indians backed away in fear, as if it were
some newfangled weapon.

Kate loosened the thumbscrews on the three legs and
lowered the telescoping extensions, then tightened the
screws and positioned the legs. Removing the lens cover,
she motioned with her arms for the villagers to gather in
front of the camera, but they either didn't understand or
were too frightened to comply. She decided to attempt a
shot anyway, praying that this new quick-shutter camera
could actually freeze action, as advertised.

While Kate stared into the focusing screen at the back
of the camera and framed the shot, a tall woman pushed
through the crowd and filled the picture. She wore a
buckskin dress, elaborately painted with a floral design of
bright green tendrils and red and yellow petals, which

covered her from the neck to below the knees. She had fringed leggings, beaded moccasins, and a wide leather belt. While most of the women wore their hair loose and cut short at the neck, her hair was long, with a braid at each temple. But what distinguished her most were the premature streaks of silver that framed her striking Anglo-Indian features.

Looking up from the camera, Kate immediately recognized the young woman as Laurel Fox Burgess.

"You are scaring them with that thing," Laurel said.

Kate surreptitiously slid the dry plate in front of the focusing screen and placed her finger on the lever that operated the shutter as she innocently replied, "Perhaps if you were to smile, they'd be reassured."

Laurel looked at her curiously and then at the camera. She seemed to read Kate's intention and, despite herself, broke into a broad grin just as Kate snapped the shutter.

"Thank you, Dr. Burgess—I presume." Kate smiled warmly as she walked forward and held out her hand.

"You know my name?" Laurel asked, accepting her hand.

"Yes. I've come from Boston to interview you. I am Kate McEwan of *New England Monthly*."

Chapter Three

It was while walking the buggy to Laurel's tipi that Kate McEwan mentioned having driven Singing Water back to the village. Upon learning of Singing Water's disheveled and disoriented state, Laurel immediately grew concerned. Leaving Kate with Three Eyes, who was attaching the last few buffalo hides to the tipi frame, Laurel grabbed her medical bag and hurried to her friend's abode.

Laurel pulled aside the handwoven blanket that covered the entranceway and entered the tipi. In the dim light, she noticed that a small fire had already been built from last night's embers in the pit near the center of the tipi. On a buffalo hide just beyond the firepit lay Singing Water, not asleep, yet not entirely awake. She was curled up on her side, wrapped in the blanket from the cabriolet, her half-closed eyes staring toward the flames.

"Singing Water?" Laurel whispered as she came around the firepit, put down her bag, and kneeled beside her friend. "Are you all right?"

It took almost a full minute for the Indian woman to respond. She slowly turned her head toward Laurel, but her expression did not register any recognition. Then she mechanically turned back toward the fire, and her eyes began to open wider, until the flames could clearly be seen upon the surface of each. As she looked back at Laurel again, the flames seemed to dance higher, until

Laurel was certain she no longer was viewing the reflected firelight but the very flame of Singing Water's soul.

"I will be fine," Singing Water calmly intoned.

Laurel reached out to touch the purplish bruise at her friend's left temple, but Singing Water lifted her hand and shielded her face.

"Let me help you," Laurel pleaded.

"It is nothing, Mountain Laurel. A fall from my horse, nothing more. I will rest and be fine."

"At least let me examine you," Laurel urged.

"There is nothing to examine. A few cuts, that is all. I will be fine."

The tipi filled briefly with light, and Laurel glanced back as the woman named Kate McEwan entered and approached. Turning back to Singing Water, she saw that the Indian woman either hadn't noticed or did not mind the presence of the white stranger.

Laurel gently pulled Singing Water's hand away from her face and checked the extent of the injuries. The Indian woman remained silent, not even protesting when Laurel pulled down the blanket and examined her bruised shoulders and chest.

"This was no fall," Laurel declared at last. "You have been beaten and scratched."

Singing Water lifted the blanket back over her chest. "It is nothing. I am a woman, and they beat me."

"Who did this to you?" Laurel asked.

"Does it matter? They were men. They were not of our people."

"How many were there?" Kate asked as she kneeled beside the two women.

Singing Water looked up and seemed to notice her for the first time. The firelight danced brighter in her eyes. "They were men—white men. I am a Ute squaw."

Laurel took her friend's hand in her own and whispered, "Did they hurt you, Singing Water? I mean, did they . . . did they—?"

"It is of no importance what was done to me," Singing Water firmly declared. "To be a woman is to know suffering. To be a woman is to find that which is born when something else dies. Do not worry about me. I will endure. I have seen thirty winters, and I will see thirty more winters—for my son . . . and for his father's brother."

As Laurel held Singing Water's hand to her lips, the Indian woman leaned her cheek upon the buffalo hide and stared at the fire, her eyelids half closed and fluttering.

Looking at the scratches across the woman's face, an image rose in Kate McEwan's mind—the picture of a band of white drifters riding north in a cloud of dust.

"Those men who attacked you," Kate cautiously began, "there were four of them, weren't there?" When Singing Water turned her head slightly to look at the white woman, Kate continued, "And you cut one of them on the face. He was skinny, with black hair and a stringy beard."

Laurel looked at Kate in surprise and then back at Singing Water, who now lifted her head from the hide and leaned forward, her eyes again wide. But it was as if the flames had contracted into two tiny points of white ice.

"They were white men," she whispered. "That is all."

"But perhaps the authorities—"

Raising her palm to cut Kate off, Singing Water turned to Laurel and said, "This woman does not understand our ways. Tell her that white law protects only the whites. It does not matter who did this to me. If that were known, it would be left to Painted Wind to hunt them down. And who would protect Painted Wind? These men would kill him—or if he succeeded, the white law would call him a murderer and make him hang. Tell her—there is nothing to be done."

"But surely there must be something . . ."

"Yes, there is," Singing Water replied. "These men came to give our people a message. They said we must give up our land—or be buried upon it. Now it is left for us to decide what we will do."

"Will you tell Painted Wind?" Laurel asked.

"He will be told of the message. But he must never learn of what they did to me. Promise you will never tell anyone."

"I am a physician—and your friend. Everything you have told me will be kept in confidence."

Singing Water turned to Kate McEwan. "And you, my white friend. You will not tell, will you?"

For a brief moment, Kate weighed her conflicting responsibilities as a journalist and as a visitor and friend. Then with a warm smile, she replied, "I will keep your secret."

Singing Water returned her smile. Lying back against the buffalo hide, she closed her eyes and ever so softly began to sing, "Hummingbird, wake to the dawn, that the flowers may bloom, that the flowers may grow. . . ."

Upon returning to her tipi, Laurel was pleased to see that Three Eyes had completed the basic structure. All that remained was to arrange the interior and decorate it with the flowers in the baskets on Singing Water's horse.

Laurel explained to Three Eyes that his mother had been injured in a riding accident but that she would be fine. Taking his leave, the boy hurried off to be with her. As soon as he was gone, Laurel invited Kate to spend the night and helped her unload her bags. As for the series of magazine articles Kate wanted to do, Laurel promised to decide in the morning the extent of her cooperation.

As the two women worked that evening finishing the tipi, Kate was struck by Laurel's calm efficiency—a trait she already had observed when they were with Singing Water, and one quite dissimilar to herself. At one point, when they were digging a small firepit in the hard-packed earthen floor, Kate banged her finger against a buried stone. With a pained cry, she threw down her small hand shovel and swore liberally, followed by several minutes of complaints about the primitive tools, the condition of the ground, the phase of the moon, and everything else that remotely pertained to the situation. However, when the same thing happened to her friend a few minutes later, she saw that Laurel merely squeezed her injured hand while breathing deeply for a few moments. Then she picked up her shovel and resumed digging.

"Well, and aren't you the sainted martyr!" Kate joked, putting on a thick brogue. "A real stoic, you are. You must have inherited that from your mother's side."

"Are you kidding?" Laurel replied. "From the stories I've heard about her, she would've been prancing around here cursing the gods for having created both rocks and fingers!" Laurel fixed Kate with a mischievous grin. "She probably would've acted like a real fool—not like either of *us*!"

"Speak for yourself, lassie. As for me, I'm more'n proud to count myself among the fools of this world! How did Shakespeare put it? 'Better a witty fool than a foolish wit.' And he was right, even if he *was* an Englishman!"

Shaking her head, Laurel said, "I prefer to take my advice from that popular old saying: 'God looks after fools, drunkards, and the United States.' And since I'm only half a citizen, I'd better be only half a fool!"

"Well, m'dear," Kate declared, "you're succeeding admirably—in a half-witted sort of way. Admirably!" She clapped Laurel on the back, and they broke into laughter.

Soon they were at work, and an hour later everything but hanging the wildflowers was finished. Laurel made a fire and prepared a stew of venison and root vegetables, which they quickly devoured. Afterward, they curled up under heavy buffalo robes and soon were asleep.

Kate awoke the next morning to the smell of cornmeal mush simmering over the fire and found Laurel already arranging the tipi with flowers. After washing and dressing, Kate filled a wooden bowl with the porridge and watched the young half-breed woman stringing the tipi poles with daisies, morning glories, cornflowers, painted cups, and forget-me-nots set among sprigs of mountain laurel.

As she ate, Kate asked about the tensions between the Ute reservation and the growing white community in southwestern Colorado. Laurel described the forced relocation of the Northern Ute during the past few years to reservations in Utah, instigated by a booming mining industry that coveted the silver-rich Indian lands. So far that fate had not befallen the Southern Ute, whose land hadn't yielded any appreciable amounts of marketable minerals. Yet mining companies continued to send geologists to the reservation in search of silver and other precious metals, but to date their unenthusiastic reports had discouraged investors.

"Still, I fear for the future of our people," Laurel admitted. "It would take only one significant strike to bring on a swarm of prospectors. Then see how quickly the government finds a way to dissolve all those treaties that guarantee this land as the Ute's permanent possession. It will take a real effort to keep that from happening."

"Is that part of the reason you have returned?"

"Exactly. Quint and I believe we can help each side better understand the other's position. That's why I've decided to participate in those magazine interviews of yours."

"Really?" Kate said, delighted. She immediately put down her bowl and got out her pencil and notebook. "How do you and Quint hope to make a difference?" she asked.

"We understand white society in a way my people never could. We realize that the Ute cannot secure the future by simply clinging to the past. We must retain the best of the past while adopting some of the advantages of the world around us. To further that end, we plan to open a school."

"A school? For the Indians?"

"Yes. While Lucas was being educated back east at a school for the deaf, Quint used the time to study methods of teaching the Indian children. In many ways, it's similar to teaching a deaf person to exist in a hearing society."

"Will Quint be the teacher?"

"Yes. I'll help all I can, but the brunt of the work will fall on his shoulders."

"But he doesn't speak Ute," Kate pointed out.

"That's unimportant. More and more Ute speak English—particularly the children, who pick it up with astonishing ease. The others will study it as their first subject."

"What do you expect will be your own biggest problem in earning your people's trust?"

"As a physician?" Laurel asked. Kate nodded, and Laurel said, "A doctor among the whites has one major obstacle—proving he isn't a charlatan, which is done by establishing a reputation over a period of time. Once people are convinced he isn't a quack, trust comes easily, because at heart people have great respect for physicians. However, there's no such established respect for the medical community among the Ute. Therefore, besides proving I'm not a charlatan, I have to educate the Ute to trust my form of medicine."

"Won't that be even more difficult, being a woman?"

"Curiously, no. That's the major obstacle for a woman physician among the whites. However, the Ute are much more willing to judge a woman by her own abilities—once she demonstrates them. So if I can convince my people to trust my medical skills, they will accept me."

"But hasn't your father already paved the way? Didn't he doctor the Ute for some thirty years or so?"

"Yes, he did, but to the Ute that was not a testimonial to modern medicine but rather a testimonial to his personal power—his *po-o-kan-te*, as the Ute call it. He was a medicine man, nothing more or less. My grandfather, Surnia, was a *pwu-au-gut*, a traditional Ute medicine man, and the people believed it was his connection to the spirits of his herbs and potions that provided the healing. Without Surnia's *po-o-kan-te* the herbs would be useless."

"So you must prove that you are a medicine woman—a *pwu-au-gut*—like your father and grandfather."

"If that's all I do, what will happen when I'm gone?" Laurel declared. "No, I must do more. I must show that my medicine is a science, and that its *po-o-kan-te* is available to all. My people must learn to use the tools of both the physician and the *pwu-au-gut* to heal themselves."

Kate looked up from her notebook. "It almost sounds as if you believe in the power of the medicine man."

"Is that so unusual?" Laurel replied with a smile. "To whites, medicine begins and ends with Hippocrates and his descendants. Do you think no one was ever healed among the Chinese or Africans or American Indians? Medicine is a natural science that evolves wherever people are interested in the meaning of life. The only reason white physicians pay no attention to the traditional Indian healing arts is because they consider it beneath them to study what they see as folk medicine. If they looked, however, they would discover a remarkable similarity between their own science and such folk medicines. In truth, there is much each culture can offer the other."

"Do you recommend setting up a program to teach other physicians some of the—?"

Kate was interrupted by the sudden appearance of a young Indian man, who stood in the entranceway waiting for permission to enter. The man wore buckskin leggings and moccasins, with an overshirt that reached to his knees. The buckskin overshirt was fringed at the neck and bottom, with the double-thickness breast piece painted a bright yellow. A black and red blanket was passed over the right shoulder and under the left, fastened around the waist by a cord. Like most Ute men, his long black hair was parted in the middle and gathered on either side in a long braid, with the last few inches wrapped in strips of beaver fur, from which were tied several bear claws.

Laurel motioned for the young man to approach, and as he headed toward her, he glanced nervously at Kate. Then he began to whisper rapidly to Laurel. Kate strained to pick up his words but soon realized he was speaking in Ute.

After a short, excited conversation, the man nodded and immediately departed. Kate stared expectantly at Laurel, burning with curiosity but not wanting to pry.

Laurel walked over to her buffalo-robe bed and picked up her small medical bag and a much larger case containing her other supplies. As she carried them toward the doorway, she turned to Kate and asked, "Are you coming?"

"Where?"

"I have my first patient."

Eagerly clutching her notebook and pencil, Kate jumped to her feet and followed Laurel outside.

As the two women rode up in the cabriolet to the small tipi—a special birthing tipi constructed a half mile north of the village—they could hear the plaintive moaning of a woman in hard labor. An old woman, wrapped in a blanket, sat cross-legged in front of the doorway, as if on guard. The young man who had summoned Laurel was pacing helplessly in front of his horse, which was tied to a nearby tree.

Laurel climbed down from the buggy, medical bag in hand, and the man rushed over and muttered in Ute. Laurel nodded and then motioned for Kate to follow. When they reached the tipi, however, the old woman stood up and blocked the way as she babbled on and on about something. The man shook his head and pointed at Laurel and Kate, but the old woman merely crossed her arms and refused to budge. Finally, the man grasped her upper arms, lifted the short woman off the ground, and stood her to the side. Irate, she started to holler, but the man paid no attention and signaled for the two women to enter.

"Laurel!" Kate gasped as the old woman suddenly grabbed her around the waist and held on.

Laurel spun around and stifled a smile as she saw the determined little woman with mouth set in a grim line, her feet planted firmly in place. Laurel spoke something in Ute, but the old woman shook her head and refused to let go. Again Laurel spoke, this time gently grasping the woman's hands and pulling them apart. The woman looked up, first at Laurel and then at Kate, her brow furrowed in angry concentration. Finally she muttered what sounded to Kate like a Ute curse and then turned her back and stalked away.

"Sings-With-Moon thought it shocking enough that Wild Elk lost faith in the midwives and sent for a half-breed doctor to attend his wife," Laurel explained, "but she simply couldn't allow a white stranger to defile the birthing tipi—even when I explained you were my assistant."

"I am?" Kate asked.

"You said you wanted to write an inside story," Laurel reminded her. "So let's get inside and begin."

The two women entered the tipi. Wild Elk, unwilling to alienate the Great Spirit further, remained just outside the entranceway, staring inside.

The peak of the tipi was open to the sky, and the morning light revealed a platform bed at the center of the

room. A heavyset young woman, apparently naked, lay
under a blanket. She was sweating profusely, and her
hands clutched at the blanket, which had fallen away from
her bare legs. Her eyes were open but rolled back, and
she seemed close to unconsciousness. Her teeth were
clamped tight on a strip of leather, which did little to
muffle her pained cries.

Near the wall at the far end of the tipi, three elderly
women sat cross-legged on the floor, staring impassively at
the platform, apparently waiting for the baby to start to
show. They had long since given up their previously futile
attempts at assisting the woman in delivering her baby
and now seemed content to let nature take its course to
either birth or death.

"She has been in labor for more than two days," Laurel
explained as she and Kate approached the woman. "I've
been aware of it, but the family wouldn't let me attend.
Wild Elk is not so superstitious, however. He hasn't forgotten the time when my father treated him as a boy for
scarlet fever, and he recovered. So when he could no
longer stand her pain, he overruled the midwives and her
family."

"Where *is* her family?"

"The midwives told them to prepare for her burial."

Laurel kneeled beside the platform and pulled the blanket away from the young woman. Despite the fact that she
was overweight, it was obvious that her belly was grossly
distended, and to Kate's untrained eye it seemed somewhat misshapen.

"There may be internal bleeding," Laurel said. "I'll
have to do an internal examination."

Laurel spoke in Ute to the three women, but they did
not respond, so she turned and repeated her words to
Wild Elk, still in the doorway. He nodded and hurried
away.

"I've sent him for water so I may wash," Laurel explained.

When the man returned, Laurel walked to the doorway
and took the bucket. As she spoke with him, he kept
glancing nervously at his wife. Finally he nodded and
called out to the midwives. The three women stood and

filed over to the door, and immediately a lively argument ensued. The women kept shaking their heads and pointing toward the platform; Kate couldn't be sure if they were indicating her or the woman in labor. Eventually the husband grabbed one of the women by the arm and pulled her from the tipi. The other two women shuffled out behind, muttering all the while.

As soon as they were gone, Laurel yanked the blanket in front of the doorway and carried the bucket back to the platform. "I had to get rid of those women," she said as she carefully washed her hands with a bar of soap from her medical bag. "They never would have sat still for an internal exam—it violates our customs."

"Does he know . . . ?"

"There wasn't any need. I said that they make me nervous, that's all. *That* he could understand."

"So can I," Kate agreed with a tense grin.

"Now, hold her shoulders gently," Laurel requested, "though I doubt she's even aware we're here."

As Kate complied, Laurel spread the woman's legs and began the exam. As expected, the woman seemed unaware of what was happening. With one hand inside and the other on the surface, Laurel painstakingly felt the woman's belly. Kate assumed she was determining the position of the baby, and from the look on her face, it was not good. At last, Laurel removed her hand and sat back, sighing deeply.

"What is it?" Kate asked.

"I'm afraid I must operate at once."

"A cesarean section," Kate surmised aloud. "Is the baby breeched?"

Laurel stared for a moment at the semiconscious woman, then turned to Kate and shook her head sadly. "If only that were all."

"What do you mean?"

"Kate, there is no baby in her womb. This woman is suffering from an ovarian tumor."

Two hours later, preparations for the operation were complete, and Kate stood ready to assist Laurel. The first

hour following Laurel's diagnosis had largely been spent
trying to convince Wild Elk to permit the operation. While
such procedures had become increasingly routine since
the first successful ovariectomy was performed in 1809,
cutting into the abdominal cavity was considered evil medicine by the Ute. The midwives urged Wild Elk to await
the return of the *pwu-au-gut*, Painted Wind, but in the
end the young husband was convinced that Laurel's way
held the only hope for his suffering wife.

Once permission had been given and the midwives sent
away, Wild Elk and the two women had quickly readied
the tipi for the operation. The platform bed was raised
waist high, with a table prepared beside it on which the
surgical instruments were laid out. Then the skins covering the entire upper quarter of the tipi were removed so
that the midday sun would fully illuminate the operating
area.

Wild Elk took up a position outside, maintaining a vigil
of prayer and making sure that no one tried to stop the
operation. Though the tribe might curse or condemn him,
they would not interfere in the decision of a husband
regarding his wife. Inside the tipi, Laurel checked the
pulse of her patient, who was not fully conscious but
seemed to be resting peacefully for the moment. Assured
that the woman's heartbeat was strong, Laurel turned to
the nearby table and began to describe each instrument
she would be using, so as to familiarize Kate with the
procedure.

"And this is a Spencer Wells forceps," Laurel said,
picking up the final instrument, which was shaped like a
small pair of scissors, but with flat blades that could cut off
a bleeding artery and with a catch near the handles to lock
it in place. "It was designed by Sir Thomas Spencer Wells,
one of the most prominent surgeons in London. He has
had a major part in perfecting this very operation, and I'll
be using the procedure he laid out in his book *Diseases of
the Ovaries*, published around 1865. Of course, his work
would have been nothing without the pioneering efforts of
a courageous Amerian doctor."

"An American?" Kate asked, suddenly more interested.

"Yes. Dr. Ephraim McDowell. In 1809 on the frontier of Kentucky, he became the first surgeon to successfully remove a diseased ovary. But let's get started." She picked up a vial of chloroform. "I'll tell you all about him as we work."

"You don't have to—"

"It helps me concentrate," Laurel explained.

Laurel removed the rubber stopper from the vial, revealing a glass spout. She laid a strip of gauze over the patient's nose and then turned the vial upside down and tapped three drops of the anesthesia onto the cloth.

"That should keep her asleep and without pain. If she starts to awaken, I want you to administer some more, drop by drop. All right?" Kate nodded, and Laurel continued, "Fine. Then we're ready."

Laurel removed the blanket and felt the woman's belly. "Give me some absorbent wool and that pan," she said, indicating a small pan of liquid on the instrument table. When Kate brought over the items and placed them on the operating table, Laurel dipped the wool into the liquid and began to wash the woman's belly.

"This is carbolic lotion—the same thing we used when we washed. It's also what I soaked the instruments in after I boiled them."

"I wondered about that," Kate said. "Why did you do that?"

"The major cause of death following an operation is infection. During the Civil War, more soldiers died from infections following surgery than from the actual wounds."

Laurel handed the pan of carbolic lotion to Kate, who returned it to the instrument table. Then Laurel walked around the operating table to a position where she could easily reach both patient and instruments. Picking up a thin-bladed scalpel in her right hand, she measured off a section of the belly with her left hand and deftly made a six-inch incision through the top layer of skin. For a moment, Kate stood immobilized at the sight of the oozing blood, but then she looked at Laurel's calm expression and quickly picked up a wad of absorbent wool. As Laurel had instructed her earlier, she moistened it in the carbolic lotion and dabbed away the blood.

As if nothing out of the ordinary was taking place, Laurel continued her lecture. "An Englishman named Lister has done some amazing work regarding the cause of infection. There's still much controversy, but apparently germs can enter a wound during surgery and lead to infection and often death. Lister espouses what he calls an antiseptic method of operation. The germs are killed by boiling all surgical instruments and treating them with carbolic acid."

Laurel made a second, somewhat longer cut, this time into the outer layers of fat.

"Dr. McDowell and his colleagues had no such knowledge in their day. It's no wonder that a procedure like this was practically considered murder. Do you know that when he first attempted this operation on the Kentucky frontier, a lynch mob gathered outside and threw rocks at his house? If he'd failed, he probably would have been strung up."

Kate became aware of the growing sound of angry voices outside the tipi and the drums beating in the distance. She imagined a fate similar to McDowell's might await them.

Laurel noticed the noise and glanced toward the closed doorway. "Don't worry," she said. "The Ute don't lynch. If I fail, I'll simply be cast out—along with Wild Elk."

The third incision cut through the final layer of fat. With a force that surprised even Laurel, the intestines were pushed up through the incision by the terrible pressure of the huge tumor, and they tumbled out onto the table. Laurel quickly gathered them in a pile, then pulled open the two sides of the incision and held them wide, making sure no damage came to the tubes where they entered the body.

"The retractors," Laurel called as calmly as she could. "Quick, the retractors," she repeated. Looking over at Kate, she saw that the woman was rigid with shock, her eyes staring at the awful sight of the intestines spilled out on the table. "Kate!" Laurel cried. "Kate, it's all right. She will be all right. But I need the retractors."

Slowly, Kate turned from the horrible sight and looked at Laurel, who nodded and said, "Please—the retractors."

Kate found herself nodding, and she numbly turned to the nearby table and picked up two of the instruments Laurel had called for.

"Put the first one here, by my right hand," Laurel said. Following her directions, Kate placed the flat, shovellike end in the open incision and pulled back the skin. "That's perfect. Hold it there." Laurel removed her right hand from the incision and took the other retractor from Kate, which she placed on the left side. "Here, take both now and keep the incision open as wide as possible."

Kate's mind cleared as she concentrated on the task at hand. When the incision was open wide, Laurel again picked up the scalpel and reached into the body cavity. Working deftly, her face beaded with sweat, Laurel cut deeper until she bared the huge tumor sac. Kate briefly turned away, but then found she couldn't keep her eyes from the eerie sight as Laurel cut the woman's Fallopian tube and freed the sac that held the gelatinous tumor.

At last the tumor was free, and Laurel reached in with both hands and pulled out the quivering, putrid-smelling sac, which she dropped into a bucket beside the table. "At least fifteen pounds," Laurel muttered in disbelief as she picked up the forceps in one hand and a needle holder in the other. She quickly tied off the Fallopian tube and several damaged blood vessels.

"Now, let's put her back together," she declared, forcing a smile.

Ever so slowly, Laurel lifted sections of the intestines and worked them back into place in the abdomen. Once she was satisfied that everything was in position, she removed the retractors and began to close the wound, using absorbable catgut ligatures for the inner layers of the incision and silk sutures for the final outer layer of skin. Finally, she covered the closed incision with a gauze bandage impregnated with cyanide of zinc and mercury, to ensure that no infection would develop.

"Will she be all right?" Kate asked.

"If that is the will of the Great Spirit."

As the two women stood in the center of the tipi, the drums and shouting voices grew ever louder. Kate shivered and crossed her arms, rubbing her shoulders.

"Don't be afraid," Laurel told her. "Perhaps I am like Ephraim McDowell. He performed an impossible operation because he believed God had a divine plan in bringing him to the frontier cabin of that suffering woman. He waited until Christmas Day to operate, believing that God's grace would then be at its highest. Like him, I cannot believe I was brought to this tipi simply to fail and be cast out of my community before my work even begins."

Laurel walked around the operating table and picked up the bucket containing the putrid tumor. "Come. Let us face them together," she said as she started toward the doorway.

"What are you doing with that?" Kate asked, pointing at the bucket.

"They must see that there was no child—that I did not destroy life, but cut away death."

With that, Laurel led the way to the covered entrance. She waited until Kate came up beside her, and then the two women stepped out into the sun and found themselves facing a crowd of over one hundred enraged Ute.

As the two women appeared, the drums fell silent and a hush fell over the assembly. Laurel took two steps forward and placed the bucket between herself and the crowd.

"The evil has been removed," she said in Ute, and then she turned to Wild Elk, who stood to the side. "If the Great Spirit wills it, your wife will be fine."

A smile born of hope lit the young man's face and eyes. He started toward the tipi, then turned back and tried to speak, but no sound would come.

Laurel motioned him toward the tipi and whispered, "He'e'e' Ahi'ni'yo'." As he nodded and disappeared inside, she turned to Kate and translated, "I told him to walk with the Spirit—to go to his wife with faith."

"He'e'e' Ahi'ni'yo'," a voice from the crowd called out,

followed by several others. Then the people began to disband and head back toward the nearby village.

"They will wait now and see if the Great Spirit smiles on what I have done," Laurel explained. "If she lives, everything will be all right."

Kate put her arm around the courageous young physician and replied, "*He'e'e' Ahi'ni'yo'*, my friend. *He'e'e' Ahi'ni'yo'*."

Chapter Four

After a large midday meal on the day after his arrival, Quint Burgess toured the compound of Halloran's Trading Post with his host. Leading the way toward one of the wood-frame outbuildings, Isaac Halloran eagerly waved his arms as he described the improvements he had made to his establishment.

"And it's all Alice's doing," he declared, "though I don't mean she's driving me like a slave or nothing. Nope, it's just that a fella starts to see the grand picture when he's got a family to think about. I want little Deborah to have the best of everything—and her mother, as well."

"Alice seems very nice," Quint said.

"Ah, that she is. Never thought I'd settle down with a woman, but I tell you—I should have done it years ago. Of course, I didn't know Alice years ago." As they reached the building, Halloran pulled open the plank door. "But enough blabbering about our womenfolk. Here it is— finished it just a few weeks ago. What do you think?"

Quint stepped into the large, empty room that comprised the building. It was thirty feet square, with a low peaked roof and a single wood-burning stove in the center, vented through a tin chimney pipe. The room smelled of fresh pine from the newly cut siding.

"It's perfect," Quint said. "Are you sure you want me to use it?"

"I'm positive. I think opening a school is a great idea.

And it's good for business. Think of all the penny candy I can sell!"

Quint walked around the room, inspecting the construction, and then returned to where Halloran was standing. Placing his arm around the older man's shoulder, he said, "This is a fine thing you're doing, Isaac. I hope you know that."

"Aw, forget it," Isaac mumbled, beaming with pride. "Just see that you turn this into the best damn school in the territory. Remember, one day my little Deborah will be a graduate."

"Don't worry. We'll give her a seat right up front."

"You'll do nothing of the sort," Halloran replied, widening his eyes with mock concern. "I won't have my daughter being spoiled by anyone but her father. You just treat her like everyone else."

Quint clapped him on the back and then walked over to check the woodstove.

"It's the best one of its size," Halloran declared. "Had it shipped in from Chicago."

"Won't you be needing it?"

"Never you mind, Quint. It was pretentious of me to order it in the first place. It's far too fancy for a storage shed. I must've sensed you'd be needing it."

"And where will you store your supplies if I use this place for the school?"

"We've been managing just fine so far," Halloran said, "and we can manage that way for a while longer. It won't take but a few weeks for me to put up another building—" he flashed a mischievous grin "—with your help, that is."

"Isaac, you couldn't keep me away!" Quint exclaimed.

"Good! Then it's settled. You'll turn this shed into the first Ute elementary school."

Quint nodded. "But you realize this is only temporary. In time I hope the Indians will permit a school to be built right at their village."

"Fine, fine. But I'm too old to be worrying about tomorrow. The thing is to make sure we've got the best damn school we can today. So, until tomorrow arrives, your school's got itself a home at Halloran's!"

The two men turned as the door creaked open. Little Bear came bounding into the room, followed by Lucas. Close on their heels came Alice Halloran, carrying her infant daughter. Alice was at least twenty years younger than her fifty-year-old husband. She was tall and plump, with soft, pleasant features and pale blue eyes. Her blond hair was pulled back in a bun, and the rolled-up sleeves of her coarse blue dress revealed strong, tanned arms that looked always ready for work. Like Halloran, she had a ready smile and a steady disposition.

"Do you think this building will meet your needs, Mr. Burgess?" she asked.

Several times already Quint had urged her to use his first name, but to no avail—despite her insistence that he call her Alice—and so he had given up trying. "It's wonderful, Alice. I am so thankful to you and your husband."

Lucas finished a complete circuit of the room and came over to the adults. Pulling at his father's sleeve to get his attention, he said, "I like this school." The words came slowly, with a faint slur.

"What do you think?" Quint asked Little Bear as he kneeled down and roughly rubbed the big dog's neck. Little Bear barked in reply. Standing back up, Quint turned to the Hallorans. "I want to thank you for putting us up in your quarters last night, but if you don't object, I'd like to move our things out here."

"But Mr. Burgess," Alice said, "there's really no reason. We have plenty of room—"

"It's not that. It's just that we've got so much to do to get the school ready, and it will go much more quickly if we stay right out here."

"Whatever you say, Quint," Halloran agreed, walking toward the door. "Whatever you say." As the others followed outside, he asked, "And how long until you head over to the reservation?"

"I'll go hunting first thing in the morning. If I'm successful, I'll bring the deer to Laurel later in the day."

"And if you're not?"

Quint smiled. "I suppose you'd have to order me a deer

from one of those catalogues, Isaac. They say you can get anything through the mail these days."

"You're quite right, Mr. Burgess," Alice declared. "That's where he got me," she added with a chuckle, and everyone—even tiny Deborah—joined in.

Quint turned his horse off the old wagon trail and rode partway into the forest. Pulling the animal to a halt, he patted its head to keep it from nickering and slipped off its bare back. He was no longer wearing his usual denims, wool shirt, and bearskin coat. Early that morning he had donned buckskins, adapted from the traditional Ute outfit, which had been handstitched by Laurel during their stay in New York. Rather than leggings and loin-cloth, however, he wore buckskin pants cut European style, with pockets and buttons. His lined leather jacket, fringed at the cuffs, shoulders, and hem, was authentic, as was the intricate beadwork design on the chest. And while he had substituted moccasins for his usual boots, he still wore his flat-crowned plainsman's hat and carried a Winchester repeating rifle slung across his back.

Tying the horse to a cottonwood branch, Quint eased the rifle over his shoulder and started cautiously through the trees. As he neared a clearing ahead, he slowly cocked the Winchester, muffling the click between his arm and chest. Keeping low behind the underbrush, he parted the branches with the barrel of the rifle and peered into the clearing, which was filled with a luminescent, early-morning mist.

Quint raised the Winchester against his shoulder and drew a bead on the deer—an eight-point buck. As he held his breath and began to squeeze the trigger, his mind silently intoned a Ute dedication:

> come to me, sacred brother
> your journey has begun
> bring us your gift, sacred brother
> your journey has begun

With a sharp explosion, the rifle bucked against Quint's shoulder. The deer leaped, staggered, and fell lifeless in the mist.

Quint entered the clearing and walked to the body of the buck. As he knelt beside the animal and watched the blood slowly drain from the bullet hole in its chest, he recalled stories Laurel had told him of how the Anasazi, the great ancestors of the Ute, were able to hunt for meat without taking the life of an animal. Through the power of a prayer of dedication, an Anasazi hunter could draw an animal to him and give it enough loving light so that its spirit would willingly pass on to the next world, leaving behind its body as a gift for the nourishment of the people.

The oral history of the Ute was not clear on how and when they came to this area. It merely was said that centuries ago many tribes were drawn to the powerful *po-o-kan-te* that remained in these valleys and canyons after the passing of the Anasazi, who lived in harmony with nature, unmolested by the other North American tribes, and mysteriously disappeared before the coming of the Ute. While Laurel was certain her people were not directly descended from this lost civilization, her people looked upon the Anasazi as their spiritual ancestors.

It was from the Anasazi that the Ute learned reverence for all life. The teachings had come through a line of medicine men unbroken since the days when the Ute first came to this land. No one knew the original source of these teachings—whether an Anasazi *pwu-au-gut* passed along his knowledge to the Ute before the ancient ones were all gone or whether the teachings came directly from the Great Spirit. But it was given for each Ute *pwu-au-gut* to initiate someone in the secret path before passing to the next world. And while Laurel had indeed studied many of the ancient ways with Surnia, she knew that she had not been fully initiated and that perhaps the secret knowledge had died with the passing of Surnia.

"Sorry I had to use a rifle," Quint whispered as he placed his right palm over the dead buck's eyes. Then he completed the prayer of dedication that had once enabled the hunter to gather food without killing:

Great Spirit in all things
bless this gift of life
that the giver and receiver
may grow and be renewed

come to me, sacred brother
your journey has begun
bring us your gift, sacred brother
your journey has begun

As Quint stood up, he heard the soft thud of hoofbeats on the forest floor to the right. Levering a cartridge into the chamber of his Winchester, he turned to the sound just as four riders appeared at the edge of the clearing. He immediately recognized them as the same men who had ridden north from the trading post when he had arrived two days before. Holding his rifle in a position where he could quickly bring it to play if necessary, he nodded as the riders cautiously approached.

The riders pulled up in a line about twenty feet from Quint, and then one of them kneed his horse a few steps forward. "Who are you?" asked the gaunt man with the stringy beard and greasy black hair.

"The name's Burgess," Quint replied, forcing a smile.

"Hell, that's a white name," one of the other men called out. "But he's all dandied up like a heathen brave."

"A damn Indian lover," a third cut in.

"Or a half-breed," the second man added, then spat a thick stream of tobacco juice at the ground.

"Shut up," the leader said over his shoulder, then turned back to Quint. "What've you got there?" He pointed at the dead animal just beyond where Quint stood.

When Quint did not reply, one of the men said, "Looks like a deer, Striker."

"Hell, it looks like our dinner," Striker replied, turning his horse to the right and heading in a circle that would bring him abreast of the deer. At the same time, the other three riders started to the left, heading to a position behind Quint and the deer.

Quint backed up until he was standing directly beside

the deer. As he slowly raised the barrel of his rifle toward the man named Striker, he heard a series of metallic clicks and knew without turning around that the other three men had drawn and cocked their revolvers and were training them on his back. Maintaining a calm composure, he said, "There's plenty of other deer in these woods."

"Then you'll have no trouble finding another, Mr. Burgess," Striker said, grinning as he stared at the rifle aimed at his chest. Making no move toward his own gun, he added, "Now, you wouldn't shoot a man whose gun is holstered, would you? Hell, my boys would drop you before you squeezed the trigger. So why not put that thing down? We've no intention of hurting a white man—we just want the deer . . . and, of course, your horse to carry him."

From behind Quint, one of the other men leaned forward in his saddle and asked, "What about his hat, Striker? I need a new one."

"And that Winchester," another called out as they all began to chuckle.

"You can try," Quint said with firm resolve, "but if any of your men makes a move, you're going down, Striker."

The gaunt man stopped grinning and stared for a long moment into Quint's eyes, then glanced beyond him at his three men. One of them had raised his revolver and was aiming it, as if to shoot Quint in the back. Striker's eyes widened, and he shook his head slightly until the man lowered his gun; somehow, Striker knew that this stranger would get off his shot even if they plugged him in the back.

"Looks like we've got a standoff," Striker said, his smile returning.

Just then a clattering noise was heard approaching through the trees from the wagon road south of the clearing. The clamor was punctuated by the plodding beat of hooves, and the combined rhythm served as a background for the voice of a man singing merrily off-key.

As Quint and the other men turned, they saw a rider coming toward the clearing through the trees, trailing a packhorse weighted down with camping gear and curious-looking mechanical equipment, all of which was banging in rhythm with the hoofbeats. The man's head was bowed, and he seemed oblivious to the gathering of men.

"If a body meet a body, coming through the rye," he sang. "If a body kiss a body . . ."

His song trailed off as he entered the clearing and looked up to see the five men with guns drawn. Apparently unaware of the danger, he broke into a broad grin and said in a thick British accent, "Good day, gentlemen. Are you having some kind of dispute?"

Quint stared incredulously at the obviously naive foreigner. He seemed a true innocent, perhaps in his late twenties, with wavy blond hair, a lean but muscular frame, and black wire-rim glasses that enlarged his riveting pale-blue eyes.

Forgetting Quint for the moment, Striker turned to the newcomer. "Just who the hell are you?" he demanded.

"The name's Paige," the young man replied with a disarming smile. He waved toward the other three mounted men, two of whom were now training their revolvers on him. "And there's no need for those things. You can see I'm unarmed." He raised his hands as he slipped down from the saddle.

"Now, hold it right there," Striker ordered as Paige started to walk toward him.

Halting, Paige said, "But if there's some disagreement over that deer, I thought I might be able to resolve it."

Paige cautiously stepped forward and held out a small leather bag that hung from his shoulder. As he shook the bag, the distinctive jingle of coins could be heard.

"I'm useless as a hunter, so I was hoping you fellows would give up your own claims to the deer and sell it to me," Paige explained with an eager grin. He reached into the leather bag and held up several gold coins, which he let slip through his fingers back into the bag. Quint stared at him in disbelief, but the young man returned his look with calm confidence, as if he were signaling Quint that everything would soon be all right.

Striker turned to one of his men. "Go see how much that idiot is carrying."

"Ah, then you are agreeable to my suggestion?" Paige asked.

"Damn fool," Striker muttered in reply. "We'll take your money *and* the deer."

"But that surely isn't sporting," Paige declared as one of the drifters dismounted and approached. Sighing in resignation, Paige again opened the shoulder bag and jangled it at the man, who holstered his gun and reached for it. With a brief nod at Quint, Paige turned sideways, drew up his right leg, and snapped it out in a brutal kick to the man's groin. As the man yelped and dropped to the ground in agony, Paige whipped a small pocket revolver out of the leather bag and aimed it directly at Striker. Simultaneously, Quint whirled around and trained his rifle on the other two men.

"Drop those guns!" Quint ordered.

After only a moment's hesitation, the men complied.

"And don't even think of trying it," Paige said, waggling his revolver at Striker, whose hand was hovering inches from his holstered gun. Reluctantly, Striker pulled his hand away and raised his arms, as directed by Paige.

Keeping his rifle on the two horsemen, Quint backed over to the man still writhing on the ground and disarmed him, tossing his gun near the deer. Then he went over to the horsemen, picked up their revolvers, and threw them over near the deer, as well. Finally, he pulled their rifles from the saddle scabbards and added them to the pile of revolvers.

As soon as Paige had disarmed Striker, Quint waved his rifle at the two horsemen and said, "Get your friend back onto his horse."

The men dismounted and hurried to their injured friend. Yanking him to his feet, they dragged him to his horse and unceremoniously lifted him into his saddle.

"Now get back on your horses and get out of here."

"But our guns . . ." Striker muttered as his men mounted up. "This is Indian country. You can't leave us without any guns."

"You should've thought of that earlier," Quint declared. "Get moving."

Striker glowered at Quint and then turned his gaze on the young stranger who held the pocket revolver on him. Cursing under his breath, Striker wheeled his horse and took off into the trees, his friends following at a gallop, with the injured man's horse in tow.

Lowering his rifle, Quint walked over to the young man named Paige and held out his hand. "My name's Quint Burgess. Thanks for your help."

As Paige slipped the revolver back into the shoulder bag and took his hand, Quint realized he was shaking badly.

"Damn," Paige exclaimed. "I can't believe I did that."

"Neither can I," Quint replied with a grin. "But it worked. Are you some kind of an actor?"

"Me? Hell, no. Just an English archaeologist out for a little adventure. Guess I got more than I bargained for."

"That's a fact. Did you think up that ruse on the spot?"

"Actually, no. When I was still a ways down the wagon trail, I heard a shot—it must have been you killing that deer—so I left my horses and came ahead on foot. I saw what those men were up to, so I hatched up a little plan to catch them off guard and went back for my animals."

"Well, it paid off real well," Quint said. "Where are you headed?"

"I've been out toward Utah studying some of the ancient Indian cultures, and I was headed to the Ute trading post to restock on supplies."

"That's where I've come from. Care to ride back with me?"

Beginning to relax, Paige smiled. "What, and miss a chance to run into those desperadoes on my own? You bet!"

"Great. Let me just tie that deer to my horse, and we'll be off."

Laurel Burgess gently grasped her patient's shoulders and tried in vain to ease her back down against the buffalo hide. "You must rest, Woman-Cheating-Death," she said in the Ute tongue, using the woman's newly chosen name. The woman, propped against a pile of blankets, refused to comply and continued her handweaving.

"How can she do that?" Kate McEwan asked, looking on from several feet away. "The operation was only yesterday."

Laurel glanced up at her friend. "After the pain she was in, she now probably feels as good as new. What amazes me is that she has any strength left at all."

"Will she fully recover?"

"If there is no serious infection. But she'll never have children."

"I'm sorry," Kate said with a frown. "How will you tell her?"

Laurel began to close her medical bag. "I don't intend to. It would serve no purpose."

"But doesn't she have a right to—?"

"Every patient has a right to know. But none of the Ute would believe it. They don't view childbirth the same way whites do. A child is a gift of the Great Spirit, who alone decides if and when a woman shall bear. My people would not believe I could know such a thing, even if I explained about the anatomy of the ovaries and how pregnancy would now be impossible for Woman-Cheating-Death. To them, it wasn't a tumor that I removed but some kind of evil spirit that was growing within her. And if the Great Spirit now deems that she should have a normal child, nothing I might say could prevent it."

Kate nodded slowly. "I think I understand."

Wiping away a strand of hair, Laurel picked up her bag and rose to her feet. "If I were to tell her, people would be convinced that I had put a curse on her to make her barren. That wouldn't help her or anyone else. It's better to let time and the Great Spirit reveal that a child is not in her future."

Laurel turned back to Woman-Cheating-Death and again urged her to rest as much as possible, promising that she would return the next day. Then she and Kate started from the tipi. At the entranceway, they were stopped by the sudden appearance of Wild Elk, who was panting after having raced from the village to the birthing tipi. He spoke hurriedly to Laurel and then headed over to be with his wife.

"What is it?" Kate asked.

Beaming with excitement, Laurel grasped her friend's forearm and said, "A rider is approaching the village from the east—a white man in Ute clothing."

"Is he carrying a deer?" Kate asked, picking up Laurel's enthusiasm.

In reply, Laurel grabbed Kate, hugged her close, and whispered, "Come. I have to be at the tipi when he arrives." Then the two women hurried out to the waiting buggy.

Children scurried into tipis or behind the skirts of their mothers as Quint Burgess rode bareback into the Ute village. He wore the buckskin outfit made by Laurel and had removed his plainsman's hat. Slung across his back was his Winchester repeating rifle, and strapped to his right calf was a sheathed bowie knife. Tied in front of him across the bay gelding was the deer he had shot earlier that morning.

Quint had been to the Ute village several times with his son, Lucas, when he had been a driver for the Durango Overland Stage Line. But today the settlement seemed subtly altered; he had the distinct feeling that he was coming home. He knew that Lucas would feel the same when he arrived in a few days. Tonight, however, was Quint's wedding night—a night for him and Laurel alone. Lucas, who had taken an immediate liking to the English archaeologist named Paige and his curious scientific equipment, would spend the night with Paige and Little Bear in the schoolhouse at Halloran's Trading Post.

Quint kneed his horse forward. Though he did not know the location of Laurel's bridal tipi, he had no trouble finding the way, for every so often one of the Ute women would dash out of her tipi and sprinkle a handful of flower petals on the ground, then disappear back inside with a nervous giggle. As Quint reached and passed the petals, another woman would appear ahead of him and repeat the process, creating a carpet of petals for him to follow.

As the last handful of petals fluttered to the ground, Quint looked ahead and saw a tipi framed in reds and

oranges by the painted evening sky. Seated cross-legged
in front of an entranceway bedecked with sprays of wildflowers was Mountain Laurel. She wore her beaded Indian dress, and her silver-streaked hair was long and loose,
with a delicate braid at each temple. She did not look up
to acknowledge Quint's approach, but continued weaving
a sash on a small hand loom that sat on the ground in front
of her.

Quint pulled his horse to a halt beside a tree about
twenty feet from the entrance to Mountain Laurel's tipi.
Slipping off its back, he tied the reins to a low branch.
Then without a word or even a glance at the woman
weaving in front of the tipi, he strode over to the entrance,
pulled aside the buffalo robe, and stepped inside.

As soon as the robe fell back in place, Mountain Laurel
looked up from her weaving. In the distance, dozens of
villagers were slowly venturing forth from their homes,
gathering in clusters and staring toward the bridal tipi as
they awaited Mountain Laurel's reaction to the white man's
proposal of marriage. With an impish smile, she picked up
the small hand shuttle and passed it through the shed
created by the crossed warp threads, then reversed the
warp and passed the shuttle back the other way. Her
action drew an audible gasp from the assembly.

With a furtive glance upward, Mountain Laurel could
see the disconcerted villagers whispering and pointing at
her. They quickly fell silent as she put down the shuttle.
When she stood and walked slowly toward Quint's horse,
there was a collective sigh, followed by a great cheer.
Then laughing jovially and slapping one another on the
back, the villagers dispersed and went back about their
business.

Following tradition, Mountain Laurel first watered the
horse and poured out a pile of oats for it to eat. Then she
untied the deer and pulled it off the animal's back. It was
a large buck, but she hardly noticed its weight as she
dragged it along the ground to a nearby outdoor cook fire.
Working adeptly with a large skinning knife, she carved a
choice section of the hindquarters and placed it on a spit
over the fire.

Half an hour later, Mountain Laurel removed the meat from the fire and cut it into pieces, which she placed in a small ceremonial basket given her by Singing Water. Covering the basket, she turned and carried it into the tipi.

Inside, Quint was seated cross-legged in front of the small central fire. Across from him sat Kate McEwan, who had been invited to participate in the role of a member of Mountain Laurel's family.

Removing the basket cover, Mountain Laurel walked to the fire, stood in front of Quint, and presented the venison. Rising, Quint reached in and took out a small piece. Kate came over and accepted the basket from Mountain Laurel, who reached in and took a portion for herself.

Kate carried the basket toward the entranceway. While Quint and Laurel completed their vows, she would take the meat to the other villagers, so that they might share in the ceremony. Then she would return to Singing Water's tipi, where she would be staying until a tipi was built beside the Burgesses' tipi for her and Lucas to use. Before departing, she paused in the entranceway and watched as the two lovers fed each other.

Holding forth her portion of venison for Quint to partake, Mountain Laurel intoned in Ute:

> *come with me, sacred brother*
> *our journey has begun*
> *take of my gift, sacred brother*
> *our journey has begun*

Quint leaned forward and took a bite of the venison held out by Mountain Laurel. Then he held forth his own piece and in English intoned:

> *come with me, sacred sister*
> *our journey has begun*
> *take of my gift, sacred sister*
> *our journey has begun*

Mountain Laurel took a bite of the meat. Then they both dropped the remaining portions into the firepit beside them. As the roasted meat began to sizzle and char, they spoke together, he in English and she in Ute:

> *our love is a flame*
> *our love is a flame*
> *may it burn and transform*
> *the lover and beloved as one*
> *the lover and beloved as one*

Laurel kissed her husband's fingers as he touched them to her lips. She caressed his face, her own fingertips touching his closed eyes and then tracing the line of his jaw to his neck and across his shoulders.

As they kissed, Quint slid his arms around her back and pulled her close. Laurel reached behind her, took Quint's hands in her own, and led him to a bed of buffalo robes and woven blankets to one side of the tipi. Standing in front of him, she slowly untied the leather thongs that held the dress closed at her neck. It slipped off her shoulders and fell to the floor.

Quint lifted his buckskin shirt over his head, then untied his pants and pulled them off. He leaned forward and kissed the front of Laurel's neck, his hands moving down along her arched back. Together they lay down upon the bed of robes, their hands and mouths searching, pressing, delighting in each other.

In the darkening village, a nightbird called to its lover, and a wooden flute picked up its plaintive call. Another flute answered, and soon others joined the melody, as interweaving layers of sweet harmony merged and diverged. Soft drums and chanting voices entered and deepened the song, which rose from the floor of the valley and filled the mountains and canyons to the farthest reaches of the Ute land.

As the sun sank in the west, the old medicine man took his place cross-legged before the *sipapu* in the floor of the *kiva* and felt the music of his people as it poured through the canyons of Mesa Verde and filled the chamber around him.

"A child is coming," the *pwu-au-gut* whispered. "That we may know one another. That we may know one another."

He'e'e' Ahi'ni'yo'.

Chapter Five

Lucas Burgess finished setting up his bedroll under the front window inside the schoolhouse building and then walked to the middle of the room, where Paige was examining and making adjustments to one of his instruments. Paige didn't hear him approach, and Lucas stood motionless and watched what the friendly young scientist was doing.

Lucas had taken an immediate liking to the easygoing man, perhaps because he sensed that Paige was a bit of an outsider, like himself. Quint had told him that Paige was from England and spoke with an accent, but from that description, he could only surmise that somehow Paige was different. The concept of an accent was still too obscure for a boy who was unable to hear even his own voice.

Lucas also was drawn to Paige's ready smile and easy laugh—the one trait that he still could recall about his mother, who had died when he was six. The similarity was enhanced by Paige's wavy blond locks, which were lighter than Lucas's sandy-colored hair but matched the descriptions he had heard of his mother's hair when she let it hang loose. In the one picture he had of his mother, her hair was pulled up in a sweep.

If she had lived, Susannah Burgess would have been twenty-eight—the same age as Paige. Lucas found himself fantasizing that Paige was her long-lost twin brother, and therefore his uncle. Maybe his mother and Paige were really English nobility, and a jealous cousin kidnapped them when they were infants to keep them from becoming heirs to the family fortune. Paige was sent to an orphanage, where he was beaten and forced to steal for his food, while Susannah was shipped off to America, never to be heard from again.

Lucas giggled at the ridiculous notion, and Paige turned from what he was doing and grinned at him.

"What is it?" Paige asked, but Lucas shook his head without replying. "Well," Paige continued, "I never thought of a surveyor's telescope as being so funny, but I guess it is a little strange looking. Here . . ."

He led Lucas over to the tripod apparatus and began to label each of its parts, speaking slowly and distinctly so that Lucas could read his lips.

"T-h-e-o-d-o-l-i-t-e," Paige spelled when Lucas didn't understand the word he was saying. "Theodolite. It's sort of a telescope used to measure angles." He pointed to a second tripod set up nearby, which held a two-foot-square, movable writing surface furnished with a flat rule with a set of sights for lining up objects. "That's a plane table, on which I record data and keep my charts." He could see that Lucas did not fully comprehend, so he mimicked the action of drawing on the table.

Lucas nodded and then asked, "What for?"

"The plane table?" Paige asked, indicating the instrument. "I take measurements, draw sketches, make maps. I'm an archaeologist." When Lucas appeared not to understand, he began to spell out the word: "A-r-c-h-a-e-o-l—"

"I know," Lucas interrupted, nodding eagerly. "You look for old places."

"Yes."

"But why?"

"To understand the new. Everything changes, yet everything stays the same. Things today aren't too different from hundreds of years ago. We just give them new names."

Though some of what Paige was saying was beyond the boy's comprehension, Lucas understood the general concept. He stared at the young scientist for a moment and then asked, "What is your name?"

"It's Paige. You know that."

"No—it's more. I am Lucas. But I am Lucas Burgess."

"You want to know my—my full name?" Paige asked somewhat hesitantly, and Lucas nodded. Paige was silent for a long while, and Lucas detected a hint of a frown. Soon it passed, and Paige put his arm around the boy's shoulders. "Will you keep a secret?" When the boy promised, he slowly intoned, "Wellington," and then spelled it out.

"Wellington," Lucas repeated, slurring the name. "Paige Wellington."

"No," Paige said. "It's Wellington Paige. I hate it. I never use it. Just plain Paige—that's what I like."

"Wellington Paige," Lucas said again. "It's nice."

Paige grinned. "You're lucky you can't hear it. It makes people laugh."

Lucas nodded with understanding. "People laugh at me sometimes—because I can't hear. But I won't laugh."

"I know you won't. That's why I told you. But you *will* keep it a secret, won't you?"

"I'll pretend I never heard it," Lucas replied with a laugh, and Paige joined in, clapping him on the back.

"Come," Paige said, leading the way over to the bedrolls. "Let's get some sleep."

From out of a deep sleep, Lucas jumped upright in his bedroll as a wet tongue darted up his cheek. In the thin moonlight that filled the single-room schoolhouse, the form of Little Bear hovered and pranced over him like a black cloud. The boy reached up and patted his dog's neck, but Little Bear immediately pulled away and ran to the nearby front window, where he lifted his paws and stood staring into the night, his body shivering in agitation.

Lucas could faintly make out the form of Wellington Paige, fast asleep in a bedroll about fifteen feet away. He quietly slipped from under the covers and hurried over to the window.

Standing beside his dog, Lucas rubbed some condensation from the windowpane and peered into the gray night. Some sort of activity was going on inside the trading post across the compound. The windows shimmered with the flickering light of at least one lantern, spilling out onto the front porch and faintly illuminating several saddled horses tied at the hitch rail—horses that had not been there when Lucas went to bed.

Though his impairment kept him from hearing anything amiss, he became aware of a discordant edge to the muffled rush of sound that usually filled his head. He covered his ears to see if indeed some noise was filtering through, but the heightened edge was unchanged, and he knew that it was not caused by sound. Instead, it reminded him of the feeling he sometimes got when the atmosphere became charged with electricity just prior to a storm.

Returning to his bedroll, Lucas tossed off his nightshirt and pulled on his pants and plaid woolen shirt, fumbling with the buttons until several were closed. While yanking his boots over his stockinged feet, he crow-hopped to the front door, where he snatched his jacket from a hook and then grabbed Little Bear's rawhide leash. The big black dog bounded over to him and eagerly pranced on all fours as he realized they were going outside.

"Shh!" Lucas whispered, kneeling down and patting the dog's neck as he hooked the leash to the collar. Little Bear seemed to understand and made an effort to calm down.

As soon as Lucas opened the door a crack, he was dragged through by Little Bear, and he had to struggle to hold the dog back while he pulled the door closed. With a few quick twists of the wrist, he wound the leash around his hand until the dog was close beside him. Then he padded across the yard to the side of the trading post. Reaching one of the dimly lit windows, he had to stand on tiptoe to peer inside.

Isaac Halloran stood in front of the service counter in heated discussion with three men. Lucas immediately recognized them as being among the four who had ridden past the wagon when he and his father had arrived at the trading post—the same men who had threatened his father early that morning when he was deer hunting. Lucas had not caught all of the story when Quint and Paige recounted it to the Hallorans, but he knew that his father had disarmed these men. They were well armed now, yet Lucas knew they could not have ridden to Durango and back in one day. Halloran would never have willingly sold these drifters weapons, so they must have sneaked inside and helped themselves to some guns before being confronted by Halloran.

As Lucas scanned the scene, he spied the fourth drifter standing to one side beside Alice Halloran, who was seated on a straight-backed chair. It was clear that she was very frightened and that this fourth man was guarding her.

One of the drifters—the gaunt one who seemed to be their leader—lifted the lantern from the counter and held it close to Isaac Halloran, as if to emphasize his words. The action served to light his face enough for Lucas to read his lips and make out part of what he was saying.

". . . give up this damned place or . . . burn it down . . . lose it either way . . . damned Indian lover!"

"We won't be run off!" Halloran declared.

"I said we'd buy you out," the man replied.

"Five hundred . . . ?" Halloran turned to his side and spat at the floor. ". . . what I think of your five hundred. Get out! . . . Get the hell out of here!"

The young drifter lowered the lantern. As he stared at the gray-bearded owner of the trading post, a malicious sneer spread across his face. He laughed abruptly and stopped just as suddenly. Placing the lantern back on the counter, he drew the revolver from his holster. For a split second he pointed it at Halloran, then he turned away and headed down the counter to where a dozen glass jars of brightly colored penny candy were lined up. With a wide sweep of his arm, he raked the revolver along the counter, knocking off half the jars.

As the jars shattered against the floor, Lucas turned and ran from the window, Little Bear close at his side. Throwing open the schoolhouse door, he raced inside and almost leaped on top of Paige.

"Whaa?" Paige blinked open his eyes and stared up at

the boy kneeling beside him and shaking him. "What is it?"

"Men! Four men!" Lucas blurted, tugging at his arm.

Putting on his wire-rim glasses, Paige pulled himself out of the bedroll and picked up his pants, but before he could put them on, he was dragged to the window, where Lucas pointed at the lights inside the trading post and the horses tied in front of the porch.

"The four men!" Lucas repeated. "They have guns!"

Paige understood at once. Yanking on his pants, he hurried over to the open front door and picked up the repeating rifle that was leaning against the wall. Levering a cartridge into the chamber, he turned to Lucas and said, "Keep away from the trading post. Understand?"

"Don't go alone!" Lucas pleaded, pulling at Paige's arm to keep him from going outside.

"I'll be careful."

"No!" Lucas cried, still holding on to Paige's sleeve.

Paige turned to the boy and kneeled in front of him. Placing his hands on Lucas's shoulders, he said, "Will you help me?" Lucas eagerly nodded. "Get Quint. Go to the village and bring Quint. I'll hold them off until you return. Can you do that?" Again Lucas nodded. "Take my horse. Can you saddle him?"

"Yes."

"Good. Don't use a lantern—you'll have to do it in the moonlight. Then ride as fast as you can and bring Quint. Just follow the road Quint took. Understand?"

"I'll bring Quint," Lucas replied firmly.

"Good. And whatever happens, don't look back—go as quick as you can." Paige pulled the boy close to him and held him for a moment. Then he released him. "Now take Little Bear and get going."

"Be careful," Lucas whispered, and Paige squeezed the boy's shoulders and smiled.

Picking up Little Bear's leash, Lucas slipped through the open doorway, turned left, and raced to the barn. As he quietly slid the barn door open, he looked back across the yard and saw Paige running toward the trading post.

Then Lucas entered the dark building and groped his way toward the horse stalls.

Paige glanced through the side window of the trading post long enough to take in the situation, then sprinted to the front of the building and up onto the porch. Without hesitation, he lifted the door latch and shouldered open the heavy plank door.

"Hold it!" he yelled as he dashed into the dimly lit room and leveled his rifle at the gaunt man named Striker, whose revolver was holstered again. The other three men had their weapons out, but like Striker, their backs were to the door as Paige burst through.

"Put down your guns!" he demanded as the outlaws turned in surprise. "Tell them to put them down!" Paige ordered Striker as the others started to bring their weapons around.

The three men stared for a moment at the intruder with the rifle, then looked uncertainly at their leader. At Striker's nod, they lowered the hammers on their revolvers and placed them on the counter.

"Now, move over against that wall." Paige waved the rifle barrel in the direction of the wall to his left. "You, too," he directed the tall, dark-haired man who had been guarding Alice.

Just then, Paige's attention was diverted by Striker, who was reaching toward the revolver still in his holster. "Take it out easy," Paige demanded as he again pointed the rifle at Striker.

Before Striker could comply, there was a sudden movement off to the side. Paige swung his rifle around just as the dark-haired outlaw leaped behind Alice Halloran's seat. The man held a six-inch boot knife at the woman's throat.

Isaac Halloran, who was moving to retrieve the revolvers on the counter, was caught midstride, and he turned back to stare in helpless anguish at his wife.

"Your turn to drop it," Striker intoned, pulling out his revolver and aiming it at Paige, whose rifle was still trained on the man with the knife at Alice's neck. "And do it quick, or I'll have Denny slit the pretty lady's throat." He punctuated the comment with a deep, guttural laugh.

Paige stared between Striker, Isaac Halloran, the two outlaws who were already picking up their revolvers from the counter, and the man with the knife at Alice's neck. He slowly lowered the barrel of the rifle and made no resistance when Striker pulled it from his grasp.

Working in the glow of the moon, Lucas Burgess reached under Paige's bay gelding and tightened the cinch strap, then looped the reins over the saddle horn. Grasping the horn, he slipped his left foot into the stirrup and was about to hoist himself up when Little Bear turned toward the trading post and began to prance excitedly.

Lucas saw that the dog was growling, and he quickly kneeled down and wrapped his arm around the dog's neck. "Shh, boy," he urged as he turned in the direction Little Bear was facing.

Looking across the compound, Lucas saw the front door of the adobe building jerk open. Someone was pushed out onto the porch, and when the man turned his face toward the light spilling from the doorway, Lucas recognized him as Isaac Halloran. Almost immediately, Alice hurried out and wrapped her arms around him, leading him over to the side of the porch. Two of the drifters came out next, their guns drawn on the Hallorans. Finally, Paige came through the doorway—without his rifle. He was being prodded by the outlaw leader, who had his revolver pressed against Paige's back, and behind them was the fourth man, who was carrying what seemed to be Paige's repeating rifle.

Some sort of an argument was going on, with Paige turning around and saying something to the outlaw leader, who shouted back in reply. Lucas could hear nothing of what was being said, and it was too far to read lips, but it was apparent that Paige had somehow been overpowered and was now a prisoner, along with the Hallorans.

Little Bear stirred beside Lucas, as if he was about to dash toward the adobe building across the way. "Easy, boy," Lucas said as he hugged the dog closer and took hold of his leash, shortening it around his hand.

Lucas stood and took a cautious step toward the trading post as he wondered what he could do to help. He had no weapon, and there were four armed men on the porch. He knew he should ride to the Ute village at once, yet he couldn't bear to leave Paige and the Hallorans in such desperate straits.

His thoughts were interrupted when the gaunt outlaw leader stepped forward and lashed out with his revolver, striking Paige across the cheek with the barrel. Lucas winced as Paige staggered backward but kept his footing. With his hand to his bruised cheek, Paige glared at the outlaw and muttered something. The outlaw merely turned to the man beside him and nodded. The man stepped forward, swung back the rifle he was carrying, and slammed the butt full force into Paige's belly.

"Paige!" Lucas blurted, stumbling forward as his friend buckled to his knees under the impact of the rifle. Beside him, Little Bear leaped against the restraining leash.

The unexpected shout turned all eyes in his direction. Though they seemed unable to make him out against the backdrop of the dark outbuildings, Lucas knew it would take but a moment for their eyes to adjust. His heart told him to run to his injured friend, but his mind prevailed.

"Stay with me," he whispered to Little Bear as he leaned down and quickly undid the leash, dropping it to the ground. Then he spun around and ran back to the waiting horse. Leaping into the saddle, he grabbed the reins and kicked the horse forward, turning him to the right toward the opening between the barn and schoolhouse.

"There he is!" Striker shouted, raising his revolver and aiming at the dark form galloping across the yard. As he thumbed back the hammer, the man lying curled at his feet suddenly sprang forward, slamming full force into his legs. The revolver fired almost straight up as Striker went down under Paige's weight. Instinctively, Striker swung the revolver down. It crashed against Paige's skull, knocking him unconscious.

"Get him!" Striker shouted at his men, waving toward the vanishing horse.

Already the others had dashed toward the edge of the porch, and the man with the rifle was drawing a bead on the back of the shadowed rider. A sudden black specter burst up from the ground below the porch and hurtled against the man's chest, sharp teeth piercing his left forearm.

The other two men jumped back in confusion as the dark form leaped back off the porch and raced off into the night. Raising their revolvers, they fired several times in unison, the explosions echoed by fierce barking that grew fainter as it blended with the sound of running hooves and then faded into the night.

Striker rolled the unconscious man off his legs and stood up. "Get him, dammit!" he shouted.

One of the men started toward the porch steps, but the man with the rifle grabbed him by the arm and stopped him. "I'll do it," he said. "The bastard's mine." As he leaped from the porch and hurried over to the hitch rail, he cradled the rifle under his right arm and rubbed his bloody left forearm.

"You okay?" Striker called out as the man untied his horse and hoisted himself aboard.

"It's nothing," he declared.

"Just don't lose that fellow, Denny."

"Don't worry, Striker. The bastard's as good as dead!"

The outlaw pulled his horse back and around, then galloped into darkness.

Wellington Paige felt his senses returning as if from a distant journey. Sound approached first, a pounding of hooves that seemed to grow louder and more distinct as it faded away, replaced by a jumbled shouting of voices. The taste of blood filtered into his consciousness, accompanied by the smell of leather, sweat, and dry dust. His eyes fluttered open, and the faint, flickering lantern light from a nearby doorway flooded his head with pain. It was then that he discovered his sense of touch, come back in the form of a nauseous knot in his belly and an explosive throbbing through his skull and across one cheek.

Memory returned, as well, and as Paige curled his legs up and tried to pull himself onto his knees, he prayed young Lucas had made it away without harm.

"Striker—he's getting up," Paige heard a voice mutter, and he turned his head and tried to focus on the figures hovering above him.

"The hell he is!" the familiar voice of the outlaw leader replied. A second later, a boot smashed into Paige's side and knocked him off his knees. Like a rock tossed into an unsettled pool, the pain stabbed at him abruptly and then flowed into the waves that already rioted across the surface, until any difference between the new and the old became indistinct. The waves threatened to carry him back to a place without feeling—without pain—and Paige struggled to remain conscious and afloat.

"Felders don't want us to kill no one," a faint voice called above the crashing waves. "Felders—"

"Shut up!" the more familiar voice shouted. "I say who dies, not Felders. And I ain't gonna kill him—just teach him a lesson!"

The boot struck Paige's head with the force of a boulder, then began to jab him in the chest and sides. This time there was no pain. Only waves of blackness. Only the whirlpool of night.

Lucas kept his horse to a full run as he crossed the rolling land between Halloran's Trading Post and the Ute village, five miles away. His eyes had adjusted quickly to the bright moonlight in the open valley, and he glanced over his shoulder every few seconds to see if he was being pursued, but so far he was alone. He could see Little Bear keeping pace beside him, and he was confident that should the dog tire and fall behind, he would have no trouble following the scent of Lucas's trail.

Lucas spied a fast-approaching line of trees just to the right of the trail. He looked over his shoulder and was about to turn back around when a dark form came rushing over a rise only a couple of hundred yards behind him. One of the outlaws was coming on fast, and Lucas had no doubt that he was gaining ground rapidly.

Realizing he was still a great distance from the Ute village, Lucas veered his horse to the right, hoping to lose his pursuer among the trees. Entering the woods, he began a meandering course to the north. He was unable to hear the rider behind him and could only pray that he had not seen Lucas turn off the trail.

As if to crush his hopes, a tiny burst of flame flashed among the trees behind him. Lucas caught sight of it over his shoulder and hunched down, expecting to feel the impact of a bullet striking his back. Instead, his horse screamed, then stumbled and fell to its knees.

As the horse went down, Lucas freed his feet from the stirrups just in time and was able to roll away, dazed but otherwise unhurt. As he sat up and shook his head to clear it, Little Bear suddenly appeared from out of the darkness and began to lick his face in concern. Fifteen feet away, Paige's horse was thrashing about in agony.

Lucas jumped to his feet and grabbed Little Bear's collar, then began to run through the trees. He could not hear the horseman approaching but was certain he could feel the ground reverberating with the crash of hooves.

Denny Whitcomb levered a fresh cartridge into the chamber of the Winchester rifle he had taken from the English dandy back at the trading post. He continued forward at a walk to where he could see a horse on its side, kicking and whinnying in agony. In all likelihood the rider had been knocked unconscious in the fall, but Whitcomb knew he must be cautious. He had no idea if the man had a gun.

The outlaw halted beside the wounded horse and looked around, his rifle raised and ready. Only faint beams of moonlight filtered through the trees, but he could see where someone had hit the ground some fifteen feet away, stirring up the undergrowth. Whitcomb walked his horse to the spot and then followed a line of trampled leaves through the trees.

As Whitcomb kneed his horse forward, he flexed the fingers of his left hand and felt the sting where the rider's dog had bitten him. "The bastard's as good as dead," he muttered.

The trail Whitcomb followed wound among the trees and bushes. Several times he reached places where the path was indistinct, but then he would pick it up a few feet later. At one such point, however, he was unable to find any more markings when the ground again became soft. He halted his horse and listened.

Whitcomb was about to start forward again when he heard a rustling of leaves behind him and to the right. Turning in his saddle, he saw a thicket of bushes near where the trail had ended. Yanking the reins around, he started back.

As he came up beside the bushes, Whitcomb raised the rifle into position. The bushes were only about four feet high, and he decided to push his horse through and take by surprise whoever was hiding on the other side. The animal resisted for a moment when he kicked it in the sides, but a sharper jab sent it plowing ahead.

Whitcomb found the man he was pursuing, huddled on the ground to his left. But as he swung the rifle around, he realized it was not a man but a boy. He hesitated only a moment, then proceeded to squeeze the trigger.

It took only that moment's hesitation for Lucas to let go of Little Bear's collar and for the huge dog to spring forward at the man with the rifle. With the leap of a mountain lion, Little Bear hurled into Whitcomb and knocked him off his horse, his rifle firing as it went spinning from his hands. The outlaw landed on his back, the wind rushing out of him, the ferocious black dog gripping his left arm in its powerful jaws.

"Let him go!" Lucas called as he raced over, the outlaw's rifle already in his hands and levered. The big dog let go of the man's arm but continued to stand over him.

"N-now, don't do anything f-foolish," Whitcomb gasped as he stared at the boy with the rifle and then at the dog straddling his legs. As he looked back at Lucas, his right hand slid toward the revolver that was still in his holster. "Just take it easy, boy," he begged as Lucas began to shake his head. "I swear, I didn't know you were only a kid." Slowly, he slipped the gun free.

Lucas was not looking at the man's lips and had no idea what he was saying. Instead, his attention was on the man's hand, and he shook his head again as he realized what the man was about to do. His own finger tightened on the trigger, his mind begging the man to leave his revolver alone.

Swiftly the man brought up the revolver. Lucas squeezed shut his eyes and pulled the trigger, and the blast of his rifle was met by a single burst from the man's weapon. Lucas felt a slight sting at his left shoulder as the bullet tore through his shirt. He opened his eyes and levered the rifle but saw at once that there was no need to fire again. The man was sprawled on his back, a fist-size hole in his chest filling with blood.

Little Bear watched Lucas drop to his knees and start to cry. The big dog turned back to the man on the ground and sniffed at the bloody wound, until he was certain the man could not hurt his master. Satisfied the man was dead, he bounded over to Lucas and began to lick his face.

"I'm all r-right," Lucas stammered as he hugged his dog. "We've got to get Quint," he added as he stood up.

Taking the reins of the outlaw's horse, Lucas lifted himself into the saddle and started back through the trees, with Little Bear trotting along at his side. A minute later he approached Paige's horse. The animal was no longer thrashing about but seemed to be in shock as he stared up at the horse and rider above him. A steady stream of blood pulsed from a gaping hole in his neck.

"Forgive me," Lucas whispered as he fought to keep from crying. Through a haze of tears, he raised the rifle with his right hand, aimed it at the animal's head, and squeezed the trigger. All the while, his left hand continued to sign, *Forgive me. God, forgive me.*

Chapter Six

Isaac Halloran kicked broken bottles and overturned shelves out of the way as he and his wife dragged the unconscious form of Wellington Paige through the main room of the trading post toward the living quarters in the back. An occasional whimpering cough came faintly from the nursery beyond their bedroom.

"She's fine," Alice reassured herself, trying to keep her voice steady and calm as she hoisted Paige's legs a little higher and struggled against his weight. "Just wanting to be fed."

"She'll be all right," Halloran replied.

"Will she?" Alice asked, and as her husband looked up at her questioning expression, he knew her thoughts went beyond the events of that night.

"They just wanted to scare me." His head nodded, taking in the damage caused when Striker had waded through the trading post with a broken-off porch rail after beating Paige senseless. "They won't be back."

"You know it's not finished," Alice replied.

Propping Paige against his knee and slipping his left arm out from around Paige's chest, Halloran reached back and opened the door to the back hall. "Hell, Alice, I've dealt with worse scum before. I'll just be ready next time."

Halloran fell silent as they brought Paige into the bedroom and placed him on the bed. He turned and stared at his wife as she stepped back from the bed and looked down at the injured man. He wanted to comfort her, and his hands lifted toward her briefly but then fell back at his sides.

Alice turned to face her husband, and she could read the pain in his eyes. She reached over and gently stroked his gray beard. "It's not your fault. There was nothing you could do—no reason for shame."

Halloran's eyes misted. "I shouldn't have let it happen. I should've been ready." His head sagged, and his shoulders shook with emotion.

"You couldn't have known," Alice whispered as she pulled her husband to her and cradled his head against her neck. "You had no idea."

"I should've known," Halloran repeated, his arms gripping around her back. "I should've . . ." He began to sob very gently.

"It's all right," Alice whispered, her hand gently caressing the back of his neck. Then she lifted his head off her shoulder, took hold of his hands, and gave him a firm smile. "I love you, Isaac. I always will."

Halloran looked up into his wife's pale-blue eyes. At a plump five foot eight, she was two inches taller than he, and though he knew that most men would not consider her looks to be anything more than pleasant, at that moment she was the most beautiful woman he had ever seen.

Halloran felt his eyes misting again. Breathing deeply and shrugging his shoulders to shake off the surge of emotions, he said, "You check on Deborah, and I'll get some hot water and bandages for Paige."

Alice pressed his hands softly, then turned from the room and headed down the hall.

Ten minutes later, Alice returned to the room to find Paige propped up against the pillows, a half smile on his bruised face. Halloran was seated beside him, wringing a strip of cloth in a pan of water that sat on the nightstand.

"Thank God you're all right," she murmured as she came up beside them.

"He's fine," Halloran said. "Just banged up a bit."

"I'm far from fine," Paige muttered with a mock frown, the words garbled by both his thick English accent and his swollen lips. "In fact, I think I'm dead. Must be, 'cause a beautiful angel of mercy just appeared."

Catching the drift of what he had said, the Hallorans laughed softly.

"Now, you lie back and rest," Alice said as she leaned over and felt his forehead.

Paige smiled, but his expression soon clouded, and he asked, "The boy . . . how is Lucas?"

Halloran glanced at his wife uncomfortably, then picked up the wet cloth and resumed wiping Paige's cheek.

Paige grasped and held Halloran's wrist with a surprisingly strong hand. "How is Lucas?" he repeated firmly.

"We don't know," Halloran replied. "It's been less than an hour. That fellow Striker and his men stuck around for fifteen, maybe twenty minutes after Lucas took off. They smashed up the place a bit and then got tired of waiting around for the man they sent after Lucas. Took off without him."

"Do you think . . . ?"

"Lucas had a good head start. I think if that fellow had caught up with Lucas and . . . well, the bastard would've been back here by now."

"Then where is Lucas?"

"I don't know. With any luck, he led that bastard right into the heart of the Ute nation. If so, Quint will be coming along soon enough."

"And if not . . . ?"

Halloran sighed. "I just don't know."

Paige pulled himself up onto one elbow and began to pull off the covers.

"What are you—?"

"I'm not going to lie around here when Lucas could be hurt or in danger out there," Paige said, rising from the bed. He felt a sudden wave of dizziness and grabbed the bedpost for support.

Alice hurried over and took hold of his arm. "You can't go out there in your condition," she insisted.

"Well, I just can't—"

"I'll go," Halloran declared. "I was only waiting until I knew you'd be all right."

"I'm fine," Paige said, giving in to his wooziness and allowing Alice to help him back onto the bed. "But hurry. Lucas may need us."

Alice turned sharply toward the window. "Shh," she ordered. "What's that?"

Halloran walked across the room, thrust open the lace curtain, and raised the window. He stared outside for a moment and then declared, "Horses. Quite a few of them."

"Striker . . ." Alice muttered, stepping to the foot of the bed and grasping the bedpost.

"I'll find out," Halloran said as he hurried from the room and rushed out into the trading post store.

Grabbing a shotgun from the rack on the wall behind the counter, Halloran yanked open a drawer in the counter and fumbled around for the shotgun shells. He stuffed a handful in his pocket, broke open the gun, and inserted a shell in each of the double barrels. Snapping the gun closed, he pulled back the hammers and headed out onto the porch.

Halloran stood with his legs spread and the shotgun raised as a half dozen riders came around the schoolhouse. Before they even crossed the yard, he knew who they were. It was the ghostly silence of their ride—or what seemed like a silence to a man used to the racket of stagecoaches and saddle tramps. There was no creak of leather or jangle of harness, merely a wave of spectral riders borne atop a phantom herd of wild mustangs, the only sounds being the snorting of horses and rhythmic pounding of hooves.

Lowering his shotgun, Halloran raised his hand in greeting the Ute braves, rifles in hand, reined in at the In the lead was Quint Burgess, still wearing his Indian outfit and riding bareback. He slipped down from the horse and hurried up the steps.

"How is—?"

"We're all okay," Halloran cut in. "Just shaken up a

bit. Paige bore the brunt of it, but he'll be fine. And Lucas . . . ?"

"He's coming along in the carriage with Laurel and Kate. He had a rough time of it. Had to kill one of them and shoot the horse he was riding."

"Good God . . ."

"But he seems to be handling it. Even insisted he was well enough to lead Laurel back to where it happened."

"Well, come on in," Halloran said, coming up beside Quint and, with an arm around his shoulder, leading him into the trading post. As they passed through the doorway, Halloran turned and waved the Ute warriors inside.

"Damn . . . look at this place," Quint exclaimed as he made his way through the overturned shelves and the debris scattered around the floor. "Striker do all this?"

"Yanked a post right off the porch rail and went to town in here while his boys kept their guns on us outside."

A figure appeared in the darkened doorway at the back of the room. "Hello, Quint." the man said.

"Paige!" Quint replied, looking up at the man in the doorway. "Thank God you're all right."

"I'm all *something*—just not sure if you'd call it all *right*." As he stepped into the light of the main room, he was grinning sardonically. It was then that Quint saw the mass of welts and bruises.

"The bastards," Quint muttered as he approached Paige. "Shouldn't you be lying down?"

"Hell, Quint, it's my face and rib cage that's hurting—not my butt."

Quint found himself grinning, despite the growing wave of anger within him. "Well, friend, when I get through with Striker and his bunch, it'll be a lot more than their butts that'll be hurting."

"That's for damn sure!" Halloran agreed as he ushered the two men through the doorway toward the family quarters.

As they passed from the main room, Halloran turned back toward the front door of the trading post. The Ute braves were huddled on the porch, staring inside but uncertain whether or not to enter. "Come on in, fellas, and make yourselves at home," he called, waving them in with a genial smile. "But pardon the mess. We weren't expecting visitors!" He spun around and disappeared down the hall.

The five Ute warriors gingerly entered the trading post and approached the aisles blocked by an assortment of cans, clothes, and brightly colored candy sticks. The man in the lead, a stocky brave in his early twenties, took a few hesitant steps into the aisle where shelves of coats and hats once stood. He carefully stepped over some jackets that had fallen in a neatly folded pile, but accidentally planted his foot inside an overturned derby with a fur band. The other braves, who were more cautious about wading into the debris, burst into a tittering laugh, as if their comrade had stepped into a bucket of bear grease.

The man spun around and scowled at his friends. Then he looked down at his feet and began to chuckle. He lifted his foot, picked up the hat, and held it in front of his face, raising his eyebrows and making exaggerated expressions of admiration as he carefully pressed out the dents made by his foot. With his friends staring in silence, he raised the hat over his head and slowly lowered it, letting it drop the last inch into place. With a look of smug superiority, he puffed up his chest and began to strut in a slow circle.

For a moment his four friends remained silent. Then they turned to one another, seeking courage to try on the clothing also. Finally, with the suddenness of Thoroughbreds breaking from the starting gate, they burst into the aisles and began scrambling for hats and gloves and coats.

It was only a little after one in the morning when Laurel finished redressing Paige's wounds. She had arrived with Lucas, Kate, and Little Bear in the cabriolet half an hour earlier, after visiting the spot where the outlaw had been shot and determining that he indeed was dead. Quint and the Ute braves would return there later to bury the body.

Though Lucas was visibly shaken by his ordeal, he had brightened upon seeing Paige, who had insisted the boy rest in the big bed with him. Now Lucas had fallen asleep, with Little Bear lying nearby on the floor.

Laurel decided to leave him with Paige while she went to the kitchen, where Kate was helping Alice prepare some food and coffee for the others. As she was about to leave the room, the door opened and Kate McEwan entered.

"How are the patients doing?" Kate whispered, nodding toward the bed where Paige and Lucas lay.

"Fine," Laurel replied. "I was just—"

"Who is it?" Paige cut in, leaning up on his elbows and picking up his black wire-rim glasses from the nightstand.

"That's right, you haven't met." Laurel motioned Kate toward the bed. "Paige, this is Kate McEwan, a correspondent for the *New England Monthly*. Kate, this is Mr. Paige . . ." She hesitated, not knowing his full name.

"Just Paige will be fine," he said. He smiled warmly at the attractive visitor and added, "Excuse me for not rising to the occasion, but my doctor has forbidden it."

Looking at him curiously, Kate said in a thick, affected brogue, "Aye, and I detect the sound of an Englishman, sure enough."

"Quite," he responded with a smile. "And are you from the northern counties?"

"Scotland, me laddie," she corrected him, "and proud to say my parents hail from Aberdeen. But, alas, I'm a Yankee, born and bred." She held out her hand. "Pleased to meet you, even if you are an Englishman."

"The pleasure is mine," he replied, taking her hand, "even though you're a Yankee—a bloody Scottish Yankee, at that." They both laughed.

Laurel headed back to the door. "If you'll excuse me, Alice wanted me to look in on the baby." When there was no immediate reply, she slipped out of the room and headed down the hall.

"So what brings an Englishman to the wilds of America?" Kate asked after Laurel had gone.

"Treasure!" Paige exclaimed in a hushed tone of mystery. "But not the gold doubloon in a treasure chest kind. I'm talking about your country's real treasure—the ruins of great civilizations lost for hundreds, even thousands of years, just waiting for an upstart English archaeologist like me to discover."

"And what will you do with your great treasure, once you discover it?"

"Study it, measure it, record it, and eventually be forced to turn it over to the journalists and bureaucrats, so that they can exploit it in the name of progress." He gave an exaggerated sigh. "Ah, well, such is the life of a dedicated Englishman of science."

"And you can bet that when the time comes, I'll be first in line, notebook and camera in hand, ready to exploit both you *and* your story. It's in my journalistic blood."

"And your Scottish breeding, no doubt. But I'm willing to overlook such flaws. Tolerance is in *my* breeding."

Kate tried to suppress her smile and look angry. "As we Yankees have discovered, the only things the English are good at breeding are revolutions."

"Truce!" Paige exclaimed. "In fact, I surrender. If the rest of the Scots were as sharp-witted as you, Miss McEwan, I'm sure we English would have granted their independence long ago."

"I accept your apology—if that's what it was—despite your sad misconceptions about my people."

"Well, it wasn't meant as an apology, but I'll make it one if you'll allow me to call you Kate, Miss McEwan."

"First, Mr. Paige, how do you know it's 'Miss'?"

"I daresay, I just assumed—"

"Perhaps you assume too much," she suggested with an impish grin.

"If so, I'm dreadfully sorry, Mrs. McEwan, and I withdraw my—"

"A typical Englishman," she cut in. "If they don't assume one thing, they assume another. To clear things up, you were right to presume the 'Miss,' where this lassie is concerned. And of course you may call me Kate."

"Or Kathleen?"

"If you wish. But we Scots prefer simple Kate to the Irish Kathleen."

"Then Kathleen it is," he mischievously declared with a

sweeping flourish of his hand, as if he were doffing an imaginary hat.

"And I'll call you Paige, if that's what you'd like," she offered, and he nodded in approval. "Though I must add you're a curious Englishman, indeed. The first one I've met without at least one title, four names, and a Roman numeral or esquire floating around somewhere near the end."

"That's because there is only one Paige," he intoned solemnly.

"And the Highland saints be preserved for that!"

They began to laugh, and Kate sat down in the chair beside the nightstand. "I'm sorry for being so feisty," she apologized. "It must be the hour. I really have nothing against the English—unless they're too pompous to be able to laugh at themselves—and you don't seem to suffer from such a weakness."

"Ah, but I have other weaknesses."

"Such as . . . ?" she asked, eyebrows raising.

"Beautiful Highland lassies."

"Thank God I'm American!"

Their laughter was interrupted by the entrance of Quint Burgess and Isaac Halloran.

"Excuse me," Quint said. "I thought we should make our plans."

"Yes," Paige agreed. "It's quite late, and I'm sure the Hallorans would like their room—"

"Nothing of the sort," Halloran cut in. "We've already set up a bed in the nursery. Alice wouldn't hear of moving you."

"But I don't want—"

"It's been decided," Halloran continued. "And if you don't object, we'll leave Lucas right where he is. Miss McEwan, you and Laurel are being put up in the guest room."

"And you, Quint?" Paige asked.

"I'm returning to the village with three of the Ute—the other two will stay here in case Striker and his bunch are foolish enough to return. We'll be setting off at dawn in search of them."

"Meanwhile, I'll send a message to Durango to see what I can drum up on that Felders person," Halloran said.

"Felders?" Kate asked.

"Yes. One of them mentioned the name—made it sound like he was in charge, or something. Did you hear, Paige?"

Kate glanced over at him, but he was staring downward, seemingly lost in thought. "Paige?" she asked. He stared at the blankets a moment longer, and when she called his name again, he finally looked up. "Paige, Mr. Halloran was asking if you had heard them mention someone named Felders."

"Felders? Why, I'm not sure."

"Of course not," Halloran put in. "It was when they were—well, you were getting it mighty bad just then."

Paige nodded absently, then looked back down.

"Perhaps we should let Paige get some rest," Quint suggested, noticing his distracted look.

Paige glanced up and smiled thinly. "Yes, I *am* a little tired just now."

"Then we'll be moving along," Halloran said, motioning the others toward the door. "You get some sleep. We'll talk in the morning."

Paige smiled again and nodded as the others passed from the room. The last to depart was Kate. She looked back and acknowledged Paige's smile, then watched for a moment as his gaze drifted. She closed the door quietly and followed the men into the main room.

Kate entered and looked around. Gone were the scattered piles of clothing and trail supplies. All the shelves had been righted, and everything was stacked neatly in place. The five Ute warriors were completing their work, piling up penny candy on the counter where the jars had once stood. The clothing they had tried on was all put away, except for the hats, which they still wore.

Seeing Halloran and the others enter, the Indians nudged one another and then headed over to the clothing section. Each removed his hat, and at a nod from the young brave who had first tried one on, they began to replace them on the shelves. It was clear from the way they reverently held each one and painstakingly brushed off the brims that they were more than taken with the fashionable headgear.

"No, no, no!" Halloran called out as he hurried down the aisle. He grabbed one of the hats from the shelf where the first brave had replaced it and thrust it back in his hands. "This is for you." He grabbed the next hat and clapped it on the second brave's head. "For you. And you," he added as, one by one, he returned each hat to the man who had been wearing it. Then he waved his hand, encompassing the entire room. "It's for the work you've done, putting my store back together."

The braves looked at one another in wonderment. They knew enough English to understand, but it took a moment for the full impact to settle in. At last they broke into broad grins and began to slap Halloran on the back in delight.

The Indians headed outside to their horses to await Quint, who walked up to Halloran and said, "We'll bury Striker's man on our way home. Laurel gave me the directions."

Halloran nodded grimly.

"Mr. Halloran," Kate said, coming over, "you were telling us the other day that this Striker fellow wanted you to sell out. Is that what he said this evening?"

"Yes, but I think he wants more."

"So do I," Kate continued. "There was an incident near the reservation. A woman named Singing Water was attacked by several men, and I'm convinced it was that same bunch. They told her that she and her people should get off the reservation or be buried on it."

"Something's brewing. That's for sure," Halloran said.

"Someone may have his eyes on the Ute land—perhaps this Felders person," Quint suggested. "We'll have to be on our guard. They may try to stir up more trouble."

"Isaac," a voice called, and they turned as Alice and Laurel entered. "Laurel is a bit concerned about Deborah."

"What is it?" Halloran asked in alarm.

"It's probably nothing," Laurel reassured him, "but she is congested and has a slight fever."

"She seemed so unsettled earlier," Alice said, "but I thought it was because of all the excitement."

"Most likely it's an ordinary cold, but we'll keep an eye on it. When I return to the village tomorrow, I'll make up some belladonna syrup for the cough. And I'll check on her every few days until it passes."

"You can't imagine what a comfort it is to have a doctor in these parts again," Halloran said. "Before you came back, it was either take care of yourself, go all the way to Durango, or put up with Painted Wind's chanting and herbs."

Turning to Kate, Laurel explained, "Painted Wind is Singing Water's brother-in-law." She looked back at Halloran. "How is he? I haven't seen him since I returned."

"He's stepped in as the new medicine man, trying to fill in the gap left by Surnia and your father. But he's no Surnia. And he's certainly no Josiah Fox."

"I heard that he's off on a journey."

"Yeah," Halloran muttered. "They say it's another of his vision quests, but I think he's in Utah."

"Utah?" Kate asked.

"Yes, to check out the new reservations," he explained. "Word is that the government's been quietly offering money and horses to some of the chiefs if they can get the Southern Ute to move to Utah and join their Northern Ute brothers. If you ask me, Painted Wind has gone west to check the lay of the land and see what's in it for him."

Halloran shook his head slightly and gave a look of disdain. "Vision quests . . . hell, I don't put much stock in such foolishness—or in Painted Wind. He's a friendly enough sort, but I seen the way his eyes light up when he looks around my store. I think his mind is too caught up in the good things of this world to have any room for visions."

Far to the west, two men sat beside a dying campfire in a grove of pine trees. Tied to a pair of trees at the edge of the circle of light, a muscular, dappled gray stallion stamped impatiently beside a smaller, though equally powerful black mustang.

"What did you think?" the man with the gray eye patch

asked. Even seated in the thin light of the campfire, he struck an imposing figure in a Confederate-gray suit coat and slacks that matched his full beard and single steel-gray eye. He was a Virginian who had fought with and tried to emulate Robert E. Lee—though only in appearance. He had lost his left eye to a Northern bayonet, and the fierce light that danced in his remaining eye came not from the campfire but from a restless flame that raged within his soul. It was a fire that made Jakob Felders a very dangerous man.

Felders was used to these long pauses, and he waited patiently for Painted Wind to reply. He squinted as the Indian stood and picked up a branch for the fire. Though Felders remained seated, he felt as if he towered over this self-styled medicine man. It was not merely their respective heights—Painted Wind was tall for a Ute at five foot ten, yet dwarfed by the six-foot-four Felders. Rather it was a state of mind. Felders was certain that he understood the complexities of a man such as Painted Wind. He was equally certain that the Ute had little notion of the kind of man he was dealing with in Jakob Felders.

After carefully positioning the branch on the fire, Painted Wind sat down and declared, "The land is worthy, but it is not Ute."

Felders was tiring of the endless circles of their conversations. Trying to maintain his composure, he said, "But it *can be* Ute land—for as long as grass grows and rivers flow. It can be Ute land if one chief is brave enough to show his people the way. Are you that man, Painted Wind?"

"The horses," the Indian said impassively.

Understanding Painted Wind's reference at once, Felders replied, "The government is offering two for each brave. Each squaw is to receive four bolts of cloth and a new iron kettle." He paused, waiting until Painted Wind looked up at him, then said, "There will be no rifles."

The Ute nodded in resignation.

"But the government's offer need not be all." Felders stood and crossed to where his saddle sat on the ground. Tied to the back was a long oilcloth package, tied with leather thongs. "The man who leads his people to a new land is truly their chief of chiefs," Felders said as he sat back down and untied the thongs. He knew that in recent years no single leader had emerged to lead the Southern Ute, and he hoped to play upon Painted Wind's obvious ambition. "You can be that leader. And such a man must have a new rifle."

Felders lifted from the oilcloth a new-model Winchester repeating rifle and handed it to Painted Wind. Seeing the eager light in the Indian's eyes, he knew he had won.

Painted Wind carefully examined the rifle. "It is true the land in Utah is plentiful with deer and fish," he said slowly. "And the water runs full and clear even during the days of the high sun."

"It is a land where a chief may graze his twenty horses and watch them grow strong and tall," Felders put in. When Painted Wind looked up at him questioningly, he added, "Yes, a Ute chief must have more than two government horses. I will add enough to make a full twenty for the chief's herd."

Painted Wind smiled. "These things are good for my people. When the chief is strong, all the Ute grow strong."

"Then you must be the chief who sees the new way and brings it to his people."

"My people must be left in peace to make this decision," Painted Wind declared.

"So it will be. It is a decision for the Ute to make, not the whites. But you must understand that our supreme chief lives far away—a ride of many weeks—and there is no leader out here to control all the whites. I'll do what I can to keep peace between our people while you're deciding, but I cannot control every white. I know there have been men who have entered the Ute lands to do harm. That's because more people crowd into Colorado every day and push these drifters closer to the Ute. You will not have this problem in Utah—it is a land beyond the eyes of my people."

"I will think on these things. You will have my answer when we meet again."

The Ute held forth the rifle, but Felders waved it away.

"The rifle is yours already, because we are friends and you speak true."

Painted Wind hesitated, then nodded briskly and pulled the Winchester to him. He turned and gazed into the low-burning fire. In the hot red and white flames, he saw the future of himself and his people. It blazed as brilliant as the summer sun.

Jakob Felders watched as the Ute stared entranced at the firelight. Then he leaned forward, grasped the end of the branch Painted Wind had placed on the fire, and stirred the embers until the branch crackled and burst into flames.

Chapter Seven

Lucas Burgess squirmed with discomfort as he looked down at his new buckskin trousers and moccasins. When he had arrived at the Indian village the previous afternoon, Laurel had surprised him with a Ute outfit that matched his father's. Though the buckskin felt surprisingly soft, the material was far heavier than his cotton denims and made him feel as if he were wearing a second layer of skin. But he loved the way the outfit looked, and he was determined to get used to the feel.

Lucas picked up his hat and started across the tipi. It was a crude, unpainted structure—used by Ute hunters in the old days when they followed the buffalo—which had been hastily erected upon their arrival from Halloran's Trading Post the day before. Lucas shared it with Paige, while Kate McEwan continued to stay at the tipi of a woman named Singing Water, whom Lucas had not yet met. Quint and Laurel's tipi stood twenty feet away, though at the moment Quint was still on the trail of Striker and his men, having left with several Ute braves at dawn the previous day, following the attack on the trading post.

As Lucas emerged into the bright late-morning sunlight, Little Bear came bounding over from the nearby woods. The boy looked up and saw Paige waving at him from the edge of the trees, where the horses were tethered.

"Lucas!" Paige called out. "Over here! Everything's loaded!"

Lucas and Little Bear ran to where Paige was adjusting the saddle on his packhorse. Only a couple of surveying instruments were attached to the pack saddle, leaving plenty of room for Lucas to ride.

"Do you still want to come?" Paige asked.

Lucas nodded his head eagerly and then said, "Are you sure you feel well enough?"

"I'm twenty-eight, boy. Don't you think I ought to know if I can stand a little riding?" He chuckled. "Hell, they hardly made a dent in me, and I've had a whole day to recuperate. Anyway, we won't be going far. I just want to get a better look at the land to the north."

Lucas was already grabbing hold of the pack saddle, and Paige hoisted him on top. The saddle was little more than a large square of leather, cinched below the horse's belly, with loops and rings to which equipment and supplies could be attached. There was neither a padded seat nor a saddle horn, so that the ride would offer little more comfort than going bareback. But seated atop the horse with the surveyor's telescope strapped to one side and the plane table to the other, Lucas looked as happy as could be.

Paige approached the black mare he would be riding and gently stroked its face. He had rented the animal from Isaac Halloran the day before and was using his own riding saddle, which the Ute had retrieved for him from the body of his dead horse.

Paige released the reins of the packhorse and handed them to Lucas, then mounted the mare. With a broad sweep of his arm, he waved Lucas and Little Bear forward and led the way north through the village.

Lucas grinned as Paige kneed the horse in a futile attempt to get it into a trot. The aging horse had its own ideas, however, and seemed to feel a gentle walk was sufficient on such a pleasant morning. As Paige began to slap the reins and kick the horse all the harder, Lucas giggled and trotted up along his right side.

"Thanks!" Paige grunted as Lucas laughed alongside him.

Lucas noticed Paige glance beyond him, as if reacting to someone's call. The boy swung around in the saddle in time to see Kate McEwan standing beside one of the tipis. She, too, was laughing, and he just managed to read her lips as she called out, "You ride like an Englishman!"

Swinging back to his left, Lucas saw Paige reply, "And how does an Englishman ride?"

"Like his boots are two sizes too small and his pants two sizes too tight!" So saying, Kate again burst into laughter and disappeared inside the tipi, leaving Paige no opportunity to reply.

"Women!" Paige muttered to Lucas as the boy turned back to face him. He slapped the reins quite vigorously and kicked the animal's sides with even greater force. Suddenly the horse reared up slightly and broke into a halfhearted gallop, which caught Paige with such surprise that he had to grab hold of the saddle horn to keep from falling.

Watching the way the young Englishman was bouncing along, his legs stiff and his rump bouncing painfully against the saddle, Lucas began to understand Kate's remark. Though he didn't know what Paige's nationality had to do with it, he found himself mumbling, "Just like an Englishman," as he kicked his own horse into a gallop.

Paige and Lucas set up the surveying telescope at the top of a rise three miles north of the Ute village, from where they could see many miles in all directions. After lowering the tripod to the boy's height, Paige showed him the various set screws and adjusting knobs and explained how to angle the theodolite horizontally and vertically. Having studied plane geometry at a school for the deaf, Lucas quickly understood the basics of how the instrument worked.

"Go ahead, take a look," Paige encouraged him.

With an eager nod, Lucas took hold of the theodolite and began to search the horizon. Catching sight of a bird soaring low to the ground, he focused in and identified it as a hawk. He tracked it to the west until it dove behind an outcropping of rocks and disappeared. He scanned to the north along the rocks, pausing to watch a jackrabbit feeding on some scrub grass. The rabbit stopped eating and sat up, raising its ears in fright. It looked so close through the telescope that for a moment Lucas thought it could see him looking at it. Then the rabbit darted away among the rocks.

Assuming it was the hawk that had scared the animal, Lucas angled up along the rocks toward the skyline. He stopped abruptly when a blurry pair of legs came into view. Focusing, he tilted upward and jumped back in surprise when he found himself looking into the lens of another telescope.

"What is it?" Paige asked, but Lucas merely motioned at the eyepiece in fright.

Paige stooped down and peered through the lens. He, too, found himself looking at a person staring back at him through another telescope. A few seconds later, he stood up and said, "There's someone over there, but we needn't worry. It seems to be a boy. Come on, let's go find out."

Paige closed the tripod and strapped the theodolite to the pack saddle. Then he mounted up and waited until Lucas did the same. With Little Bear leading the way, they cautiously approached the outcropping of rocks a quarter mile away.

Nearing the rocks, Paige raised his arm and called a friendly hello, but they saw no sign of the boy with the telescope. They dismounted at the base of the ten-foot-high outcropping, and Paige shouted again. They spun around in surprise when a voice called, "Hello," from behind them.

Paige and Lucas found themselves facing a muscular Ute, perhaps fourteen years old, who stood with his right hand raised in greeting. Hanging from a leather thong around his neck was a brass spyglass engraved with the words "U.S. Army."

"Hello," Paige repeated, smiling again. "I am Paige, and this is—"

"Lucas," the stranger completed. "I know of you. I am Three Eyes—son of Singing Water, nephew of Painted Wind."

"You speak English," Paige declared in surprise.

Breaking into a mischievous grin, Three Eyes replied,

"I must be speaking English. You sure as hell not speaking Ute." Seeing their startled expressions, the boy continued, "Learn it from traders. Uncle and I travel many times with packtrains. Lead them to Navaho land—sometimes beyond. Learn mighty damn good English." Turning to one side, he spat at the ground like a man chewing tobacco.

Three Eyes walked over to Lucas, who was standing next to the packhorse with Little Bear. Though the boys were the same height, the Indian was at least twenty pounds heavier.

"They say this one not speak. Not hear song of birds. Pretty damn bad." He looked with genuine sympathy at Lucas.

"I hear with my eyes," Lucas said in as clear a tone as he could manage.

"Son of a bitch!" Three Eyes whispered in astonishment, his eyes opening wide.

"You've had quite a liberal education," Paige said, trying not to smile. When the Indian boy turned back to look at him, Paige pointed at the brass spyglass around his neck and said, "Is that why they call you Three Eyes?"

The boy's face lit with excitement. "This glass eye a gift of my father. He took it from the body of a bluecoat whose spirit he released in the old days—the days of war."

"Is your father—?"

"My father has gone. He walks now with the bluecoat brother who left him this gift."

Three Eyes walked over to the packhorse and reached toward the surveyor's telescope, but then pulled back his hand.

"Would you like to look?" Paige asked. Though the boy did not reply, Paige could see the eager light in his eyes.

Three Eyes watched in fascination as Paige unstrapped the instrument, opened the tripod, and focused on a distant tree. When Paige stood back up and motioned for Three Eyes to look, the Indian seemed hesitant, as if to look through the telescope would be to usurp someone else's *po-o-kan-te*. He wavered, anxious to examine this elaborate glass eye, yet not wanting to trespass where he didn't belong. At last he resolved the issue by removing his brass spyglass and handing it to Paige, indicating that Paige should try it. By sharing each other's power, neither would be diminished.

As Paige looked through the old army spyglass, he glanced out of the corner of his eye at Three Eyes, who seemed captivated by the detail afforded by the surveying telescope, which had almost double the power of the spyglass. When at last the boy stood away from the telescope, he adopted a serious expression and declared, "That one hell of a glass eye."

"But it is so heavy to carry," Paige replied. "Your telescope is much better for traveling. Perhaps someday I will be lucky enough to have one like yours."

As Paige handed back the spyglass, Three Eyes caressed it with pride and muttered, "It *is* damn good. Pretty damn good." Again he spat at the ground.

"Would you like to ride back to the village with us?" Paige asked.

Three Eyes looked uncertainly at Lucas, who nodded eagerly. Smiling, the Indian boy declared, "You bet your boots, mister!"

Paige and Lucas walked their horses as they followed Three Eyes around the outcropping of rock to where his horse was tethered. The Appaloosa was drinking from water that had collected in a ten-foot-square stone structure, composed of four low walls, one of which was in bad disrepair.

"What's this?" Paige asked in excitement as he hurried over and began to examine the stone walls.

"Water catcher," Three Eyes replied offhandedly. "Been here since the days of the ancient ones."

"It's a cistern," Paige announced, growing more animated. "You say it's been here a long time?"

"Since the old days. There was a village here once."

Paige glanced around and began to make out signs of an old stone village, in such ruin that it almost blended with the rocky terrain. Rushing over to the packhorse, he removed the theodolite and quickly set it up beside the cistern. He scanned to the left and right and took a few notes in a pad that he produced from his pocket.

"This is fantastic," he declared. "I'll have to return with the rest of my equipment."

Lucas came over and touched Paige's sleeve. Getting his attention, Lucas said, "What is this place?"

Carefully pronouncing the words so that the deaf boy would understand, he replied, "The ruins of a village built by the people who lived in this area before the Ute."

"The ancient ones," Three Eyes put in, though he stood in a position where Lucas could not see him.

"The Ute call them the ancient ones," Paige continued. "They were the Anasazi Indians. We know very little about them, except that they lived around here for hundreds of years and disappeared at least five hundred years ago."

Three Eyes stepped closer and asked, "Why do you care about old stone walls?" He kicked the cistern. "No damn good. Hardly hold water to drown a rat."

"I'm an archaeologist," Paige explained. Seeing Three Eyes' confused expression, he added, "I study those who lived before."

"Why the hell do that? We live today, not before."

"By understanding what people did before us, we may not make the same mistakes they made. Then our villages will not end up in ruins, and our people will not become ghosts."

Three Eyes nodded, apparently accepting the concept, though not fully comprehending it. Then he squinted his eyes curiously and asked, "Are you one of the ancient ones, come back in the skin of a white man to unleash the *po-o-kan-te* of Mesa Verde?"

"Mesa Verde?" Paige asked. "What is that?"

"The sacred home of the ancient ones. In the cliffs to the west."

"I thought they lived around here, in stone villages like this one."

Three Eyes scowled and shook his head, then spat. "No, this place give up the ghost. Not enough *po-o-kan-te*. Ancients build new cities hidden in the cliffs. Big houses. More *po-o-kan-te* than you can shake a stick."

"Cliff houses . . ." Paige mused. He had heard rumors

of cliff dwellings throughout the Southwest, and several such ruins had been discovered in the Navaho lands to the south. Each had been an important archaeological find—as would be the discovery of Anasazi cliff dwellings.

"No one must know of these things," Three Eyes said earnestly. "The whites must not defile the land."

Paige wondered why the Indian boy was telling him these things if it was supposed to be a secret from the whites, and he assumed it was because they shared a personal power—or *po-o-kan-te*, as the Ute called it—in their telescopes.

"Have you seen this Mesa Verde?" he asked cautiously.

"We do not go there, but all our people know where the sacred land lies. It is where we journey when we die."

Paige was not sure whether Three Eyes was referring to an actual journey his people made to the site of these supposed cliff dwellings—perhaps to a burial site—or to some spiritual odyssey the Ute expected to make after death. For the moment he decided not to press the boy, but to work at slowly gaining his trust.

"It would be good to see this Mesa Verde," Paige declared solemnly as he packed up the surveying telescope and prepared to depart for the Ute village. "It would be a good thing to see it with our glass eyes."

"It would!" Three Eyes exclaimed as he leaped atop his Appaloosa. "Son of a bitch, it would!"

With a piercing *"He'e'e'!"* Three Eyes kicked his horse into a gallop and wheeled it in the direction of home.

Two days later, Paige stood outside Halloran's Trading Post, his packhorse weighted down with his equipment and new supplies, the rented black mare saddled and ready to go. As he was saying good-bye to Isaac and Alice Halloran, a buckboard arrived from the Ute village, bearing Laurel, Kate, Lucas, and Little Bear. Driving the wagon was Quint Burgess.

"Hello, Quint!" Paige called as the wagon entered the yard. "I see you got back all right. Any sign of Striker?"

"None," Quint said as he pulled the wagon team to a halt. He stood and helped the women down.

"Think they're still in the area?" Halloran asked.

"We tracked them north almost to Durango. At the Animas River they turned east. Who knows? Maybe they went clear to Denver."

"Getting ready to leave?" Kate asked as she approached Paige.

"Just about. I was planning to stop at the village and say good-bye—and give you all my thanks."

"No thanks needed," Laurel assured him. "We're just thankful you were here to watch out for Lucas." As she spoke, the boy walked over and smiled at Paige, who placed a hand on his shoulder.

"Not to mention what you did for me," Quint put in.

"And for us," Alice Halloran added.

"Well, I suppose we all have each other to thank," Paige said, smiling at each of his new friends.

"I hope your work is as rewarding as you desire," Laurel said as she went over and shook his hand. "If you'll excuse me, I'd like to look in on little Deborah." She said a final good-bye and then followed Alice into the building.

Quint approached next. "Lucas and I had best be getting to work on our schoolhouse. Thanks again, Paige."

The two men shook hands, then Quint motioned for Lucas to say good-bye and come with him.

Lucas turned to Paige. "Thank you," he said aloud, mouthing but not speaking the additional word, "Wellington." Paige grinned and tousled his hair.

"Come on," Quint said, heading toward the schoolhouse.

Lucas gave Paige a quick hug and followed after his father, leaving Halloran and Kate standing with Paige.

"Uh, er, I think I better be seeing if Quint needs anything," said Halloran. "That is, if you've got everything you need."

"I do," Paige replied, his eyes remaining on Kate.

"Then it's good-bye from me, too. But you hurry back as soon as you finish whatever it is you're doing out there in the wilderness."

"I will." Paige turned to Halloran. "And thanks, Isaac."

Halloran mumbled something unintelligible and then headed after Quint and Lucas. Little Bear seemed to realize he, too, was unwanted, and he trotted off beside Halloran.

"So you're really going back out there," Kate said once they were alone. "Even with that Striker bunch still on the loose?"

"They won't bother me," Paige insisted. "What would they want with a skinny Englishman?" He gave a self-deprecating grin.

"They just might think you're off hunting buried treasure. Is that what you're really up to, by any chance?"

"Buried civilizations, that's my treasure."

"Are you sure that's all there is to it?"

"What do you mean?" Paige asked.

"Quint says you have a lot of books on geology."

"Knowing the geological features of an area is a big part of archaeology."

"It's also a big part of mining," Kate said pointedly.

"I don't see—"

"I really have no desire to pry," Kate cut in, "but I thought it best to clear the air. After all you've done for Quint and Laurel, they would never ask directly."

"But leave it to a Scot," Paige interjected, forcing a chuckle.

"No, leave it to a journalist—and a friend. There's been a lot of talk about the mining companies wanting to come onto the reservation—maybe even force out the Ute. It would stand to reason that first they would want to know how profitable the land might be."

"And you think I'm working for those mining companies?"

"I don't know, and I don't intend to ask."

"That doesn't sound like a journalist—a female journalist, yet."

"What do you mean *female*?" Kate asked, her temper flaring. "I should've known an Englishman would have such a backward attitude about the so-called proper role of women."

Paige began to laugh and blurted out, "I'd be a real Union Jackass if I thought that I—or anybody else, for that matter—could fit Kate McEwan into any sort of *proper role*. The man doesn't exist who could tame the likes of you, Miss McEwan, and I'd be the last to try."

"Well, that's one burden off my mind, Mr. Paige," she replied. "That is *Mr*. Paige, is it not? Or is Paige your first name? Oh, yes, I remember that we decided not to ask about that little mystery, either. A real man of mystery, you are." She stared at him closely. "Or perhaps a man with something to hide?"

"With the likes of a journalist like you, I'd say we all have something to hide," Paige declared, turning away under the intensity of her gaze.

As Paige walked to his horse and lifted himself into the saddle, Kate came over and stared up at him.

"I daresay you're blushing, *Mr*. Paige," she mocked. "Why, your face is all red."

Paige looked unusually uncomfortable, and indeed his pale skin had the ruddy tone of a sunburn. Forcing a less-than-easy laugh, he replied, "If I'm red, it's not from having something to hide. It's just the natural reaction of an Englishman to a bloody-tempered Scot. Good day, Miss McEwan." He kneed his horse forward and led the packhorse toward the west.

Kate stood for a moment watching him leave. Feeling suddenly ashamed of the way she had prodded him, she ran toward him and shouted, "Paige, I'm sorry." When he pulled up and turned in the saddle, she continued, "You're right—it's my Scottish temper. It always gets me in trouble."

"Thank God you're only half Scottish," Paige declared, laughing softly. "We'd really need those Highland saints of yours to protect us if you were certified, one hundred percent!"

Kate joined his laughter, then raised and shook her fist. "Well, don't ever forget who you're dealing with, Mr. English Archaeologist. I may be only half Scottish, but I pack twice the punch of any bottle of certified, one hundred proof Scotch you'll ever encounter!"

"That's why I stick to sherry. Far more civilized."

"And far more dull!"

Paige gave a broad frown and then suddenly burst into laughter again. "You're a bloody original, Kate!" he shouted as he kicked his horse into a feeble trot and continued on his way. "A genuine, one hundred percent, bloody original!"

Sitting on his horse atop a rise a mile west of Halloran's Trading Post, Three Eyes held his brass spyglass steady as he tracked the white rider with the wavy, golden hair. The man's packhorse was fully laden with satchels, pots and pans, and that mysterious three-legged glass eye; it was clear that he was embarking on a journey that would take him far beyond the Ute village.

"Mesa Verde," Three Eyes whispered, lowering the spyglass and letting it hang against his chest. He imagined himself standing among the sacred cliff dwellings with this man and his unusual seeing device. He could already feel the *po-o-kan-te* flowing through him, and the spyglass given to him by his father seemed to vibrate with this new energy.

"Mesa Verde," he repeated, grasping the reins of his horse. "You bet your boots, mister!"

Three Eyes kicked his horse into a run and went racing down the slope toward Wellington Paige, the brass spyglass bouncing against his chest.

"Smallpox."

Alice Halloran looked up in fear as Laurel made the pronouncement. "Are you certain?" she asked.

"It's just a possibility. But we must be prepared."

Alice laid her sleeping eight-month-old daughter in the crib. "But her cough has eased," she pointed out, "and her cheeks are so rosy. I had thought she was on the mend."

"Her temperature is up, and her rosy cheeks aren't a good sign." Laurel raised the baby's shirt, revealing a swath of pink across her belly. "Neither is this. A rash like this is one of the indications of smallpox."

Alice's eyes filled with tears, and her lips trembled.

"Let's not worry when we may not have to," Laurel said. "A rash is sometimes merely that—just a rash. But to be safe, I'm going to send to Durango for some vaccine."

"Medicine?" Alice asked.

"Not in the usual sense. If Deborah has smallpox, I'm afraid there is little we can do but wait it out and treat the symptoms. The vaccine is for everyone who comes in contact with her. It keeps them from coming down with it."

"But what about Debbie?"

"She is strong, and there's every reason to expect a full recovery. Babies handle this thing very well—much better than the rest of us. It's the older children that I'm worried about—and the adults."

"But there aren't any older children—"

"Smallpox is extremely contagious," Laurel explained. "If Deborah has it, then you and your husband will have to be vaccinated as soon as possible. Even so, you already may have passed it along to some of the Indians who come to the trading post. We could have an epidemic in a matter of weeks if we don't check its spread at once."

"Will this . . . vaccine help?"

"Yes, but only if the Ute allow me to administer it," Laurel pronounced somberly.

"But why wouldn't they?"

"Smallpox is a white man's disease. The Ute may not trust white man's medicine to deal with it."

Alice covered her daughter with a blanket and led the way from the room. At the door, she paused and asked, "Is there anything we can do . . . for Debbie?"

"Yes. I'll write out exactly what to do, and I'll come back tomorrow to check on her. Meanwhile, I'll check for any signs of smallpox among the Ute. The vaccine should arrive in a few days, and by then we'll know for sure what Deborah has. Until then, you must keep her quiet and comfortable, and make sure no one else enters her room."

"Even Isaac?"

"I'm afraid so. For now, it would be best for you alone to care for Deborah, while Isaac handles the customers. And until you're vaccinated, it would be a good idea for you to move into the nursery. Perhaps if we take enough precautions, we can keep this thing from spreading."

Alice fought back her tears. "Smallpox . . ." she muttered, shaking her head in disbelief. She began to cry.

"I may be wrong, but you'd best be prepared," Laurel whispered. "I'm sorry." She wrapped her arms around Alice's shoulders and held the sobbing woman tight.

Chapter Eight

Even before Painted Wind saw the Ute village in the valley beyond, he could smell the familiar cottonwood and pine of the cook fires and the pungent scent of buffalo and deer hide stretched over lodge poles or drying on racks in the sun. Topping the final rise, he pulled his black mustang to a halt and stared down at the tipis below.

Painted Wind slid to the ground and opened one of the pair of leather bags slung over the back of the mustang. He took out a buckskin shirt, beaded and painted with a representation of a rainbow wind sweeping down from the sky, and pulled it over his head, covering his bare chest. Next he removed a pair of buckskin leggings and stepped into them, attaching them to the waistband of his loincloth. Finally he unwrapped the new Winchester repeating rifle given him by Jakob Felders and slung it across his back. He leaped back onto his horse and started down into the valley.

Though it was warm enough for him to have remained in his loincloth, Painted Wind viewed his return to the village as a ceremonial occasion. At only thirty-nine, he was already considered a spiritual leader of the Ute—a role he adopted upon the disappearance of Surnia two years previously. But there were those who remembered that the revered Surnia had turned him away as an apprentice, and they were less willing to accept him as *pwu-au-gut*, awaiting some clear sign that he was touched by the *po-o-kan-te* of the medicine man.

It was true that he understood the secrets of plants and herbs, and many Ute sought his counsel on matters of health, but others had lost faith in the ancient healing arts, transferring that faith to the medicine of the white man, brought to them by Josiah "Silver" Fox.

Painted Wind knew that the *po-o-kan-te* of Silver Fox lay not in pills and potions but in the people's faith and respect. But now Silver Fox was in that heaven proclaimed by his people, just as Surnia had passed to the Spirit World. There was only one other whom the people held in respect as a healer—Mountain Laurel, who had been trained by both Surnia and Silver Fox—and she had given up the way of her mother's people to live in the land of her father.

Painted Wind had been patient, but he saw now that *his* time had come. In leading the Ute to a new home in the west beyond the influence of the whites, he would bring peace forever to his people and claim the heritage that rightfully was his—the way of the supreme *pwu-au-gut*—a heritage forfeited by Surnia when he allowed a white physician to enter the land and blind his people to the true way.

Keeping his horse at a high-stepping gait as he rode among the tipis, Painted Wind looked neither left nor right and did not acknowledge the greetings of the men and women who witnessed his arrival. Neither did he slow his horse or change direction to dodge the exuberant youngsters who swarmed in front of him. Like a ship cutting through the sea, he headed for his tipi, where he knew his brother's wife would have his bed prepared and a hot meal waiting.

Painted Wind felt a warm surge of pride at the love and respect shown him by his people. It was a fitting thing for a man of great *po-o-kan-te* such as he, and it was a good thing for the people.

Yes, he reminded himself, *when the chief is strong, all the Ute grow strong*.

*   *   *

Singing Water sat in her tipi staring at the fire, her sewing untouched upon her lap, her thoughts on her brother-in-law and her son. Painted Wind was overdue from his journey to Utah, and she worried that he would be displeased to find out that she had allowed Three Eyes to travel west with a white man. Unable to concentrate on her work, she was about to throw it down in frustration when the door covering was thrust aside and a man entered.

Looking up in surprise, she saw Painted Wind framed by the sunlight spilling through the open doorway. Her heart leaped with joy, but she allowed herself only a restrained smile. As she listened to him speak, his deep voice gave the Ute words the rich tone of the evening wind pouring through the opening at the peak of the tipi. She almost did not hear what he said, but instead envisioned herself lying each evening by the fire, her brother-in-law holding her in his arms as they listened to the wind.

"It is good to be home," Painted Wind repeated when at first Singing Water did not respond.

"We are glad you are back," she finally replied.

"Where is the boy?" he asked as he came forward and kneeled in front of the fire. "I did not see his horse when I tethered mine."

Singing Water looked down. "He journeyed west. I thought perhaps you would pass along the trail."

"No. I took the trail north of the canyons. Was he looking for me?"

Her eyes glanced up at him in fear. "No. He is traveling as a guide . . . for a white man."

"A white?" Painted Wind asked, scowling. "What is this thing he is doing? Is it a wagon trader he is guiding?"

"No, it is not a trader. This white man travels with a packhorse and many strange machines with which to see and measure the ancient villages. He carries a giant glass eye, like my son's, but which stands upon three legs."

"A *surveyor*," Painted Wind concluded, using the English word.

"I do not know of these things. I only know that this man is a friend of the people. A friend . . ." She hesitated, trying to guess her brother-in-law's reaction. "A friend of Mountain Laurel."

"Mountain Laurel," he said without emotion, as if he wasn't surprised to hear her name. "Then she has returned."

"Yes."

"And she brings her white medicine?" he asked.

"She has taken her father's place."

"But not her grandfather's," he said, more a statement than a question.

"She does not speak of her grandfather or of the old ways. She speaks of new ways, and she comes with a new family." She waited until Painted Wind was looking up at her. "She has returned with a husband, the man who drove the stagecoach, and his son, the boy who does not hear."

Like the rest of the Ute, Painted Wind had heard that Laurel had chosen a white husband while she was living in the East. "Then she no longer is one of the people," he declared solemnly.

"But her mother—"

"She has chosen her father's path." Painted Wind stood and smiled. "It is as it should be. I have returned to lead our people to a new home, but first I must face this test. Mountain Laurel will not stop me. I will prove myself worthy in the eyes of the Great Spirit and the people."

Painted Wind headed back to the tipi entrance. Before departing, he turned around and said, "I will be sitting in my tipi, receiving visitors." He looked around at the flowers that adorned the tipi and added in a soft voice, "Your tipi looks very pretty, my little sister."

Singing Water nodded as he left. As soon as the tipi flap was closed again, she allowed herself to smile. "My little sister," she repeated, warmed by his gentle tone.

It was nearly dark outside when Singing Water returned to her brother-in-law's tipi to clean up the dinner she had served him earlier. He was in a somber mood as she went about gathering the serving pot and other dishes.

"I have heard strange things," he said, looking up and

fixing her with a heavy gaze. "You will tell me of these things Mountain Laurel is doing to my people."

"I do not understand," Singing Water replied, putting down the dishes and coming up beside Painted Wind, who sat cross-legged by the fire. "She is only following—"

He reached up and grasped her wrist, pulling her down until she was kneeling beside him. "You will tell me what she has done—how she has used her knives to cut the flesh of Wild Elk's woman. He has told me of her white man's medicine, and he says it is a great gift to the people."

"Yes, it is so," Singing Water replied with a tentative smile. "It is true that after the cutting and the evil thing was removed, Woman-Cheating-Death was healed and—"

"You will not call her that!" Painted Wind demanded, clutching her wrist tighter. "It is an evil name, and it is an evil thing Mountain Laurel has done."

"But the woman got better after Mountain Laurel removed this thing growing within her that was not a child."

"It was a trick," he insisted. "She killed the baby and mutilated it so it would not look like a child."

Singing Water gasped in horror. "But Mountain Laurel would never—"

"She is no longer one of the people. She is in league with dark spirits, and if she did not mutilate the child, then the spirits did it and fooled her as well. The people do not cut into one another. It goes against the way."

"But if one of our people is shot, don't we remove the bullet?" Singing Water asked.

"What man puts into the body, man may take out. But a gift of the Great Spirit must be left to the Great Spirit to bring forth." Painted Wind abruptly let go of her hand and turned to the fire.

In a gentle tone, Singing Water asked, "Have you spoken to Mountain Laurel of these things?"

"I sent for her, but she is not here. They say she has gone to work her medicine on the little white baby at the trading post. She is there with her family and the white woman with the Spirit Catcher picture machine."

"When she returns, she will explain what she has done, and you will see these things are good."

"No," he declared abruptly, "it is a bad thing for our village. This is bad medicine Mountain Laurel has brought our people. If Wild Elk's woman seems better, it is a trick of the evil spirits Mountain Laurel has conjured. I know these things to be true, and I will prove it to my people."

"But how?" she asked timorously.

Painted Wind's eyes narrowed as he continued to gaze at the flames. "I will chant the Song of Renewal and drive out the spirits infesting Wild Elk's woman. I will prove these things I say. The people will see that when the spirits have gone, the health of Wild Elk's woman will decline."

"B-but she could die," Singing Water stammered.

"She is dead already!" Painted Wind exclaimed. "Her only hope is to free herself of the evil spirits and allow me to restore her to life."

Singing Water stood up and backed away from her brother-in-law. "What if you are wrong?" she asked. "This is a dangerous thing you do."

"You doubt that I am right?" he asked incredulously. "Then be gone from me, woman. You will see that I have spoken the truth and that Wild Elk's woman suffers the delusion of being healed. I will prove all that I say, and the shadow will be lifted from my people's eyes."

In the final thin light of day, Wellington Paige and Three Eyes entered a sheltered valley and approached the ruins of an ancient stone city that Paige had been using as a home base for his operations.

"We almost near to Mesa Verde," Three Eyes announced. "Cliff houses in canyons to the west."

"I've been in those canyons, but I never saw any cliff dwellings."

"How one Englishman to find houses hidden from white eyes for hundreds of summers? If you do that, you one smart fisherman, mister!"

Paige grinned at the likable boy. "Well, at least this

fisherman was able to find a well-preserved village with some interesting artifacts in it out here in the valley."

"Yeah, out here for anybody to stumble into, even with eyes closed," Three Eyes said with a smile. "And it seem you not the only one to find it. See?"

Paige looked ahead to where Three Eyes was pointing and saw the light of a campfire. He opened the satchel that hung by his side and took out his small pocket revolver.

"Maybe you'd better wait here," he said.

"Three Eyes will stay with the Englishman," the boy declared, kneeing his mount forward. "Who knows what trouble you might find?"

As they skirted the low walls that marked the edge of the village, Paige made out the form of a man seated beside the campfire. Beyond the fire, Paige's large supply tent and smaller pup tent were still pitched where he had left them while going for supplies at the trading post. When the man looked up at them through the firelight, Paige clearly saw his well-trimmed gray beard and matching gray eye patch.

"Wellington!" Jakob Felders called as he rose and waved in greeting.

Cringing at both the sound of his first name and this unexpected meeting, Paige returned the revolver to his bag and dismounted near the fire. "Jakob," he said without emotion, accepting the big man's hand. "What brings you here?"

"I was returning to Durango from Utah and thought I'd stop by and see how your investigation is coming." He pointed at the Indian boy. "Who's the young heathen?"

"His name is Three Eyes."

"Does he understand English?" he asked gruffly.

Paige gave Three Eyes a very sharp look, then turned to Felders and replied. "Not really. Just a few words."

Three Eyes seemed to accept that Paige did not want this man to know he understood what was being said, and so he crossed to the fire and kneeled down to warm himself. Though he was listening closely, he pretended to be disinterested in their conversation.

"Did you have any trouble finding the campsite again?" Paige asked.

"No, though it was a little trickier finding it from the west than when we came out here last month from Durango. I got in this afternoon. You left the tents set up, so I figured you were out in the field somewhere. Find anything yet that would be of interest to me?"

"No gold or silver or other precious metals. The geological features of the area aren't right."

"There must be something of worth out here."

"Only coal. I've found extensive deposits slightly to the southwest."

"Then coal it will be," Felders declared. "These days it's as good as gold. As soon as we come to terms with the Ute, we'll get the operation started."

"Just how do you intend to deal with the Ute?" Paige asked. "It is their land—their coal."

"I'm well aware of that," Felders said, dismissing Paige's concerns with a wave of the hand. "And you can be certain their interests are being considered. But you leave those matters to me. Your job is to determine the mining potential of the region." Felders glanced about and with a sweep of his arm took in the ruins around them. "I know you're interested in archaeology, but I hired you because you're a top geologist. Now, if you want to use your spare time to search out these worthless old villages, be my guest. But remember that it's your geological findings that are paying the way and making this hobby of yours possible."

"I'm just concerned that the interests of the Ute—"

"Well, don't be concerned," Felders said abruptly. "They'll be well taken care of. Hell, nobody wants an Indian war or the kinds of problems we had when the Ute to the north were forced to relocate. All we're trying to do is show them that a move to Utah is in their best interests. You know, they're not all against relocation. In fact, I've just been to Utah with one of their leaders who's quite agreeable to the idea—a man by the name of Painted Wind."

"Painted Wind?" Three Eyes asked animatedly, forgetting that he was not supposed to understand.

"What?" Felders said in surprise, glancing at the boy.

Paige kneeled beside Three Eyes and laid a restraining hand on his shoulder. "Three Eyes heard you mention Painted Wind. The man is his uncle."

"Really?" Felders said with a smirk. "And a typical heathen half-wit he is. I don't know which he liked more—the land in Utah or the fine Winchester I gave him with promises of horses to come." Felders laughed curtly. "So don't worry yourself over the Ute, Wellington. If a Ute leader like Painted Wind sees promise in Utah, I'm sure the rest of his people will agree."

"And if they don't?"

"Then I'm sure we can come up with other arrangements."

"Like Striker?" Paige asked pointedly as he stood up.

"Striker?"

"Yes. A pleasant chap. I know he works for you. I had a little run-in with the fellow. He tried to kill me."

"Be serious."

"I am. He tried to run Isaac Halloran off his trading post, and I got in the way. One of his men mentioned your name." There was a long pause, each man waiting for the other to speak. Finally Paige continued, "You aren't going to deny it, are you?"

"That I know Wade Striker? Of course I know him. But I had nothing to do with any attack on the trading post."

"A man like Striker wouldn't act on his own."

Felders was furious at the veiled accusation, and he had to control his voice as he said, "I'm looking to buy out Halloran, that's all. I'd be a fool not to. That place will be worth a lot more once our mining operation is under way. Striker must've gotten a bit too eager to get the job done, that's all. But don't worry. When I get back to Durango, I'll make it up to Halloran—and I'll pay off Striker and send him packing."

"It may be too late," Paige said.

"What do you mean?"

"One of his men is dead. He was killed when they attacked the trading post."

"Damn!" Felders exclaimed. "Those damn fools!"

Felders started toward the tents and then turned and

called, "I'll be spending the night. First thing tomorrow I'll be on my way to Durango to take care of those idiots. I'll return two weeks from today for a full geological report and to see those coal deposits of yours. Understand?" Without awaiting a reply, he spun around and stalked away.

As soon as the tall man disappeared into the pup tent, Three Eyes stood up and turned to Paige. "I do not like this friend of yours."

"I'm beginning to feel the same way," Paige replied.

"He does not have the true tongue. Painted Wind must hear these things he has said about him and our people. Tomorrow I will show you in which canyons to search for the cliffs of Mesa Verde, and then I must return to my village."

Paige nodded in agreement. "And I want you to take a message to Quint and Laurel. Will you do that?"

"You darn tootin'!"

Laurel Burgess had already opened the small wooden crate and was examining the glass vials inside by the time the stagecoach that had delivered it pulled out. Quint came up onto the porch to where she was standing by a lantern, holding one of the vials to the light. Kate sat in a chair nearby, her notepad in her lap.

"You're convinced Deborah has smallpox?" Quint asked.

"Yes. She now has all the symptoms. Thank God there was vaccine available in Durango." She handed him the vial.

"Doesn't look like much more than water, does it?" he said, giving it back to her.

"No." She smiled as she replaced the vial in the crate. "But suspended unseen in that liquid is the diseased matter taken from a cow suffering from a form of the pox. Transferring it to the arm of a person will produce a localized smallpox eruption that will render him immune to the disease for many years."

Kate looked up from her notepad. "How long have we been inoculating people against smallpox?"

"Actually, this isn't inoculation, which was a much earlier and far more dangerous method of inducing immunity. Inoculation used diseased matter from the sores of someone actually suffering from smallpox. This was done in ancient China, in which the crusts of smallpox sores were pulverized and inhaled through a tube into the nose. For some reason, the left nostril was used for men and the right nostril for women. The inoculated person would contract the disease—hopefully a mild case—rendering him immune. However, a severe attack was not uncommon, and the inoculated person was himself contagious during the treatment. And while inoculation rarely resulted in death, it often left the patient as disfigured as if he'd caught smallpox naturally."

"So now we use cows," Quint said, bemused.

"Yes. The reaction to cowpox is far less severe but still results in immunity to smallpox. The procedure was developed in the 1790s by Dr. Edward Jenner in England."

"You sure that wasn't Scotland?" Kate asked hopefully.

"Sorry, Kate, but this one goes to the English."

"Well, when do we get started, and how do we begin?" Kate asked.

"First I want to vaccinate you and the Hallorans. Quint, Lucas, and I were vaccinated back east. Then I plan to return to the village and start vaccinating the Ute."

"First thing in the morning, we can—"

"No," Laurel said, cutting off Quint. "I'm returning tonight. The rest of you can follow tomorrow in the wagon."

"How exactly do you administer that stuff?" Kate asked.

"It's really very simple. All we have to do is make some pin pricks on your arm and smear some of the vaccine over it. In a couple of days you'll develop a sore, and maybe a slight headache or even a touch of fever. But those are the only side effects—I promise."

"Then let's get started," Kate said, standing and rolling up her sleeve.

The rhythmic beat of a drum reverberated across the valley beyond the Ute village. As Laurel entered the village, the wooden crate of vaccine strapped in front of her on the Appaloosa, she recognized the eerie medicine chant of a *pwu-au-gut*. She turned her horse away from her tipi and headed toward the sound. Even as she rode, she knew the Song of Renewal came from the tipi of Woman-Cheating-Death. She knew, as well, that Painted Wind had returned:

> *the wind stirs the willows*
> *and paints us its song*
> *the whirlwind comes gliding*
> *and paints us its song*

> *the evil is broken*
> *the Great Spirit is singing*
> *and paints us its song*
> *and paints us its song*

Laurel tethered her horse and approached Painted Wind, who sat with his drum on the ground in front of the tipi of Woman-Cheating-Death. As he looked up at her, his eyes narrowing in recognition, he continued to repeat the verses of his song, the drum never missing a beat. Laurel knew he had been sitting there since sundown and that he would be there when dawn broke, the monotonous rhythm of his song eventually merging with and becoming a part of the night and the souls of all who listened.

"I had hoped we could work together," she said in Ute.

". . . the wind stirs the willows . . . and paints us its song," was his only reply.

"This will not affect my medicine," she proclaimed.

". . . the whirlwind comes gliding . . . and paints us its song."

Realizing the futility of such a conversation, Laurel turned from Painted Wind and headed to the tipi entrance. She thrust aside the buffalo hide covering but found her way blocked by Wild Elk.

"I must see Woman-Cheating-Death," she insisted.

"No, you must not see her!" the man cried in obvious fright. "You must see her no more!"

"But that is crazy. The song of Painted Wind can have

no effect on your wife's recovery. My only concern is that she may become hysterical and—"

"But yes, yes, it is as Painted Wind has said. It is evil spirits that have made her feel well. He is chasing them away, and now she suffers. The spirits fight for her soul, and she will die if Painted Wind cannot defeat them."

"*Aiieeee!*" a voice shrieked from across the tipi.

Pushing Wild Elk to one side, Laurel looked to where Woman-Cheating-Death was lying on her bed, held down by four elderly women. She had pulled herself upright, her eyes wide with terror as she stared at Laurel.

"*Aiieeee!*" she screamed again in pain and delirium, then fell back against the buffalo robes.

Wild Elk grabbed Laurel by the shoulders and forced her from the tipi. "You must not return," he demanded. "You must take your medicine away from our village. Painted Wind has returned, and he will make these things right."

Laurel stood stunned in front of the tipi as Wild Elk spun around and disappeared inside. Behind her, a hypnotic voice chanted, ". . . the evil is broken . . . the Great Spirit is singing . . . and paints us its song . . ."

Seated in the darkness by the *sipapu* hole in the *kiva* at Mesa Verde, Surnia closed his eyes and listened to the Song of Renewal. The music was sharp and discordant, and he felt the clash of two great singers, two opposing songs.

"It has begun," he whispered as the images of Painted Wind and Mountain Laurel rose before him in his mind's eye. "The seeds that have been planted must now bear fruit. May the Great Spirit that is within all things bless this garden with water and with life."

Surnia listened to Painted Wind's harsh tones and felt the equally harsh energy of Mountain Laurel's own silent song. Placing his hands on his chest, he began a deep, calm chant. As he continued to sing, his chant blended with the songs of Painted Wind and Mountain Laurel, tempering their discordant harmony with his own Song of Life Returning.

> *in the whirlwind a child is born*
> *that we may know one another*
> *that we may know one another*

Chapter Nine

Quint Burgess drove the buckboard wagon through the seemingly deserted Ute village and pulled it to a halt in the central clearing. Beside him sat Lucas, an expectant smile on his face. At eight in the morning, the village was usually alive with activity, but today no one was in sight. All was silent, and the only movement was the lapping of buffalo-hide tipi coverings in the gentle breeze.

"Go ahead," Quint said, nodding at his son. "It's time for the first day of school to begin."

Lucas picked up a cowbell from beside him on the seat, stood up, and began to ring it. Though he could not hear the clanging, he felt the buckboard shake as Little Bear barked and wagged his tail in the wagonbed behind.

After a while, Quint placed his hand on his son's arm. As Lucas sat down, Quint said solemnly, "They won't come."

Reading his father's lips, Lucas asked, "But why?"

"They have lost faith. They're frightened."

Lucas had been told of how Painted Wind had returned two days earlier and had held some sort of mystical ceremony to turn the Ute against Laurel and her medicine. That ceremony had unnerved Woman-Cheating-Death to the extent that her health had declined rapidly. She was now in a state of delirium, and nothing Laurel did or said would convince the woman's family that her condition was self-induced. As a result, many Ute had concluded that

Painted Wind was right and that Laurel's medicine was the work of evil spirits. The rest were waiting to see what would happen in the contest of wills between Laurel and Painted Wind before committing themselves to either side.

As yet, the controversy remained focused on Laurel's medicine, not on herself. She still was respected among her people, who revered her grandfather, Surnia, and remembered that he had chosen her as an apprentice and had rejected Painted Wind. The general opinion was that she had lost the true path of her people—a view promoted by Painted Wind, who was astute enough not to attack her personally but instead encouraged the Ute to pray that she would reject the evil ways of the white world and come back into the fold.

As a result of the controversy, few Ute were willing to be treated with Laurel's smallpox vaccine. They could not understand the strange idea of infecting themselves with the very disease they were trying to avoid.

As Lucas looked around at the quiet, seemingly empty village, he realized that his stepmother's medical practice wasn't the only casualty of the latest series of events. It was apparent that Painted Wind had also convinced the Ute to keep their children from attending the school at Halloran's Trading Post, which had been scheduled to open that morning.

"Let's get started," Quint said cheerfully. "We've got a school to open."

"But there are no students," Lucas pointed out.

"What do you mean? I've got at least one. You weren't planning on playing hooky, were you?"

"But the others . . ."

"Today's the first day of class," Quint declared. "The Ute must see that we aren't about to give up. We will open as scheduled, and in time hopefully others will come." He slapped the reins and started back toward the trading post.

"Dad!" Lucas cried, twisting in his seat and tugging at Quint's arm. "Someone's coming."

Quint pulled the team to a halt and spun around. A boy

on horseback was passing among the tipis, approaching them.

"It's Three Eyes," Lucas said excitedly, then began to wave and call out, "Three Eyes! Over here!"

The Ute boy rode up to the wagon and halted.

"Are you here for school?" Quint asked pleasantly.

"School?" Three Eyes asked.

"Yes. Today is our first day."

"I have been away from the village," the boy explained. "I have returned to see my uncle."

Quint's expression darkened. Forcing a smile, he said, "Painted Wind has returned. He will be pleased to see you."

Three Eyes turned to Lucas. "It is good to see you, my friend. Can you still hear me with your eyes?"

"Yes. And it's good to see you, too."

"It is a great gift you have. Perhaps you can teach me this language of the lips, and I can teach you the language of my people."

"If you attended school with Lucas, you could study those things together," Quint suggested.

"I would like that," the boy replied. "I must ask my uncle about these things."

Quint picked up the reins and smiled. "If you decide to attend our school, you can ride with us each day. We will ring our bell here every morning."

"I will listen for your sound," Three Eyes replied. He turned his horse and headed toward his mother's tipi.

Across the village, Laurel and Kate sat in Singing Water's tipi, waiting for her to consider Laurel's request.

"I do not believe what my husband's brother says about you, Mountain Laurel," she said at last. "But I cannot go against his wishes and do this thing you ask of me."

"It is not harmful to you, and Painted Wind need never know," Laurel insisted.

"But I would know. And in time, he would see the mark." She pointed at her shoulder.

"I can put the vaccination mark higher, where your clothing would cover it. Then he will never see."

As she said the words, Laurel immediately saw the look of concern in the Indian woman's eyes and realized this was a topic she could not pursue. She was well aware that Singing Water wished desperately to live with Painted Wind as husband and wife. And were that to happen, indeed Painted Wind might one day discover the mark. But this was something a Ute would never discuss—even with a close friend.

"It will be as you wish," Laurel said in resignation, standing and motioning to Kate that they would leave. "I only hope that the people see the wisdom of my medicine before the smallpox spreads throughout our tribe."

"But does it not spread by the very medicine you give our people?" Singing Water asked.

"No," Laurel replied. "There is only a little discomfort, and then you will never catch the disease."

"But Painted Wind says the people you have treated suffer with smallpox. They have the redness, the fever."

Laurel sighed and sat back down. "It is true that there is a reaction from this medicine, but it is not smallpox. There is a mild rash and sometimes a little fever, and that is what causes the body to create its own medicine, which will keep out the smallpox."

Singing Water shook her head. "I do not understand, Mountain Laurel. But I know you will not hurt our people."

"Can you talk to Painted Wind? He won't listen to me."

"He takes only his own counsel these days—and the counsel of the Great Spirit. But I will speak for you."

"Thank you, my friend," Laurel said, standing and starting across the tipi.

"Mountain Laurel," Singing Water called.

Laurel turned back at the entranceway. "Yes?"

"You no longer need worry about what those men did to me. There is no child within me."

"Are you certain?" Laurel asked, and Singing Water nodded. Laurel smiled and led Kate from the tipi.

As they stepped outside, Kate asked, "How will you get others to be vaccinated, if even Singing Water won't agree?"

"I don't know. The first few who were vaccinated did so before they knew Painted Wind would oppose it. Now he's used their mild, perfectly normal reaction to further convince the others not to be treated. If there were only some way to show Painted Wind that this is for the good of the tribe. He is the key to convincing the others."

As they started to walk away from Singing Water's tipi, Three Eyes rode up and dismounted.

"Welcome home," Laurel said in greeting. "I heard that you traveled west with Paige. Is that so?"

"I have just returned. He sent a message for you."

The boy reached into a small bag attached to his loin-cloth and produced a piece of paper, which he handed to Laurel.

As Laurel unfolded it and read, Kate asked Three Eyes, "How's Paige?"

"He is fine."

"I've been worried about him," she continued. "When he left, his skin looked red, and I thought he might have a fever. I was afraid he might be getting the smallpox."

"Yes, I saw this redness, but I am sure it was from the sun. His skin does not like our summer."

When Laurel finished reading, Kate turned to her and asked, "What is it? Is he all right?"

"Yes. It is something else—about that man named Striker and the people he works for."

"I'm concerned about him," Kate said.

"Who? Striker?"

"No, Paige. His skin seemed awfully red when he left—either sunburn or a rash. I didn't think much at the time, but now that we know Deborah has smallpox, I'm beginning to wonder if he isn't coming down with it, as well."

Laurel turned to Three Eyes and questioned him closely about Paige's condition, after which she said, "It doesn't sound like anything to be concerned about, but we can't be sure. Perhaps I should ride out there—"

"I thought I might do that," Kate cut in. "I can take some vaccine, and you can teach me how to administer it."

"If he has smallpox, it wouldn't help."

"But if he doesn't, he ought to be vaccinated. And if he's sick, I can bring him back to the trading post."

"It's a long ride, and you don't know where he is."

Three Eyes stepped forward and said, "I will show the woman how to reach his campsite."

"Are you sure you're up to it?" Laurel asked Kate.

"I'd enjoy it. And I'd like to see some of the ruins he's told me about. It would be good for my articles."

"All right," Laurel agreed. "I'll help you get packed, and you can leave later this morning."

"Is that all right with you?" Kate asked Three Eyes.

"I must first see my mother and uncle. Then I can take you west to the trail that will lead you to where he is staying." The Indian boy nodded, then turned and headed for his mother's tipi.

As soon as Three Eyes was gone, Laurel turned to Kate and said, "There is something more I want you to do."

"What is it?"

"I'd like you to try to vaccinate Three Eyes after the two of you leave the village. He wasn't here the past couple of days, and he may not know what's going on."

"But Painted Wind—"

"I'll worry about him. The important thing is that the boy be protected."

Two hours later, Kate was ready for the journey to Paige's campsite. She had fitted Laurel's Appaloosa with a saddle, on the back of which was tied a small carpetbag of clothes and Kate's tripod camera.

Laurel checked to make sure the cinch and other straps were securely fastened. "Everything's ready," she said as she pulled the last strap tight. "With Three Eyes as your guide, you should have no trouble finding Paige."

"I'll be fine," Kate reassured her. "And I'll get to the bottom of that note he sent," she added, briefly pulling the note from her pocket and then stuffing it away.

"It seems pretty clear that he wanted to warn us about this Jakob Felders person he mentions."

"Then why didn't he say so when he was here?" Kate asked, her Scottish temper rising.

"The note says that he met up with Felders out there at the ruins," Laurel pointed out.

"Yes, but it's also perfectly clear that he already knew him. And he denied that before."

"He must have had his reasons."

"And I intend to find out what they are." Kate grabbed hold of the saddle horn, stepped into the stirrup, and hoisted herself into the saddle.

Laurel reached up and took Kate's hand. "Just remember the reason you're going is to make sure Paige is all right."

"Is that what I'm doing?" Kate asked with a mischievous grin. "Well, he'd better be all right, 'cause he's got a bit of explaining to do. And the saints preserve him if he's in cahoots with that Striker fellow and his friends."

"Kate, you don't really believe that, do you? After all, they beat him savagely."

"Laurel, I'd believe most anything of an Englishman. And if he and that Felders are cooking up any trouble for the Ute, he'll soon learn that he hasn't been savagely beaten till he's been beaten by a Scot!"

With a brusque wave of her hand, Kate kicked the horse into motion and turned it toward Singing Water's tipi.

Laurel sat alone in her tipi, her thoughts scattered and confused. She had been bitterly disappointed at the ease with which Painted Wind had turned the people against her. It was obvious that she did not command the respect either her father, Josiah Fox, or her grandfather, Surnia, had received.

I must make them see, she told herself. *I must find the middle path between the old and new ways.*

It always had been Laurel's dream to bridge the chasm between the worlds of the Indian and white. She did not want to see the Ute absorbed by the white culture, yet she was convinced that the only way the Ute could survive the inevitable changes ahead was to understand the white ways and incorporate those things that were good. It was that process of evolution that had allowed the Ute to learn and grow from earlier civilizations, such as the Anasazi.

Yet now Laurel had been frustrated in her attempt before she had really begun. And though she couldn't help but feel a sense of bitterness toward Painted Wind, she well understood the power of suggestion, and she gave him credit for the way he had turned around her earlier success.

As Laurel stared into the fire, concerned about her people's welfare and overwhelmed by her inability to help, a shiver ran through her, as if a cool breeze was circling the tipi. The fire reacted, as well, flickering as a spiraling wind poured through the opening in the peak, causing the hides covering the tipi to flap lightly. Laurel listened, and it was as if a gentle voice were singing in the wind. It was the Song of Life Returning, which her grandfather had sung so often when she sat with him in his cave. But he was gone now—his voice would sing no more.

This was not the first time Laurel had thought she heard Surnia's song. In fact, the past few mornings she had discovered the chant playing in her mind, as if an unseen singer were walking within her.

"I am Ute," Mountain Laurel found herself saying. "And I am white."

Suddenly she realized she had not been following the middle path—the combiner of two cultures. She'd come home so enthusiastic about the gifts of white medicine that she had forgotten that her patients, first and always, were Ute.

"The whirlwind comes gliding," she intoned with a smile as she stood and walked across the tipi. She opened her medical bag and removed a very small bottle of liquid. Then she reached into the carpetbag beside her bed and took out a leather pouch intricately painted with the image of an owl. Opening the pouch, she dropped the bottle inside. Then she closed it and hung it around her neck. Reaching back into the carpetbag, she lifted out a cloth robe, embroidered with symbols of earth, air, fire, and water. It hung nearly to the ground as she placed it over her shoulders.

Laurel turned and gazed into the fire a final time. She recalled the words Surnia had said at their parting:

"It is time for our people to choose their own way. Silver Fox will go in one direction, Surnia in another. It is now for the Southern Ute to decide. If they seek, they will find their answer—their future. Just as you will discover the path you must walk.

"Many teachers will come, if you have the eyes to see. It does not matter whether you are in the land of the Ute or of your father. But only by seeking within will the next teacher appear—perhaps taking the form of an eagle or teaching through the lips of a child. You may even discover his voice in the whispering of the wind."

A soft wind blew again, and it seemed to whisper, "That we may know one another, know one another, one another."

Laurel touched the pouch at her chest. It was the medicine bag of her grandfather, Surnia, which he gave her when she left the people to return east and study medicine.

"*He'e'e' Ahi'ni'yo',*" she whispered. Then without hesitation, she crossed the tipi and stepped out into the afternoon light, the ceremonial robe of the *pwu-au-gut* trailing behind her in the breeze.

Wild Elk held his wife's shoulders as she doubled up in pain and then fell back against the buffalo robes, her eyes fluttering open and closed as she moaned in agony. As soon as he sensed the spasm had subsided, he tried to pull free a strip of cloth that she held clamped between her teeth. At first Woman-Cheating-Death would not release it, but at last she yielded and opened her mouth. Wild Elk quickly unfolded the cloth and dipped it in a pot of water. Lifting it back up, he wrung it out, twisted it lengthwise, and stretched it between her jaws. She immediately clamped down, moaning as another wave of pain coursed through her belly. Nearby, two old women mumbled a chant with little enthusiasm.

"It will be all right," Wild Elk tried to assure his wife. "Painted Wind will soon return. You will get well."

Suddenly the old women fell silent as a shaft of light

spilled into the darkened tipi. Wild Elk spun around to see the silhouette of Mountain Laurel standing in the doorway.

"You must not come here!" the young man cried as he leaped up and hurried across the room. "You must be gone!"

Wild Elk reached out to push Mountain Laurel back through the entranceway, but then he abruptly pulled back his hand. Hanging from a leather thong against her ceremonial medicine robe was a pouch on which was painted the symbol of an owl. Wild Elk recognized the symbol and the bag at once; it belonged to Surnia, whose name was Spanish for hawk owl.

"My grandfather has sent me," Mountain Laurel said, touching the bag as she walked to the buffalo-robe bed. The two women rose, ready to object, but they too saw that she was wearing both the robe of a *pwu-au-gut* and the medicine bag of Surnia—an object of great magic.

Wild Elk, stunned by the sudden appearance of Mountain Laurel, started toward his wife's bed and said, "But he cannot send you. He has passed beyond our world."

Removing the pouch from her neck, Mountain Laurel held it aloft. "This is the medicine of the one true *pwu-au-gut*. With it, he has bequeathed me his *po-o-kan-te*—the true *po-o-kan-te* of our people. I have come to show you that I have not left the path of our people, but have been called to combine the two great paths of the Ute and the white."

"But Painted Wind has said—"

"Painted Wind is not the true medicine teacher of his people unless his *po-o-kan-te* can surpass that of the true *pwu-au-gut*." She waved Surnia's medicine pouch.

The old women backed away as Mountain Laurel knelt beside Woman-Cheating-Death, who stared unseeing toward the ceiling as she bit down on the dampened cloth and moaned. She seemed unaware of Mountain Laurel's presence.

"I will prove all that I say. I will call on Surnia's power to deliver this pain of Woman-Cheating-Death into the hands of the Great Spirit."

Chanting softly, Mountain Laurel opened the pouch and removed the small glass vial and some packets of herbs. With great ceremony she sprinkled some of the herbs on the woman's forehead. Slipping a finger into the side of the woman's mouth, she eased her jaw open and removed the cloth, which she quickly opened and spread over her face. She sprinkled a handful of herbs onto the cloth and then poured some of the liquid onto the spot directly above her lips.

After a few minutes, Mountain Laurel removed the cloth and dropped it into the pot of water. Placing her hands on the woman's cheeks, she began to rub gently, all the while keeping up the soothing rhythmic chant.

A few minutes passed, and then slowly the woman's eyes stopped fluttering, and she looked up at Laurel.

"You are free of your pain," Laurel told her. "The gift of the *pwu-au-gut* has released you."

Woman-Cheating-Death opened her eyes wider in astonishment. She no longer felt the spasms of pain that had struck her belly. Instead her head felt as if it was floating peacefully, her entire body as light as a cloud.

"I . . . I do not feel the pain," Woman-Cheating-Death exclaimed, turning to stare at her husband. As she spoke, her voice sounded to her as if it came from a distant place.

Wild Elk rushed over and knelt at his wife's side. "It is true?" he asked. "You have no pain?"

"I am better," Woman-Cheating-Death replied, closing her eyes and smiling with bliss.

"She is better. . . ." Wild Elk muttered, turning to stare at the two old women. Suddenly he was up and running from the tipi, shouting, "She is better! She is better!"

"The *po-o-kan-te* . . ." one of the women whispered, nodding her head as she approached Mountain Laurel. She reached out but was afraid to touch Surnia's pouch. "The medicine of the true *pwu-au-gut* has healed her."

My grandfather's medicine, Mountain Laurel thought with a smile. *With some help from my father's morphine.*

By the time Laurel left Wild Elk's tipi an hour later, Woman-Cheating-Death was walking about cheerfully, no longer suffering from her self-induced pain. Her entire family was on hand to celebrate, and they were more than willing to be vaccinated, eager to share any magic Laurel had to offer.

Laurel hurried back to her own tipi and opened the wooden crate of vaccine. Removing one of the half-dozen vials, she snatched up her medical bag and headed outside. She found herself face to face with Painted Wind.

"I have been to the tipi of Wild Elk," he calmly stated without a trace of anger. "I have seen all you have done."

"It was the *po-o-kan-te* of my grandfather."

"It was a white man's trick," he declared.

"I don't want to fight you, Painted Wind."

"You are indeed a great *pwu-au-gut*, Mountain Laurel. I thought you a fool for turning your back on the old ways of the Ute, yet still you have the gift. You do not have the true *po-o-kan-te*, but you have the gift of making the people see *po-o-kan-te* where there is nothing but air."

"I must go," Laurel told him. "A sickness threatens all of our people, and I have the gift to heal it."

"With that?" He sneered, pointing at the vial in her hand. "You make people sick and say they are well."

"It is a natural reaction to—"

"I will not speak of these white man things. Go, Mountain Laurel. But you will not succeed. The people will see that your bottle contains nothing but sickness and lies."

Painted Wind turned his back on her and stood with his arms folded over his chest. She looked at him for a moment and then hurried across the village toward Wild Elk's tipi.

As she disappeared among the tipis, Painted Wind turned and stared in the direction she had gone. A great sadness fell over him as he thought of how this half-breed woman had blinded his people to the truth. And now she was going to cut up their arms and smear her poison into their skin.

"I must not let her do this thing," he whispered. "I must take her evil far from the land of my people."

Glancing around to make sure no one was watching, he slipped inside Laurel's tipi and found the crate containing the vaccine. He fleetingly considered stealing the bottles, but he knew she would merely send for more.

Painted Wind held up one of the vials. The contents looked harmless—like pure water. He unstoppered it and sniffed the contents, then with his finger touched some to his lips. Confident he would remember the aroma and bitter taste, he put back the stopper, replaced the vial, and left.

When Painted Wind returned twenty minutes later, he carried two small jugs, one empty and one filled with a clear liquid made from the extracts of bitter herbs. Placing the jugs beside the crate of vaccine, he opened one of the vials and again touched a drop to his mouth, comparing it to the liquid he had prepared. Satisfied that they were similar, he poured the contents of the vial into the empty jug and refilled it with the harmless herbal liquid.

Painted Wind emptied and refilled each vial. When all were stoppered and replaced in the crate, he picked up the two jugs—one empty, the other with the smallpox vaccine—and slipped out of the tipi. He would hide the medicine until he could take it far from the village; he would not allow the evil liquid to even touch his sacred ground.

After making a circle of pinpricks on Wild Elk's arm, Laurel used a flat metal applicator to spread some of the vaccine over the cuts. She wiped off the applicator and pressed the stopper back into the mouth of the now-empty bottle. She had vaccinated about twenty Indians, and there were still more who wanted the treatment. Realizing that the initial enthusiasm might wane once the current group of vaccinated Indians began to show side effects, she decided to continue the procedure as long as possible.

"You must all come to my tipi," she declared to the gathered throng. "I have more medicine there."

The crowd started to break up, with some returning home and others heading for Laurel's tipi. One of the last left was Singing Water, who had watched the proceedings from a distance and now hesitantly approached Laurel.

"Will you allow me to vaccinate you?" Laurel asked as she finished packing her medical bag.

"I cannot go against the wishes of my brother-in-law," Singing Water said. "But I want you to know that I think it is a good thing you are doing."

"Then you must convince Painted Wind to let you be treated, as well," Laurel insisted. "Or else you must go against his wishes and do what your heart tells you."

"I cannot do that," she declared. "But I will speak to Painted Wind." With that she nodded and walked away.

Laurel picked up her bag and made her way across the village to where a small crowd had gathered at her tipi. She went inside and brought out another vial, then sat down in front of the entranceway. One by one, the Ute came forward and sat before her to receive this new *po-o-kan-te*.

After vaccinating almost a dozen more Indians, Laurel was surprised to see Painted Wind approaching with Singing Water at his side. She prayed that he had not come to disrupt what she was doing, and she was pleased when he offered a respectful greeting.

"I do not like this thing you are doing, Mountain Laurel," Painted Wind began after she had returned his greeting. "But the people must follow the *po-o-kan-te* they believe in, even if it blinds them to the true power. In time they will discover that the Great Spirit chooses who suffers and who stays well—not your . . . your medicine." He pointed at the vial in Laurel's hand.

"Then you will not interfere?" Laurel asked.

"I will not try to stop you. The people will discover that your medicine is worthless—your *po-o-kan-te* a lie."

Laurel turned to Singing Water. "Will you let me vaccinate you now?"

Singing Water glanced uncomfortably at Painted Wind and then looked back at Laurel. "I will not go against the wishes of my brother-in-law," she said once again.

Painted Wind turned to Singing Water and shook his head. "You have already gone against me in your heart," he declared firmly but without bitterness. "Let it also be so in your actions."

Before Singing Water could react, she found herself being dragged forward by Painted Wind, who pulled her down to her knees in front of Laurel.

"Go ahead now," Painted Wind said, nodding at Laurel as he tightly gripped Singing Water's shoulders. "Do this thing and be done with it." He grabbed hold of Singing Water's sleeve and tore it open at the shoulder. "Do it!" he shouted as his sister-in-law began to whimper.

Without hesitation, Laurel made a series of pinpricks and smeared some liquid from the vial over the cuts. When the vaccination was finished, Painted Wind let go of Singing Water, who hurried away in shame, clutching her torn sleeve.

Laurel stared up at Painted Wind, who stood with his arms crossed over his chest, a thin smile upon his lips. "Why did you do that?" she asked.

"Does it matter?" he replied. "It is done." Then he turned and walked away.

Chapter Ten

Three Eyes sat on his horse and tried to hold it steady while Kate McEwan adjusted her Spirit Catcher. The tripod camera reminded him of Paige's glass-eye machine, but when Kate had allowed him to look through the focusing screen, he had been surprised to discover that it made the world smaller, rather than larger. It was a curious device, and he wondered why anyone would want to shrink the world so that it was more difficult to see. He assumed it was the only way to make the big world fit inside such a tiny black box.

The Ute teenager knew that most of his people would not allow their spirits to be caught inside such a contraption, but Three Eyes—owner of a white man's brass spyglass—prided himself on understanding and being unafraid of the new things of the world. He knew that it was not his soul that would be captured forever on a piece of paper. It was merely his image, seen through a glass lens and burned in place on the special plate inside the box.

"That's very good," Kate called, standing up from the tripod. "Now just hold steady for a moment." She glanced over her shoulder and gauged the fading afternoon sun, then looked back through the focusing screen. "That's it."

Three Eyes heard a click, after which Kate said, "Got it. Now let's just hope there was enough light."

Three Eyes watched as Kate shut the tripod and strapped the camera back on the horse. This was a curious woman, he thought. She wore the trousers and suit jacket of a white man, yet the frilly lace of her blouse, combined with the soft curves of her body, made the outfit anything but masculine. She was not Ute, yet even to a fourteen-year-old boy she was beautiful. This was a woman of great strength and tenderness—a woman who would warm any Ute tipi.

During the past day, this woman named Kate had asked numerous questions about the Englishman, Wellington Paige—including whether he knew Paige's full name. Three Eyes had managed to keep his friend's secret, deftly turning aside the question without being forced to lie. It was apparent that Kate had great interest in Paige, yet her comments often had a sharp or sarcastic tone, as if she was unwilling to admit even to herself that she might like this man.

"We will soon be at Paige's camp," Three Eyes said as Kate mounted back up and walked her horse over to his.

"This trail runs straight to the old ruins?" she asked, and he nodded. "There's no need for you to ride all the way with me," she repeated for perhaps the tenth time that day.

Just as he had on previous occasions, the boy replied, "I will see you to the camp and then return to my village."

As Kate nodded in reply, the boy wondered if she had offered to let him return home because she would rather see Paige alone. He knew she need not worry, since he had no intention of remaining with the two adults any longer than necessary. But he would not leave a white woman alone in the vastness of the Ute lands.

The two riders continued west, discussing Paige's work, the customs of the Ute, and the legendary cliff houses of Mesa Verde that lay hidden in the canyons at the edge of the Ute lands. An hour later, as the sun was setting, they reached the ruins of the old stone village.

Paige came running to greet them even as they were entering the village. He wore blue, dirt-stained work clothes and had on his battered gray-felt hat, which he held in place as he ran over to them.

"My God! What the bloody hell are you doing here?" he

shouted at Kate in surprise, his broad grin revealing that he wasn't at all displeased to see her.

"Is that a typical English greeting?" Kate asked as Paige stopped in front of her horse and took hold of its bridle. "I would have expected, 'What a pleasure to see you, ma'am,' or 'Care for a spot of tea?' "

"Do you?" he asked, leading the horse to the campsite.

"Do I what?"

"Care for a spot of tea?"

"How about coffee?"

"Why, certainly. I think I still have a tin I bought back east. I'll put some on to steep."

"Steep?" Kate repeated. She was about to remark that coffee is brewed, not steeped, and that a tin purchased when he was back east would probably brew up like a fresh pot of shoe leather, but his genuinely innocent smile made her hold her tongue. "Actually, tea sounds like just the thing," she finally replied, taking care not to elaborate on just what thing she was referring to.

"Delightful," Paige said, offering his hand.

"Quite," she added with the hint of an English accent. As she accepted his hand and dismounted, she had to struggle not to giggle at the notion of an unkempt archaeologist, a Scottish-American journalist, and a Ute teenager sitting around a campfire in the middle of nowhere having a "typically English" tea.

Three Eyes dismounted also and shook hands with Paige. Insisting on taking charge of the two horses, he led them away to be watered and fed. Meanwhile, Kate and Paige headed to the campfire, where he prepared the tea. As they drank, they discussed the smallpox outbreak at the trading post and Laurel's concern about it spreading to the Ute.

"Then none of the Indians have actually contracted the disease as yet?" Paige asked.

"Laurel isn't certain. There are a couple of people with some of the early symptoms. That's why I came out here—to make sure you haven't come down with it."

"Well, you can see I'm perfectly fine," he said, breathing in deeply and pounding on his chest.

"You didn't look well when you left."

"Are you referring to my health or my looks in general?"

Kate grinned. "You do look a little pale and skinny, and your hair could use a trim. But yes, I meant your health. It was probably just a sunburn."

"The English don't sunburn," Paige insisted.

"What do you call that?" She pointed at his reddened cheeks.

"A ruddy complexion," he stated with conviction.

"A ruddy load of bull," she replied, starting to laugh.

"That, too," he agreed, joining her laughter. "But a healthy load of bull. So you can go back to the village and let everyone know I'm all right."

"Not so quickly. There are a few things I plan to do here, first."

"Like what?"

"Like help you find Mesa Verde."

"Who told you—?"

"I'm a reporter, remember? And Three Eyes is not at all shy about being interviewed."

"Well, I don't know what he's been telling you, but I haven't been able to find any mysterious, hidden cliff houses. No one's seen Mesa Verde—has he told you that?"

"He said he hasn't seen it but that other Indians have."

"Have you ever met one?" Paige pressed. "Has Three Eyes ever met one? Not that I know of. As far as I'm concerned, it's just a myth."

"So when are you going back to look?" she asked.

"What do you mean?"

"Myths—the stuff from which an archaeologist's fortune is made. So don't try to convince me you aren't interested."

"Of course I'm interested, but—"

"So when do you start the hunt?"

Paige sighed in resignation. "I've looked every day."

"Tomorrow, also?"

"Probably."

"I'm going with you. I can sleep in your supply tent."

"But—"

"I could always follow you on my own," she pointed out. "The way I see it, we might as well work together."

"I wouldn't want to work against you, that's for sure."

"Precisely." She smiled smugly.

"You won't write the story prematurely?"

"I want the full story. As long as there isn't a crowd of reporters on your trail, I won't do anything in haste."

"Fine. Then we might as well work together."

"On one condition," she added.

"What's that?"

"I want you to explain this." She pulled from her pocket his note to Laurel and handed it to him.

"What about it?" he asked.

"You send word warning that this Jakob Felders is maneuvering to take over the Ute lands. Yet you denied knowing him back at the trading post. Why?"

"I'm afraid I work for Jakob Felders," Paige admitted.

"You *what*?"

"You heard me. But I had no idea he was trying to take advantage of the Ute or that he employed people like Striker and his bunch."

"How could you?" she asked incredulously.

"I fancy myself an archaeologist, but not many people have ancient ruins they want uncovered. So I make my living as a geologist. I was hired to survey this area and determine whether it has any potential for mining."

"But it's Ute land."

"I was under the assumption it was uninhabited, with very little game—useless even to the Ute. And I must say it appears to be so. I was told the Ute would be offered a percentage of the profit—that they would actually benefit."

"Have you ever heard of any Indian sharing in a percentage of any white man's profits?" Kate asked.

"We don't have Indians in England."

"Just lords and serfs," she muttered.

"You're perfectly right. Maybe I *was* naive, but as it turns out, the land doesn't show much potential for gold or anything else that would result in a land rush. Just coal."

"Great," she said facetiously. "Coal. Black gold. It'll be the same thing."

"It doesn't have to be. Coal is of no interest to miners

and prospectors. It would take a big company with plenty of capital, and it would be a controlled operation. There is no reason why the Ute couldn't benefit."

"From a man like Jakob Felders?" she asked. "A man who hires thugs to drive decent families from their homes?"

"I realize that now. That's why I sent the warning."

"I suppose we'll just have to figure out a way to put a stop to Felders and his friends. But now we have a more immediate concern—getting you and Three Eyes vaccinated."

"But Laurel's all the way back at—"

"We don't need Laurel," Kate said, grinning.

"No? But who's going to—?"

"I am."

"You're going to stick a needle—?"

"It's not a shot. It's just a pin, and I only have to poke you about twenty times."

"You're joking!"

Her smile broadened. "It may seem like a joke, but I promise you won't laugh."

Soon after Three Eyes started back for the Ute village the next morning, Kate and Paige loaded the packhorse and rode west into the labyrinth of canyons in which the boy was certain they would discover Mesa Verde. As they searched, their banter grew less belligerent, though they found it hard to resist teasing each other when the opportunity arose.

At one point, Kate was humming an old Scottish ballad and then, in a thick and lilting brogue, began to sing:

> "Gin a body meet a body,
>   Comin' thro' the rye;
> Gin a body kiss a body,
>   Need a body cry?
> Ev'ry lassie has her laddie,
>   Nane, they say, hae I!
> Yet a' the laddies smile at me,
>   When comin' thro' the rye."

Suddenly Paige pulled his horse up short and declared, "What kind of bleedin' song is that? Is that a Ute love chant or something?"

"What do you mean?" Kate said, taken aback.

"Well it bloody hell doesn't sound like English. 'Gin a body'? What is that supposed to mean?"

"It's Scottish for 'if somebody.' "

"Then on God's good earth, why not sing it that way?"

She kicked her horse forward and shouted, "I'll sing it any bloody way I like!" Raising her voice, she continued:

> "Amang the train there is a swain
>   I dearly lo'e mysel';
> But whaur his hame, or what his name,
>   I dinna care to tell."

Meanwhile, Paige trotted up beside her and at top voice broke into his own Anglicized rendition of the Robert Burns classic:

> "Every laddie has his lassie,
>   None, they say, have I!
> Yet all the lassies smile at me,
>   When coming through the rye."

For a few verses they competed with each other, until they were fairly screaming the words. Finally Kate burst into laughter and declared, "God, you sound awful!"

"Only when I sing a *Scottish* ballad."

"I'll take your word for it—just don't break into a chorus of 'God Save the Queen'!"

"Agreed." Paige looked up at the darkening sky and then glanced at his watch. "We ought to be heading back. The way those clouds are rolling in, it'll get dark early."

It grew chillier as they started back through the canyons, and soon a light drizzle began to fall, punctuated by an occasional distant clap of thunder. As the rain got heavier, they pulled up and donned oilcloth ponchos.

Estimating that they were less than an hour from camp, they decided to push on without seeking shelter. During the next fifteen minutes, however, the rain built steadily and the lightning grew ever closer. They soon found themselves in a furious downpour, which obscured the canyon walls on either side. The lightning grew increasingly violent, with little gap between the sharp bolts of light and the clashes of thunder that reverberated through the canyon.

"We'd better find shelter!" Paige shouted, riding up beside Kate. "A cave, some large rocks!"

But the cover of storm clouds turned the afternoon into night, and they could hardly see each other, let alone the land features around them. They stayed close together, with Paige and the packhorse slightly in the lead as they came up over a small rise at the base of the south wall of the canyon.

Kate glanced to the north as the sky flickered with light. For a moment she thought she saw a cave high up on the opposing canyon wall, and she halted her horse and awaited another bolt of light. It came with a fierce intensity—a long, zigzagging beam that struck the upper rim of the canyon and fleetingly lit the entire cliff, followed immediately by a thunderclap. The bolt nearly blinded Kate and left the afterimage of a city of tall buildings floating in an alcove on the face of the cliff.

"Paige!" she shouted into the storm, waving ahead at the other horses, which had gone down off the rise and were now quite a bit in front. "Paige! The cliff house!"

Kate thought she saw the horses halt and the rider turn in her direction, when suddenly the world flashed a brilliant white. Her entire body seemed to explode from within, and she felt herself propelled into an endless black abyss.

Surnia stood at the window of one of the towers of Cliff House and prepared to head down to the *kiva* below. Though not yet sundown, it was nearly as dark as midnight. The storm had come unusually fast, and he knew it would pass just as quickly. He also knew that he would be well protected from the firebolts of the Great Spirit in the underground chamber not far from the edge of the alcove.

As Surnia looked out the window, a bolt of lightning lit

the sky, illuminating the canyon below. As the light dimmed, his eyes retained the picture of a horse standing near the base of the opposing cliff. He peered into the darkness, trying to focus on the spot where he had seen the animal. Several more bolts lit the canyon, leaving the clear image of three horses and two riders.

These were the first people Surnia had seen during the past two years. He knew they were lost and that they must have shelter from the storm. Putting on a deerskin robe, treated with oils to protect against water, he hurried from the tower and down the crumbling steps to the base of the alcove, where a hidden trail led to the floor of the canyon.

The rain was easing, the lightning passing to the east, as Surnia crossed the canyon floor. As the thin afternoon light returned, he could see a man kneeling on the ground beside his horse, his back to Surnia. Nearby, an Appaloosa lay without movement, its fur scorched and smoking, its head cleaved open not from a fall but from a bolt of fire.

Hurrying to where the man was kneeling, Surnia noticed that there was another body on the small rise at the base of the cliff. The second rider had been thrown from the dead horse and seemed lifeless as well.

Stepping up unnoticed behind the kneeling figure, Surnia touched his shoulder. As the startled man turned around, the old Indian pulled back his hand in surprise. The stranger was a white man with curly blond hair and black wire-rim glasses—the man of Surnia's visions.

"I will help," Surnia said, stooping beside the body.

The white man opened his mouth and tried to speak, but no sound came. He seemed in shock, and he made no effort to stop Surnia from examining the victim of the thunderbolt.

Surnia placed his head against the chest of the person lying on the ground—and he was startled to discover it was a woman in man's clothing. He listened carefully and then touched his fingers to the woman's throat. Finally he opened her mouth and placed his cheek in front of it.

"She is alive," he said. "We must take her from the storm. There is a building nearby."

"Mesa Verde . . ." the white man whispered, coming out of his stupor. The old Indian heard but did not reply.

Surnia directed the white man to carry the injured woman, and then taking the reins of the riding horse and packhorse, he led the way across the canyon to the base of the north wall. Rather than heading up the trail to Cliff House, he turned into a hidden gully and made his way along a dry streambed to a tiny stone building. Most of the roof had caved in years before, but enough was left to provide adequate shelter.

After tying up the horses and helping the white man place the woman on the ground in a corner of the building, the old Indian removed his deerskin robe and took a large leather bag from around his neck. Again he listened to the woman's heart, then turned to the man and asked, "What is her name?"

"Kate McEwan."

"And you?"

"Paige."

"Your woman has been touched by the fire from the sky. Her heart does not beat true, and it wants to stop. Here—you can feel." He placed Paige's fingers against Kate's neck and helped him find the pulse. Indeed, it was irregular and weak.

"What can we do?" Paige asked.

"We must jolt it again—jolt it back to life."

Paige looked at him curiously. "I don't understand."

"We must jolt her from within."

"That sounds crazy."

"It is the way."

The old man opened his bag and looked inside, finally removing a small bundle of leaves tied with thread. "These will strengthen her heart and set it right." Pressing a few of the leaves into his mouth, he began to chew.

"This *is* crazy," Paige declared, looking at the Indian like he had lost his senses.

Surnia smiled. "I am not crazy, young man. But your

friend is in no condition to chew. I will chew for her. My own heart is so old and feeble, it can use a little jolt."

After chewing on the leaves for some time, Surnia extracted the moist remains and squeezed them between his fingers. Prying open Kate's lips, he pressed the mixture into her mouth. Then he sat back, closed his eyes, and began to hum. Paige assumed it was an ancient Ute chant, yet it seemed curiously familiar.

After a few minutes, the old man stopped humming and checked Kate's pulse. He nodded slightly, then removed some more leaves from the bag and repeated the process of chewing and feeding the mash to Kate. After a third treatment, Surnia again hummed his song and then listened to the pulse. This time a broad grin spread across his face.

"She likes my leaves," he declared. "She does not wish to die."

Paige checked Kate's pulse; it was regular and strong.

"Now we must let her sleep," Surnia said, leaning back against the wall of the small building. Sensing Paige's continued concern, he added, "Do not worry. She will live."

Paige stared at the mysterious old Indian for a long time and finally asked, "Who are you?"

"My name is Surnia."

"Surnia?" Paige asked. "I heard that name at the Ute village. Do you know Laurel Burgess?"

Closing his eyes, Surnia whispered, "Mountain Laurel."

"Yes," Paige said excitedly. "That's the Indian name of Laurel Fox Burgess."

"She has married a white man," Surnia said.

"Quint Burgess."

"And there is a young boy, is there not?"

"Yes. Lucas."

"The one who does not hear?" the old man asked, and Paige nodded. "My great-grandson," Surnia added. "I am the grandfather of Mountain Laurel."

A sudden shock of recognition struck Paige. "But you're dead, aren't you?"

Surnia smiled. "You had better hope not, because you are in the same place as me."

"Where have you been the past two years?"

Surnia knew why this white man had come to the canyon—that it was the will of the Great Spirit—and so he solemnly declared, "Mesa Verde."

"Then it's true. Mesa Verde exists."

"This building was used to store jugs with which water from the streambed was carried to the alcove above. This moment you are sitting below Cliff House—the biggest of the Mesa Verde dwellings. You will be the first white man to walk among those buildings. Soon other whites will come, and then the power of Mesa Verde will be no more."

Paige leaned against the wall, stunned. Finally he turned to the old Indian and asked, "Why did you tell me, if you believe my people will desecrate this sacred site?"

"I cannot change what will be. And I have seen you standing at Cliff House, just as I have seen another man—a tall, gray-haired man with one eye."

"Felders . . ."

"I do not believe you wish to harm this place, but there are men around you who do not understand the beauty of what has come before. This one-eyed man would destroy the beauty that is Mesa Verde."

"I still don't understand why you'd tell me this."

"Because it is the will of the Great Spirit that you be the one to first set foot upon our Mesa Verde."

"Is it also ordained that I be the one who causes the desecration?"

Surnia closed his eyes for a moment and then replied, "I cannot see that far. Perhaps this knowledge is not for me to know. But you will stand in Cliff House as surely as dawn will follow this night. What you choose to do beyond that dawn is a part of your destiny, not mine."

The old Ute leaned over and made sure Kate was sleeping peacefully, and then he turned back to Paige. "It is time. There is still light, and before the day ends you must stand among those sacred stones." He stood and walked to the broken-down doorway through which they had entered the building. "Come. The rain has stopped. I will tell you how to find the path that will lead you to your destiny."

"But Kate . . ."

"I will stay with your woman. This time is for you."

Paige went to the doorway, and Surnia described how to find the hidden trail that would take him to Cliff House. Paige nodded, understanding the old man's words, though they sounded as if they came from another world. Without knowing clearly what he was doing, Paige started through the doorway, then turned and watched as Surnia walked back and sat beside Kate. The old man closed his eyes and again began to hum the curiously familiar melody.

"That song," Paige said. "I've heard it before. Why do you sing it?"

"It is a song of great *po-o-kan-te*," Surnia declared, opening his eyes. "I sing it because it vibrates with the energy of this woman. It is a song that binds the two of you together."

"Is it a Ute chant?"

Surnia grinned. "Do you not recognize your own medicine song? It is the song I have heard your spirit sing when I have seen you standing in Mesa Verde. I do not understand the words, but they have great energy. Perhaps you can teach me the meaning of these words."

Surnia closed his eyes and again began to hum, but then he added the lyrics that went with the familiar chant:

> "Gin a body meet a body,
> Comin' thro' the rye;
> Gin a body kiss a body,
> Need a body cry?"

Paige listened for a moment, then started to laugh softly. "It's just a song," he said as the old man continued to sing. "It's just a bloody Scottish song!" Joining in, he turned and walked from the building.

Surnia opened his eyes and smiled as the young man's voice disappeared into the distance. Reaching over, he placed his hand on the young woman's forehead and continued the song.

Chapter Eleven

Most of the cook fires had been doused by the time Three Eyes reached the Ute village. He hobbled his horse in a grassy meadow just beyond the outer perimeter of tipis, where it could graze during the night. Then he entered the village and made his way to the tipi he shared with his mother. As he moved through the darkness, a shadow stirred to his left and a voice called his name.

"Uncle?" the boy asked tentatively.

"We will talk in my tipi."

Three Eyes took it as a command and immediately changed course and headed for the slightly larger tipi that stood next door. As the door covering was thrust aside, he saw in the entranceway the imposing figure of Painted Wind silhouetted against the small fire at the center of the tipi.

"Let us sit," his uncle said, leading him to the fire.

Three Eyes removed his buckskin overshirt and sat down quietly, waiting for Painted Wind to begin the conversation. After what seemed an endless time, his uncle said, "It is your mother. I am worried for her."

"Is she sick?" the boy asked in fear. "The smallpox?"

"You will not speak of that white man's disease," Painted Wind replied firmly but without anger. "I do not think she is ill, but something is troubling her. She will not speak of it to me. Perhaps to a son . . ."

"I will speak with her," the boy promised.

"Good. You come from a line of great leaders—first your father and now your uncle. But if the family of a Ute leader is not at peace, the people sense this disharmony and they, too, cannot find peace. It is then that false leaders rise and lead our people into dark canyons. I will lead them into the light, and my family must stand beside me."

Three Eyes nodded.

"Then it will be so," his uncle continued. "You will speak with your mother, and you will tell me why she is troubled and why she will not stand beside me in all things. It was a great sadness to me when my brother's wife allowed the evil mark to be placed upon her arm."

Painted Wind leaned over and touched his nephew's arm on the spot where Singing Water had been vaccinated. Suddenly he recoiled in horror as he saw the same mark on the boy's arm. It was already blistered over and slightly swollen in reaction to the vaccine.

"What is this thing you have done? Has your mother—?"

"No," Three Eyes cut in. "The woman named Kate gave me the medicine at the camp of the white man with the glass-eye machine. It is to protect from smallpox."

"It is the mark of evil spirits!" Painted Wind shouted. "How could you allow a white woman to defile you like that?"

Surprised by his uncle's unexpected rage, Three Eyes remained silent as the tirade continued.

"You have heard me speak against the medicine of Mountain Laurel. Yet you allowed a white woman to cut your skin and pour the white poison into your soul. Look!" Again he touched the scab. "Already the poison has marked you with the sign of a Ute who does not follow the true path of his people. You ask to be a man, but you prove yourself a boy."

Searching for words with which to defend himself, Three Eyes opened his mouth to speak, but Painted Wind cut him off with a raise of his hand. "Be gone from my tipi! You belong in the tipi of your mother—the place for young boys!"

Tears welled up in the boy's eyes, and in shame he ran from the tipi. Racing into his own tipi, he was surprised—and pleased—that no fire was lit. At least his mother need not see that he had been crying.

At first Three Eyes thought the tipi was empty, but then he heard a cough, followed by the rasping sound of someone struggling to breathe.

"Mother?" he called, approaching her buffalo-robe bed. Leaning over the bed, he was shocked to find Singing Water curled up, sweating profusely as she coughed.

She rolled over, looked up at her son, and forced a smile. "You are . . . home," she finally managed to say.

"Mother, what is wrong?" He touched her cheek. Her face seemed far thinner than he had ever seen.

"It is nothing," she tried to assure him.

"You are sick. You have the smallpox."

"No!" Singing Water shouted, bolting upright in bed.

"I must get Painted Wind."

"No!" she repeated. "With sleep, I will be fine."

"Then let me get Mountain Laurel."

"You will stay with me while I sleep. If I am not well tomorrow, then you may bring Mountain Laurel."

Three Eyes nodded; he would do as she wished.

"And Three Eyes," she whispered, reaching up and taking his hand. "You must not tell Painted Wind. Promise me you will not tell Painted Wind."

"I will do as you ask."

Singing Water smiled and leaned back against the bed. A few minutes later, she had drifted into a restless sleep.

It was the third morning of school, and Lucas was used to the fact that none of the Ute children would be responding to his bell. Whereas the first morning the entire village had remained indoors and the area had seemed deserted, now people went about their business and paid no attention to the buckboard wagon or the boy ringing the bell.

"Let's go," Lucas said, forcing a smile to show his father that he was not disheartened.

Quint tousled his son's hair and then started the wagon

toward the trading post. He had not driven far when another wagon came into view, entering the village from the east. It was moving quite rapidly, and as it drew closer, Quint recognized the occupants as Isaac Halloran and his family.

Halting his wagon, Quint waited until the Hallorans came up alongside.

"Hello, Isaac . . ." Quint began, the words trailing off as he saw his friend's swollen left eye and the large purple welt that covered his left cheek. Alice Halloran's eyes were also swollen—from crying—and she was clutching her baby close to her chest.

"Get Laurel," Quint told his son. Lucas nodded and quickly leaped from the wagon, Little Bear racing close behind. Turning to Halloran, Quint asked, "What happened?"

"Striker."

"But the Ute guards—"

"I sent them home last night," Halloran replied, shaking his head in disgust. "I'm a damn fool."

"Are you all right?"

"Me? Hell, Quint, you been around me long enough to know it would take more than a little roughing up by the likes of that Striker fellow to put a dent in my noggin!"

"I'll get some people to help straighten up your place. Then I'll round up some others and set off on his trail."

"No need to straighten up—leastwise, not right now," Halloran said. "That's what we come to tell you. Alice and me figure we'll take Deborah north to Durango until things settle down. If it was just us, we'd stick it out. But with a daughter . . ."

"I understand. But what about the smallpox?"

Alice turned her baby around and pulled back the blanket that covered her face. "She's much better," she said, smiling at last. "The sores are all gone, and so is the fever. We were hoping Laurel could check her and make sure she's well enough for the journey."

Just then Laurel came running up, medical bag in hand. Seeing Halloran's bruised face, she came around the wagon to examine him, but he waved her away, insisting that

Deborah be attended to first. It took only a few minutes for Laurel to give the baby a nearly clean bill of health. She was well on her way to recovery, and there would be no problem taking her to Durango, as long as they checked in with the local doctor upon their arrival. Since Halloran's bruises were superficial, Laurel let him go with a stern warning that he take things as easily as possible—which was not very likely with a man like him, she realized.

As Halloran prepared to pull out, he turned to Quint a final time. "There's one other thing I need to tell you, Quint. About the school." He paused a moment, trying to find the right words. In the end, he simply blurted out, "Striker burned it to the ground."

Halloran knew there was nothing more he could say. Leaving the Burgesses in stunned silence, he whipped up the wagon team and headed for Durango.

When Quint, Laurel, and Lucas returned to their tipi, they found Three Eyes waiting for them. "My mother is very sick," he told them. "She would not let me tell my uncle or come for you last night, and today she is worse."

Laurel headed off with Three Eyes, leaving Quint and Lucas to round up some braves to help track the men who had attacked the trading post. At Singing Water's tipi, she quickly determined that the Indian woman was indeed suffering from smallpox. In addition, she was dehydrated and nearly delirious from a high fever.

"You must tell Painted Wind about his sister-in-law," Laurel insisted. "But first bring plenty of water."

When Three Eyes returned with his uncle, Laurel was forcing Singing Water to drink some of the liquid. Laurel looked up at the tall Ute leader, expecting Painted Wind to be enraged at her presence, but he said nothing.

"I don't understand how she could get smallpox after being vaccinated," Laurel said, more to herself than for Painted Wind's sake. "Perhaps she already had it when I vaccinated her. But look at her arm." She lifted the upper arm and pointed at the place where the mark should be. "There is nothing—no reaction at all. Even if she already had smallpox, she should have reacted to the vaccine."

Painted Wind came over and carefully examined the faint scratch marks on his sister-in-law's arm where Laurel had cut her with the pin and smeared the medicine. Unlike his nephew's mark, this one showed no sign of redness or a scab.

"We must use the old ways," he said at last. "Perhaps your medicine is good for white people, but we are Ute. I will begin the prayers." He sat nearby and began to chant.

Laurel knew that praying could do no harm and might even help, if Singing Water heard and drew faith, and so she joined in, chanting softly as she cared for the sick woman. She was pleased that for once she and Painted Wind could work together. After all, she could claim no more effective treatment of smallpox than making the patient comfortable and keeping the fever from getting dangerously high.

The water seemed to be helping Singing Water, who was no longer babbling incoherently but was still sweating and shivering. Laurel covered her and was about to give her more water when Quint came rushing in.

"It's not only her," he cryptically announced, pausing to catch his breath. "Two other Ute just showed up at our tipi, and it looks like smallpox."

"Had they been vaccinated?" Laurel asked, and Quint nodded affirmatively.

Painted Wind took little notice as Laurel hurried from the tipi. He sat chanting beside his sister-in-law and held her hand as he struggled to figure out what was happening to his people. He knew that Singing Water and most of the other Ute had not been treated with real vaccine, but not for a moment did he think that had any connection with their now coming down with the disease. Believing that the power of a healer is largely derived from his ability to make others believe in him, Painted Wind assumed that Laurel's medicine treatment was her own method of convincing the Ute that they were protected from this smallpox. His own action in replacing the vaccine was to keep his people from being defiled by the "white poison." But the current outbreak of smallpox must be the will of the Great Spirit, which neither Laurel's vaccine nor his own medicine chants could prevent.

"The Great Spirit is angry," Painted Wind concluded, cutting off his chant. "He is displeased with my people, and so my prayers go unheard."

Three Eyes moved closer to his uncle and mother. "It will be all right."

Painted Wind wrapped his arm around the boy's shoulder and smiled. Together they resumed the chant.

As they sat with Singing Water, her fever seemed to increase. She tossed from side to side, sweat pouring from her forehead, and began to mutter in her delirium.

"Hummingbird . . . bring home my love . . . that the flowers may bloom . . ."

"Easy, now," Painted Wind whispered, leaning over and slipping his arm under her neck.

"That the flowers may grow . . ."

Singing Water suddenly opened her eyes and looked up at her brother-in-law. "Painted Wind has returned! And look! A deer—he brings me a deer! My weaving . . . where is my weaving?" Her hands began to move, as if working a shuttle. "There. I must not look. But he will see the flowers and know that I love him. Oh, Painted Wind, take me to your tipi!" Her eyes closed, and her head lolled to the side.

Easing her down against the buffalo robes, Painted Wind leaned back from the bed. "Singing Water?" he whispered. "She loves me?" Glancing at his nephew, he saw the boy was nodding. "I did not know."

"She has always loved you."

"The flowers?" he asked, remembering the way Singing Water's tipi had been decorated when he returned from Utah.

"For you."

Painted Wind caressed his sister-in-law's cheek. "You will get better. I will help you get better."

The Ute woman abruptly pulled her head away, as if cringing from his touch. "*No!*" she shrieked. "Do not touch me!"

She lashed out, flailing away at some unseen attacker.

Painted Wind grabbed her wrists and tried to hold her steady.

"No! You will not defile me! I will live for my son! For Painted Wind!" She began to moan and writhe on the bed, as if being attacked. "You can rape my body, but you will not touch my spirit!" Her body suddenly went limp. "I m-must not t-tell Painted Wind," she stammered in a barely audible whisper. "He cannot love a woman touched by the whites." She let out a wail and then began to sob.

Painted Wind held her tight, moved by her unexpected declaration of love and by the pain she had been suffering in silence. "Are these things true?" he asked no one in particular, and as he turned around, he saw that Quint and Laurel had returned to the tipi and were standing nearby.

"We believe she was raped by the same men who attacked the trading post," Laurel said, coming up beside him. "She didn't want anyone to know."

Painted Wind let go of Singing Water and stood up. "Will you take care of her, Mountain Laurel?" he asked.

She looked at him in surprise, then touched his forearm and nodded.

"I must find these men," he declared. "There will be justice."

Quint stepped forward. "I'm about to head out on their trail with some of the braves. Will you join us?"

Painted Wind stared at the white man for a long moment, then said, "We will go alone—I to avenge my brother's wife, and you for your white friends. We need no other braves."

Quint was about to protest, but he saw the look of determination in the eyes of the Ute warrior. Realizing that the two of them might be more effective than a large contingent of braves, he nodded in agreement.

With a brief glance at Singing Water, Painted Wind turned and headed from the tipi. He retrieved his new Winchester rifle from his own tipi and then prepared his horse. As he mounted up, Three Eyes came to him.

"Let me ride with you," the boy asked.

"This is for men to do," Painted Wind declared.

"I am fourteen," Three Eyes replied. "This was my mother they hurt."

"You must stay with Singing Water. If I do not return, my tipi will become your tipi." With a brisk nod, he kicked his horse into a gallop and rode away.

Lucas and Little Bear approached Three Eyes, who was readying his horse to ride. Lucas noticed that in addition to the brass spyglass around his neck, his Ute friend had his uncle's old single-shot rifle slung over his shoulder.

"Where are you going?" Lucas asked.

Without smiling, Three Eyes replied, "Damned if I will stay behind. I will find the men who hurt my mother."

"But my father and your uncle are on their trail."

"I am Three Eyes. I can see where they cannot."

"What will you do if you find them?"

"I will kill them."

"But there are at least three of them."

Three Eyes stared at the younger boy and finally gave a slight smile. "Do not worry, my friend. I will not do this alone. I will find them, and then I will get my uncle."

Three Eyes leaped upon his horse and was about to ride off, but Lucas grabbed hold of the bridle. "You promise you won't act on your own?" As the Ute boy nodded in reply, Lucas saw a flicker of indecision in his eyes. "Wait for me," Lucas said impulsively. "I will come along."

"This is for the Ute—"

"They hurt my friends the Hallorans and also Paige. And they burned down my father's school."

Three Eyes looked down at the white boy who could hear with his eyes. He nodded solemnly. "But you must hurry. Get a horse and meet me at the north edge of the village."

After fruitless hours of searching, the boys returned later that afternoon to the outcropping of rocks where they had first met each other. They tied their horses below out of sight and took up a position hidden among the boulders.

Lucas patted Little Bear's head to keep him quiet as Three Eyes pointed to a large stand of trees just beyond the wagon road to the northeast and said, "That is where we gathered lodge poles. That must be where my mother . . ." His voice trailed off, and Lucas nodded in understanding.

Three Eyes raised the spyglass and scanned the trees for several minutes, then frowned and handed it to Lucas. "I suppose we should return to the village," he muttered in resignation as Lucas looked through the glass.

Three Eyes began to stand, but Lucas suddenly pulled him back down and waved toward the trees. "A campfire!" he said in excitement. "Look!"

Three Eyes took the spyglass and focused on the spot Lucas was indicating. After a short search, he picked out the flicker of flames, then looked up to find the thin gray smoke against the equally gray sky.

"Do you think it's them?" Lucas asked.

"The white men are too sure of themselves," Three Eyes replied. "They will be damn sorry."

"It might be someone else," Lucas suggested.

"My uncle and your father would not be building a fire. Only the white outlaws are such fools. But I will go closer and make certain."

"You can't," Lucas insisted. "We must get help."

"I will not bring my uncle unless I am sure. I will not be proved a silly boy."

"Then I'm coming with you."

"You will not. An Indian can walk more quietly alone. You will wait here with the horses, and when I return, we will ride for the village."

Three Eyes opened the pouch at his waist and removed a cartridge, which he loaded into his rifle. Then he held forth the spyglass. "Here," he said, handing it to his friend. "You can watch with this. And if anything should happen to me, this glass eye is yours."

As the Ute boy stood and started down from the rocks, Lucas called, "You won't go in there alone, will you?"

"I will only do what must be done," Three Eyes replied. He scrambled down toward the wagon road beyond.

For several minutes Lucas watched Three Eyes cautiously make his way across the wagon road toward the thick stand of trees to the northeast. Periodically, Lucas turned around and glanced at the two horses waiting below.

He will look and then hurry back, the boy spelled out with his fingers. *He said he will only do what must be done*.

Suddenly Lucas leaped up and started racing down to where the horses were tied, Little Bear close on his heels. "We're going for help!" Lucas shouted as he ran up to his horse and untied it. Leaving Three Eyes' horse behind, he set off at a gallop toward the Ute village to the south.

I am a Ute, Three Eyes told himself as he stared through the trees at the two unkempt men sitting by the fire. *I will avenge my mother*.

The boy sat with his finger on the trigger and scanned the clearing. As soon as he determined the position of the third outlaw, he would leap from the trees and dispatch each one as if he were a rabid dog. He mentally prepared himself, working through what he must rapidly do in order to fire the rifle, eject the cartridge, reload, and fire again.

Three Eyes heard only the whisper of leaves rustling behind him. Before he could spin around, there was a whooshing sound as something swung through the air and struck the back of his head. Then all flashed into blackness.

As his head began to clear, he heard a voice declare, "Well, I'll be damned! Where'd he come from?"

"I dunno," a closer voice replied. "Heard something when I was off relievin' myself, and this is what I found."

"Who is he?" a third voice asked.

"Damned if I know," the first voice replied. "Tie him by the fire, and we'll beat it out of him when he comes to."

Three Eyes was about to raise his head but thought better of it. He made no effort to struggle as they picked up his limp body and carried him away.

Halfway to the Ute village, Lucas came upon his father and Painted Wind, who were returning home in the gathering darkness. After quickly describing the situation, Lucas and Little Bear led the way back to the outcropping of rocks from where the campfire had been seen. Three

Eyes' horse was still tied below, and they left their own horses with it and climbed up into the rocks.

"The fire's still going," Quint said, lowering the brass spyglass. "But I see no sign of your nephew."

Painted Wind took the spyglass and scanned the trees beyond the wagon road. Then he declared, "I will take a closer look," and Quint nodded in agreement. Fifteen minutes later, he returned to where Quint and Lucas were waiting.

"He has been taken prisoner," Painted Wind declared. "Three men are guarding him."

Quint turned to his son. "You'll wait here while we go in and get Three Eyes."

Lucas immediately began shaking his head. "I want to help. He's my friend."

"It's too dangerous."

"But you need to take them by surprise," Lucas argued. "There's a way I can help."

When Quint began to object, Painted Wind put up his hand. "Let us hear the young boy's plan."

It was nearly dark when Lucas started into the woods, Little Bear close at his side. As he approached the clearing where the campfire was burning, he began to shout the name of his friend.

"Three Eyes! Are you there?" he called again as he stepped from the trees. Across the clearing, the three outlaws had already leaped to their feet and were yanking their weapons from their holsters. Beside them on the ground, Three Eyes opened his eyes and stared in horror at his young white friend.

"Hold it right there!" Quint shouted as he stepped from the trees at the far side of the clearing, his rifle trained on the backs of the outlaws. Twenty feet away, Painted Wind also appeared, rifle at the ready.

Unexpectedly, one of the outlaws spun around and fired. His partner dropped to his knees and began firing, as well. They were met by a hail of bullets from Quint and Painted Wind. Striker, meanwhile, leaped for the ground and rolled toward the boy across the way. As he came up, his gun was trained on Lucas. While the men with the rifles were still occupied with the other two outlaws, Striker grabbed hold of the young boy and pressed the revolver to his head.

Little Bear, however, paid no attention to the revolver and leaped at the man who was attacking his master. Angling the gun down, Striker fired, and Little Bear fell in a heap.

"Stay back!" Striker shouted at the two riflemen, who stood now beside the motionless bodies of his friends. Before they had time to react, he dragged Lucas to his horse, which was tethered nearby at the edge of the clearing. He hoisted the boy on top, being careful to keep the horse between himself and the men with the rifles. Aiming the revolver at the boy's head, he lifted his left foot into the stirrup and started to climb up behind.

Twenty feet away, Little Bear raised his head and looked up at Lucas on the horse. He saw the man with the gun and knew that his master was in trouble. Disregarding the stabbing pain in his side, Little Bear pulled himself to his feet and charged.

Striker had just raised his right foot from the ground when the big black dog came barreling into him, sinking its teeth into his calf and knocking him off balance. Yelping with pain, Striker slipped from the stirrup and was forced to let go of Lucas. Immediately the boy slid off the other side of the horse and ran toward his father.

Struggling to free his leg from the animal's jaws, Striker swung his revolver around and fired. The bullet tore into the dog's back, and it gave up its hold and fell to the ground.

Striker grabbed hold of the saddle horn and hoisted one leg over the top, but stayed hanging on the other side of the horse. He heard the sudden crack of rifle shots and felt the sting of a bullet creasing his thigh as he spurred his horse into the trees and rode into the night.

The forest had grown silent as Lucas sat beside his beloved dog, holding its head in his lap. The dog's breath came in short gasps as it struggled to open its eyes.

"Rest easy, boy," Lucas whispered. He clutched the animal to him, burying his face in the dog's fur.

Little Bear whimpered, then barked lightly a final time. At last the shallow breathing stopped.

Lucas felt hands at his shoulder, and he glanced around to see Quint and Three Eyes looking down at him.

"He's resting," Lucas said, forcing a smile. "He's just resting." Lucas hugged Little Bear and began to cry.

Chapter Twelve

Kate McEwan became aware of sound and opened her eyes, and for a moment she thought it was night. But the air around her held a faint green luminescence, and as she focused, she realized it was the glow of sunlight filtering through some sort of cloth material. Her head felt thick and heavy as she struggled to make out the sound that had awakened her, but it was distorted, as if she were listening inside a pot. Slowly the reverberations diminished, and she could make out a voice:

> "Amang the train there is a dame
>   I dearly lo'e mysel';
> But whaur her hame, or what her name,
>   I dinna care to tell."

Kate pushed aside the blanket and sat bolt upright, then grabbed the back of her neck as a dull pain began to throb in her head.

"You're awake!" the voice said excitedly.

Kate turned to her left and in the dim light made out the form of a man sitting beside her. "Paige?" she whispered. "Where am I?"

"Back at our campsite—inside the supply tent," he replied.

Kate looked around and realized the dull glow came from sunlight playing upon the green canvas. She glanced

down, suddenly afraid that she might not be dressed, and
was relieved to see that she was fully clothed.

"What happened?" she asked as the throbbing faded.

"Your horse was struck by lightning. You took quite a
jolt, but you came through just fine."

"Last night . . . the storm," she muttered, remembering their journey through the canyons.

"Yes, the storm," Paige answered. "But not last night.
It was the night before. You've been asleep since then."

"You're kidding," she said, but as her eyes grew accus-
tomed to the light, she was able to make out his face and
could see that he was serious. "The cliff house," she
continued. "Did you see it?"

"See what?"

"The alcove—a great cavern up on the cliffside. It was
lit by lightning, and I saw the cliff house."

"There was no cliff house," Paige said emotionlessly.

"But I saw—"

"You were delirious. You kept babbling on and on about
having seen a cliff house, but before I brought you back
here I stood right where you were struck, and there was
nothing. It must have been a hallucination."

Kate lay back on the bedroll, her head pounding again.
"I'm sure I saw it," she insisted, rubbing her temples.

"Why not get some more rest," Paige urged her. "I'll fix
you something to eat."

"It seemed so real," she whispered as he left the tent.

An hour later, Paige had a pot of soup prepared. He was
debating whether to call Kate or let her rest some more,
when she suddenly appeared at the entrance of the tent,
looking remarkably better. Her auburn hair was neatly
brushed, and she wore a fresh blouse and pair of pants.

"Feeling better?" he asked, filling a bowl with soup.

"Much—but I'm starving, and that smells wonderful."
She came over to the campfire and sat beside him. "I
heard you earlier," she added, taking the bowl.

"You did?" he said, afraid that she had remembered
being cared for by Surnia. He was not ready to tell her
about the discovery, lest she prematurely report the find.

"Yes, and you have a lovely singing voice—when you're not trying to drown me out."

Paige relaxed. "I didn't know you were listening."

"No doubt. If you did, you wouldn't have been singing in Scottish." Smiling, she reached out and gently touched his arm. "It sounded nice—even with an English accent. It made me want to wake up."

"I suppose that's better than putting people to sleep." He looked down nervously. "I'm glad you wanted to wake up."

"And I'm feeling much better," she assured him. "So much so that I want you to continue your explorations."

"I don't think you should consider—"

"Not me. I'll spend the day resting right here. But I'd feel terrible if I kept you from your work any longer."

"I really didn't mind . . ."

"I know, Paige. And thank you. But now I want you to get on with your work. Perhaps tomorrow I can join you."

"I *have* been itching to get started again," he admitted. "There are some canyons farther south that I haven't explored yet."

"Yes," Kate said eagerly. "That sounds like a great idea. We didn't have much luck the other day. Perhaps in a new location . . ."

"I agree," he said, relieved that she had not brought up the subject of the cliff house she thought she had seen during the storm. "I'll get started right after we eat."

An hour later, Kate waved good-bye and watched as Paige rode off to the southwest, leaving behind his packhorse—at her suggestion—in case she needed it in an emergency. As soon as he was gone, she hurried into the tipi and brought out her saddle, which Paige had recovered from her dead horse. She saddled the packhorse and strapped her tripod camera to the saddle horn, then mounted up and headed west.

Kate was convinced she had seen a cliff house and that she could find it again. She would photograph it, and then Paige would see that a Scottish journalist made a better detective than an English archaeologist.

It took less than two hours to find the spot where her horse had been struck by lightning. The animal was gone, and a nearby mound of earth showed where it had been buried.

Seated on the packhorse at the top of the rise, Kate scanned the northern cliff face for an alcove large enough to hold a cliff dwelling. At first she saw no sign of such a cavern among the sandstone formations of the cliff. She was giving up hope when her eye returned to one particular area along a nearly horizontal fault line. As she followed the line, she realized that the section of rock above it might really be dozens of feet beyond.

Keeping her eyes on the line, Kate rode to one side. As she had suspected, the stone directly above the fault moved at a slower rate than the stone below—indicating that it was indeed farther away. Focusing on the upper area, she thought she saw rectangular patterns—perhaps man-made—but the angle of the sun created a mix of shadows and bright light that made it virtually impossible to see clearly.

Kate rode down off the rise and crossed to the opposing canyon wall. For a half hour she rode up and down along the wall, wondering how anyone could have made it up so steep an incline. She was getting ready to give up the search and head back to camp when she noticed a place where a small wash of stones had tumbled down from behind an outcropping of boulders, perhaps carried by the storm runoff.

On impulse, she dismounted, tethered her horse, and scrambled up the embankment that led behind the boulders. At the top, she found herself standing on a three-foot-wide plateau that seemed carved by hands, not the effects of time and weather. Leading off the plateau was a slightly narrower trail that ran up along the face of the canyon wall.

Climbing down to her horse, Kate unstrapped the camera, hoisted it over her shoulder, and started back up the trail.

Quint sat in his tipi with Lucas, who had spent the morning in bed, refusing both breakfast and lunch. He tried to talk with his son about Little Bear, but the boy would not be consoled. And yet, except during the first moments following Little Bear's death, Lucas had not cried.

Laurel came up behind Quint and placed her hand on his shoulder. "He will be all right. He just needs some rest."

"I know," Quint said, standing up and allowing Laurel to lead him from the tipi. "And you must need some rest, too. You didn't come in at all last night, did you?"

"There were still more cases of smallpox," she explained. "I had to do what I could—what they'd let me."

"How did they act toward you?" he asked.

"They're confused. They no longer trust me, but they know I've been caring for Singing Water and that Painted Wind hasn't stopped me. I think they're waiting to see what he does. Anyway, there really isn't much I can do for the ones who have already come down with it."

"If only they'd have let you vaccinate them sooner."

"I'm not sure that's the problem. You know, that vaccine had to come a long way, and it's quite unstable."

"Do you think it was no good?"

"Some of it, at least."

Quint took his wife in his arms and held her close. "I know you're doing all you can."

"Which isn't much." She leaned up and kissed him, then pulled back slightly and said, "And how are you doing?"

"I'll feel a lot better when I get my hands on Striker— and on that Felders fellow who hired him."

"Any ideas how to do that?"

"After Striker got away, one of his friends lived long enough to admit they were working for Felders. And Painted Wind knows him—Felders took him to Utah to convince him to relocate the Ute out there. It seems Felders was playing all the angles at once—trying to buy off the Ute through Painted Wind while at the same time putting pressure on them through Striker. He made promises to share mining profits with the Ute, but never planned to follow through."

"What does Painted Wind say about this?" Laurel asked.

"He's determined to kill him—especially after Three Eyes told us about meeting Felders at Paige's camp. Apparently Paige has been working for him as a geologist."

"I can't believe it. He sent that note to warn us about Felders."

"Maybe he's beginning to see what his boss is really like. In any case, Three Eyes told us that Felders and Paige arranged to meet again out there in two weeks, which I figure to be next Sunday. I plan to be there."

Just then a deep voice spoke behind Quint and Laurel, and they turned to see Painted Wind, dressed in a ceremonial robe and feathered headdress. "I will be there with you, my white brother," he said. "But first there is something we must do. Is the young boy inside?"

Quint nodded, and Painted Wind walked over and entered the tipi. Quint and Laurel looked curiously at one another and then followed him inside.

Painted Wind stepped up to the bed where Lucas was lying. The boy looked up in surprise as the Indian said, "Come, my young friend. It is time for us to go."

Lucas leaned up on one elbow, not sure what to do.

"It is time," Painted Wind solemnly declared. "Little Bear needs your help so that his spirit may begin its final journey. Come—we must speak the words of passage."

Somewhat dazed, Lucas stood and followed the imposing-looking Indian outside. There he found Three Eyes seated on his horse, holding the reins of two other horses. Painted Wind waved Lucas toward one of the animals, and numbly he climbed up onto the horse's bare back.

Laurel came over and touched her son's hand. "Do you want us to come?" she asked.

Lucas glanced at his father and then turned to the two Indians, who were mounted and waiting. "No," he replied. "I will be all right."

Laurel nodded, and she and Quint watched as Lucas rode from the village.

Upon reaching the rock outcropping from where he and Three Eyes had discovered the outlaws, Lucas saw that a ten-foot-high platform had been built at the top. The platform was draped with animal hides, which he knew were covering the body of Little Bear. Numerous feathers, beaded necklaces, and even a bow and arrow were hanging along the edge of the platform and down the wooden stilts.

The three riders dismounted and climbed up to the platform. As they stood beside it, Painted Wind took from under his robe a beautifully carved stone pipe, which he lit and passed to Lucas. The boy was hesitant at first, but Painted Wind motioned him to smoke. He took a deep draw, and tears came to his eyes as he forced himself not to cough. He exhaled the smoke and handed the pipe to Three Eyes.

When the pipe returned to Painted Wind, he hung it, still smoking, on one of the platform legs. "He'e'e' Ahi'ni'yo'," he intoned, and the boys repeated the phrase.

"Little Bear is a fierce warrior and loyal friend. He will be welcomed by the Great Spirit," Painted Wind declared. "He has given his own life so that his master may live." Painted Wind looked directly at Lucas and said, "And you will live and grow strong, my young brother. You will do this for Little Bear."

The tears came again, and Lucas nodded.

Painted Wind raised his arms, first to the platform and then to the sun. In a deep tone that sounded like the voice of the Great Spirit itself, he chanted:

> Great Spirit that is in all things
> bless this gift of life
> that the giver and receiver
> may grow and be renewed

Joining in, Three Eyes spoke the chant, while Lucas signed it with his hands:

> come to me, sacred brother
> your journey has begun
> bring us your gift, sacred brother
> your journey has begun

Painted Wind and Three Eyes left Lucas at the platform and went down to where the horses were tied. As they mounted up and waited for Lucas, Three Eyes turned to his uncle and said, "I am afraid I have failed you."

"How have you done this?" Painted Wind asked.

"I wanted to be a man but acted like a foolish boy. If I had not gone alone against those men, Little Bear would be alive, and perhaps their leader would not have escaped."

Painted Wind smiled. "If you had not found those men, two of them would still be alive to hurt our people. You sought to avenge the wrong done to your mother. You acted like a true Ute brave, and I am proud of you. It is I who should be ashamed."

"What have you done?" Three Eyes asked.

"I would have given away our sacred land—for a few horses and some empty promises. It was my nephew who hunted down and unmasked those men. You have saved me from a terrible mistake, for without your actions, I might have led my people into a bitter future, cast adrift without a home."

Painted Wind leaned across and clasped the boy's forearm, then looked up to see Lucas climbing down toward them. He had been crying but now seemed at peace.

"Come," Painted Wind said, releasing his nephew's arm. "There is more I must do to right my wrongs."

An hour later, they reentered the Ute village. Painted Wind sent Lucas home, then told Three Eyes to have all the villagers assemble at Laurel's tipi. He continued alone to his own tipi, and a few minutes later he emerged and started to walk through the village.

Laurel and Quint were outside with Lucas as Painted Wind approached. He was still wearing his headdress and ceremonial robe, and in his hand he held a jug. Following him was a large crowd of villagers.

Holding forth the jug, Painted Wind said, "I have come to return your medicine, Mountain Laurel. I removed it from your bottle and replaced it with herbal water. I do not know if this medicine of yours works, but I have learned that I have not followed the straight path and no longer have the true *po-o-kan-te* of my people. It is for you to show us the way."

Dumbfounded, Laurel accepted the jug of vaccine and touched some to her lips.

Painted Wind reached behind his neck and untied the leather thongs of his medicine pouch. Removing his feather headdress, he held forth the two objects and declared, "You must have these, as well."

Laurel waved the items away. "It takes a great leader to see that he has taken a wrong path and to lead his people onto a new one. You are truly such a leader. I am only a half-breed physician, and I can't hope to do my work without the help of men like you, Painted Wind, leader of the Ute."

Painted Wind looked at her for a long time and then put his headdress back on and placed the pouch around his neck. Stepping closer, he bared his left arm and said, "Then you will begin your work by giving me this medicine of yours."

As Laurel hurried inside and brought out her medical supplies, the rest of the Ute lined up behind Painted Wind, awaiting their turns to receive the vaccine.

Painted Wind did not flinch as his arm was pricked with the needle and the medicine was applied. As soon as it was finished, he started back toward his tipi. Making his way past the gathered crowd, he saw that his sister-in-law was standing alone beside a nearby tipi. She looked pale and weak, and it was apparent that she still had a fever.

"You must not be out here," Painted Wind declared as he hurried over and took hold of her arm. "You are not well."

Singing Water smiled at her brother-in-law, and tears ran down her cheeks. "I have seen all that you have done and heard all that you have said," she told him, her voice faltering. "It has made me feel far better than any medicine could have done." She reached up and touched his face. "You are wrong, my dear brother. You have the true *po-o-kan-te*—in your heart."

*   *   *

Kate McEwan scrambled up the last section of the trail and came over the top. She nearly dropped her camera in shock as she looked up to see the imposing stone buildings of Cliff House. To her left, the wide floor of the immense alcove led to a sheer drop of several hundred feet. Set back in the alcove was not the ruins of a few stone buildings, as she had expected, but a gigantic city of stone in almost perfect condition, complete with towers and plazas.

"God . . . what will Paige think when he sees this?" she mumbled as she hurried across the alcove to one of the stairways leading into the fortresslike city.

At the top she found herself in a stone courtyard, surrounded by individual buildings that were built one against the other so that they formed a single structure. For a few minutes she stood looking at the impressive sight, amazed that anyone could have constructed such a place in such an inaccessible location.

Suddenly she remembered the camera she was carrying. She spread the tripod, then removed the sealed dry-plate holder so that she could focus the shot. Taking off the lens cap, she opened the back of the camera and looked at the image on the focusing screen. She turned the camera and framed a suitable shot of one section of the ruins, then rotated the lens until the picture came into focus. While looking through the focusing screen, she prepared to lower the dry-plate holder into the slot, but a movement in the screen caused her to stop. As she stared, a man leading a horse walked forward into focus.

"Paige!" she declared, snapping her head up as he approached. "How did you get here?"

"I could ask the same thing. I thought you were at—"

"You didn't believe I saw anything, so I decided to find this place myself and prove it to you. But how did you get up here with that horse?"

"On the trail, just like you. You really didn't have to walk—it's wide enough and not too steep to ride."

"But how did you find it?"

"It's a long story."

"We Scots aren't known for our patience . . . so you'd better get started."

Paige sat near Kate on one of the walls and described the events following her injury, including the appearance of the old medicine man and how he had saved her life, and how he had then told Paige where to find the cliff dwelling.

Kate listened calmly, then suddenly frowned and said, "You weren't going to tell me, were you?"

"I was—but not yet."

"Why the hell not? I thought we were friends."

"We are," Paige insisted. "It's . . . it's just . . . well, look around you. This is one of the most important archaeological discoveries of the century. When word gets out, this place will be crawling with fortune hunters. They'll strip it bare."

"And that's what you take me for—a fortune hunter?"

"No, Kate, not at all. But you're a damn good journalist, and I'd expect you to do your job."

"Then you *weren't* going to tell me."

"I just needed some time. When I first came up here while Surnia was watching you, I felt as if something really important had been given to me—that I held the fate of Mesa Verde in my hands. I needed time to decide what I was going to do about it."

"And do you know yet?"

"I'm not certain. But I will."

"And what about me?" Kate asked.

"I don't understand—"

"Me, dammit! You're not the only one involved in this. You may not care to admit it, but I saw this place first—and almost lost my life in the process. Don't I have a right to be in on this thing?"

"You're right. I'm sorry."

Kate sat down on the wall and stared at the ground for a while. She looked at Paige and started to chuckle.

"What is it?" he asked.

"Just me, that's all. Here I am berating you for leaving me out, when that's exactly what I was doing to you. I planned to tell you as soon as I found this place, but who knows what I actually would have done? I guess I'll just have to believe that sooner or later you'd have told me."

"I would have, Kate. I . . . I care too much about what you think of me."

"You do?" Kate asked, looking at him closely. She saw genuine affection in his eyes, as well as caution. "Then by all the Highland saints, why don't you prove it?"

Paige looked flustered. "I don't understand. . . ."

"Well, I don't know about England, but this is how we prove it in Scotland."

Leaning close to him, Kate reached around his neck and softly kissed his cheek. For a moment Paige sat there, not sure how to respond. Then he took her in his arms, pressed his lips against hers, and pulled her close.

From a tower window high above, Surnia watched as the young couple kissed and then walked arm in arm to her Spirit Catcher. He was pleased that the woman felt better and that their individual songs were beginning to merge into one.

As the woman turned the tripod and framed the man in the shot, Surnia backed into the shadows so that his spirit would not be caught by the picture machine. A frown touched his face as he realized that many whites might see her picture and learn about Mesa Verde. He knew that she could not trap all the *po-o-kan-te* of Mesa Verde in her tiny machine, but he also knew that the whites would come like locusts, trampling the stones until no more *po-o-kan-te* was left.

"I must prepare the ground," Surnia whispered as he stepped back to the window and looked outside again. The woman had closed her Spirit Catcher, and she and the man were heading back to the trail that led down off the alcove.

"The energy is changing," he exclaimed. "The ground must be prepared."

Chapter Thirteen

The following Saturday, the day before Felders and Paige were to meet, Quint and Painted Wind assembled the party that would ride to Paige's camp. Laurel, concerned about Paige and Kate, insisted upon going along. During the past week, there had been no new cases of smallpox, and even Singing Water had improved to the point where she could be left on her own. Laurel was convinced the worst was over and that she could leave the village for a few days. Three Eyes would be their guide, and after much debate it was agreed that Lucas would go, as well.

Through the long day, the party headed west and at sundown came to the campsite that Paige had been using as a base of operations. They found the tents still set up but no one there. The boys went to work taking care of the horses, while the men built a fire and Laurel prepared dinner.

It was almost dark when Paige and Kate arrived. They could be heard long before they were seen, their voices carrying across the desolate landscape:

> "And here's a hand, my trusty fiere,
>   And gie's a hand o' thine;
> And we'll tak a right guid willie-waught,
>   For auld lang syne. . . ."

The voices trailed off as the riders realized someone was at their campsite. Riding up to the fire, Paige called tentatively, "Felders, is that you?"

"No," Quint replied, "but he's the reason we've come."

"Laurel, it's so good to see you!" Kate shouted as she leaped from her horse and ran to give her friend a hug.

"What's up?" Paige asked, dismounting and offering his hand to Quint. He noticed Quint's cool reaction, and he rephrased his question, "What's wrong?"

"We're here about Felders," Quint said. "There are a few things we'd like you to explain."

Paige nodded. "Yes, it's about time, I'd say."

Everyone gathered around the campfire, and Paige told how he had been hired to do a geological study of the western region of the Ute reservation. Periodically, Kate interrupted to point out that Paige had not known there was anything wrong with what Felders was doing, and that as soon as he was certain, he had admitted what he knew. Furthermore, she described her injury in the storm, the appearance of Surnia, and the subsequent discovery of Mesa Verde.

"My grandfather is alive?" Laurel said in astonishment. "Are you certain, Kate?"

"I didn't actually see him—"

"But I did," Paige cut in. "And it was no ghost. He's out there somewhere in Mesa Verde—he wouldn't say why."

"He's gone there to die," Laurel said quietly.

"Well, he saved my life," Kate put in. "I'd like to thank him someday."

Quint turned to Paige. "Three Eyes told us that Felders plans to return here tomorrow to meet with you."

"That's right," Paige admitted. "He said tomorrow, but I can't be certain."

"What will you do?" Laurel asked.

"He's coming for a report on the mining potential of the area and to see the coal deposits I've found."

"But don't worry," Kate put in. "Paige says he has no intention of showing Felders anything."

"That may not be such a good idea," Quint said. "He'll just hire some other geologist to do the same thing."

Painted Wind stood up and walked to the far side of the fire, then turned to face the others. "It does not matter what any of you do. Tomorrow this white man will be dead."

"You can't kill him," Quint said.

"I will do this thing. He will never again make trouble for our people."

"But we don't know who else is involved." Quint turned to Paige. "Felders heads a large organization, doesn't he?"

"Yes, a mining consortium. There must be a dozen mining companies that are a part of it."

"So killing Felders will merely postpone this problem," Quint pointed out. "By now Felders has told others about the coal deposits. His death will only bring on an investigation and more pressure to move the Ute off their land."

"There must be another way," Laurel mused. "We need to get rid of Felders and his bunch and at the same time make sure no one else tries the same thing."

Everyone fell silent, until Kate jumped up and shouted, "Mesa Verde!" When the others looked at her as if she had lost her mind, she pointed to the west and said, "Don't you see? We've got Mesa Verde out there, and if we play our cards right, we can use it to get Felders off our backs."

Paige and Three Eyes were alone at the camp when Jakob Felders approached from the east the next afternoon. The boy lowered his spyglass as soon as he saw the man with the eye patch and said, "Big trouble. There is a second rider."

Paige grabbed the spyglass, focused it on the two riders, and immediately recognized Wade Striker. "Damn!" he muttered. "We'll have to proceed, anyway. Okay?"

"Yes. But the man named Striker saw me when his men were killed. He will remember."

Paige gazed at the approaching riders, then back at Three Eyes. "Not necessarily," he said mysteriously. "Wait here." He raced to the pup tent and returned with a small box. "These are paints for my maps. Color your face."

"You darn tootin'!" Three Eyes declared as he yanked open the wooden box. Choosing the red and black bottles, he quickly dabbed some across his cheeks and the bridge of his nose. "The colors of a warrior," he said. "Is it good?"

Paige stood back and inspected. "Perfect. Now let's just hope that all Indians look the same to Striker."

A few minutes later, the two men rode into camp.

"See you've still got your little Indian friend," Felders said with a smirk as he dismounted. "What's with all the paint? Is he on the warpath, or something?"

"No," Paige said, coming up and shaking hands with Felders. "He's just afraid of the spirits."

"Aren't they all!" Felders chuckled. He turned and nodded at Striker, who stayed on his horse and paid little attention to either Three Eyes or Paige. "I think you two met already—under not the best of circumstances."

Striker glanced at Paige but betrayed no emotion. Paige frowned slightly, then turned to Felders. "We met."

"All that trouble's been cleared up. I hope it won't cause any ill feeling between you two."

"Not on my part," Paige said. Striker merely grunted.

"Good. Then let's get on with your report. I want to see that coal of yours."

Paige stooped down and picked up a small backpack from the ground. "There's plenty of coal," he said. "I've got some choice samples in here for you to take back to Durango. But forget about coal. I've found something far better."

"What do you mean?"

"Gold."

"You mean there's gold in these hills after all?" Felders said with growing excitement. Even Striker sat up and looked more alert.

"Tons of it, and you don't even have to mine it. Just go in and carry it out."

"What?"

"You asked why the boy is all painted up. Well, he's afraid we've upset the spirits by stumbling onto a secret that's been hidden for centuries."

"What are you talking about?" Felders asked, growing more impatient.

"I'm talking about Cibola—the Seven Cities of Gold. This stupid little Indian has led me to the fabled cities of gold, and they're ours for the taking!"

"Have you gone crazy?"

"Here—look." Kneeling, Paige pulled from his pocket a piece of paper, which he unfolded and spread on the ground.

"What is it?" Felders asked skeptically as he knelt beside him and examined the sketches.

"It's the city that I just finished surveying. No one ever found it because it was built in a hidden alcove in one of the canyons west of here." Paige glanced up at Felders. "Surely you've heard rumors of cliff dwellings around here."

Felders hesitated a moment and then replied, "Yes, I think so. But no one's ever seen them."

"I damn well came close to missing them, too. Even the Indians don't like to go there."

Three Eyes stepped forward, pointed at the sketch of Cliff House, and said, "They are cursed."

Paige began to laugh. "Cursed, all right. Cursed with untold wealth for any man bold enough to take it."

"Is this some kind of joke?" Felders demanded.

"I've seen it, Jakob, with my own eyes! The walls are plated with gold an inch thick. Most of the stone is crumbling, but that just makes it easier to get at the gold. It's real, all right, and I'll prove it to you right now."

Paige stuffed the drawing in his pocket, then went to his horse and hoisted the backpack of coal samples over the saddle horn. He and Three Eyes mounted up and led Felders and Striker west into the canyons. As they rode, Paige gave a running lecture about the legend of Cibola and the people who had tried to find the mysterious cities of gold.

"It's said that anyone who desecrates one of the cities will go mad. It's the curse of Cibola." He began to laugh and added, "Hey, look at me. I've already desecrated the place, and I'm not mad—at least not yet! Still, the legend persists. At least four Spanish expeditions went in search of Cibola, and each ended in the death of nearly all the members. The few who made it home had invariably gone mad from wandering alone in the desert, which is probably how the legend began. They babbled on and on about cities of gold floating in the sky, and eventually people decided it was just a myth. But I've seen them, and they exist!"

Paige led the way into the canyon in which Cliff House was located. Nearing the hidden trail, he pointed upward and shouted, "Look! It's up on that cliff. Do you see it?"

Felders and Striker shielded their eyes and stared up at the north wall of the canyon. "There's nothing up there," Felders said, growing increasingly annoyed.

"That's what I mean. You can't see it until you are on top of it. Watch."

Paige rode to where the narrow trail wound up along the canyon wall. He urged his horse up the steep incline to the small plateau atop the outcropping of boulders. Looking back down, he said, "From down there it looks like nothing, but this is the gateway to heaven. Come on!"

Felders stared in disbelieving amazement as Paige slapped his reins and disappeared behind the boulders. A moment later, he reappeared farther up the wall. Felders could not make out the trail upon which he was riding—it was as if horse and rider were floating in the air.

Three Eyes kicked his own mount forward and made his way up along the trail. As soon as he disappeared from sight, Felders turned to Striker, who merely shrugged his shoulders. With a confused shake of his head, Felders kneed his horse and started up the trail, Striker close behind.

For ten minutes they followed Paige and the boy along the switchback trail. Finally they came up over the top and found themselves confronted by an immense city of stone.

Paige and Three Eyes were sitting on their horses halfway across the alcove, and Paige turned to them and shouted, "Have you ever seen such gold in your life?"

Felders looked around, but all that he saw was stone. He turned to Striker, who muttered, "What's going on?"

Across the alcove, Paige leaped from his horse and, with arms raised high, raced to one of the nearby walls. He almost seemed drunk as he clawed at the stone. Loosening a large chunk, he held it aloft and yelled, "Pure gold for the taking! And it's all ours!"

"He's crazy!" Striker shouted.

Felders stared in amazement as Paige staggered back to his horse, waving the worthless rock in his hand. Reaching with his free hand into the backpack on his saddle, Paige produced another rock, equally worthless.

"Who cares about all this coal, when there's so much gold for the taking!" he fairly screamed as he came up to Felders and waved the stones under the man's nose. "Which do you prefer?" he asked. "Gold?" He shook the first rock. "Or this coal?" And then he shook the rock from the backpack. "Cibola! We've found Cibola!" he shrieked.

"He's mad!" Striker repeated, drawing his revolver, intent on putting an end to the charade just as soon as Jakob Felders was out of the line of fire.

Quint stood with his friends behind a high stone wall at the top of the steps that led from the alcove floor to Cliff House. They watched as Paige carried out the ruse designed to convince Felders that there was neither gold nor coal in the area—that it had all been the delusions of a man who had spent too much time in the wilderness.

Striker had been an unexpected arrival, and Quint was on guard for trouble. As soon as Striker drew his revolver, Quint raised his Winchester to fire.

"Stop!" a voice called out, and Quint and the others spun around to see an old Indian approaching from behind.

"Surnia . . ." Laurel whispered, and Quint momentarily lowered his rifle.

As Quint turned around and began to raise the rifle again, Surnia said, "I will handle those men." Quint glanced questioningly at his wife, and she nodded that he should do as her grandfather wished.

Below, Striker was trying to get a clear shot at Paige, who stood tugging at Felders' leg. As Felders tried to kick the crazed man away, his horse stamped nervously in place.

Striker kneed his horse forward and began to come around Felders, so that he could get a bead on Paige, when suddenly a deep voice shouted, "Enough! It is finished!"

The two men twisted around on their saddles and looked up at the cliff dwelling. An old Indian was slowly descending the stairs toward them. Striker raised his revolver, then turned to Felders, uncertain whether or not to fire.

"Who are you?" Felders called to the old man.

"I am the guardian spirit of Cibola! I have come to avenge the desecration of my city!"

"It's a damn Indian!" Striker shouted. He quickly aimed his revolver and fired.

Laurel watched her grandfather stagger, then glanced over as Quint raised his rifle again. When she saw Surnia straighten up again, she suddenly leaned over and pushed down the barrel of Quint's gun. Without understanding her own actions, she said, "Leave this to my grandfather."

Laurel and the others stood transfixed as Surnia continued down the steps. Nearby, Striker's horse was in a panic from the reverberating noise of the gunshot, and it began to rear and spin in circles. Striker tried to steady the horse, and he managed a second and third shot at the old man, who kept walking, apparently unharmed.

"You cannot shoot a spirit!" Surnia shouted as Striker rode closer to the steps and again fired without effect.

Laurel watched in fear as her grandfather reached the bottom of the steps, then walked right past Striker and out across the alcove. Striker seemed unnerved by the haunting specter, who stood now at the very edge of the cliff, one hand against his stomach, the other raised portentously.

"We must meet our destiny," the medicine man intoned as he beckoned Striker toward him. "We are waiting."

The outlaw raised his revolver and fired, again without effect. He pulled the trigger a second time, but the hammer fell on an empty chamber. He tried once more but again was met with the sharp click of the hammer. Enraged, he threw the gun at the old man, but it went sailing over his head. Finally, Striker gave a blood-chilling scream and kicked his spurs into his skittish horse—forcing it into a run directly toward the man at the edge of the cliff.

Laurel grabbed Quint's arm and choked back a scream as the horse went charging at her grandfather, who stood without flinching, still beckoning toward Striker. Just when it seemed as if the horse would barrel into him and carry him over the cliff, the animal pulled itself up short and came to a shuddering halt. With no time to react, Striker was catapulted from the saddle and propelled far out over the abyss. His scream echoed off the canyon walls. Then there was a dull thud, and all was silent.

Laurel gasped with relief as she saw her grandfather standing unhurt, one hand still resting on his stomach while the other stroked the neck of Striker's horse. Then he patted the horse away from him and turned to Felders, who was still sitting on his horse beside Paige.

"We are waiting," the old man said, raising his arm and beckoning at the gray-bearded man with the eye patch.

Felders twisted wildly in his saddle, as if searching for a means of escape. He wore a revolver at his hip, but made no effort to go for it. Instead, he glanced down at Paige, who was still holding the two worthless rocks, then looked back at the old, beckoning Indian.

"*No!*" he screamed, fear vividly etched on his face. "No! No! No!" He pulled at the reins, as if fighting to keep from hurtling over the abyss himself. At last he managed to yank the horse around and kick him into a run across the alcove away from the old man. In a few seconds he reached the trail that led down to the canyon floor, and he disappeared from sight.

Laurel ran down the steps and over to where her grandfather was standing. She threw her arms around him and hugged him tight. As he pulled away, she saw that his smile was pained, and then she looked down and discovered that the front of her dress was smeared with his blood. The blood was flowing freely now from beneath the hand that he held against his stomach. A second wound bled at his side.

"Grandfather!" she gasped as he staggered and dropped to one knee.

Still smiling, Surnia said, "It is so good to see you again, my child."

At Surnia's insistence, Quint and Painted Wind carried him down into the central *kiva* of Cliff House. As they stood to one side with Kate, Paige, and the two boys, Laurel kneeled beside her grandfather and examined the wounds.

"I must operate," she said, but he shook his head.

"It is my time," he declared. "Your surgery would do me no good. The first bullet struck my stomach before coming to rest in my pelvis. The bullet at my side glanced off my ribs and angled upward through my left lung. So you see, I cannot live." Seeing the surprised expression on Laurel's face, he smiled up at her and said, "I am a *pwu-au-gut*. I need not cut into the body to know what is inside."

Laurel nodded and found herself smiling back at him. "There must be something—"

"It is finished. It is the will of the Great Spirit."

Paige came hesitantly forward and looked down at the old man. "You saved my life, just as you saved Kate's. Why did you do it?"

"It was my destiny, just as you have yours." Surnia began to cough, and blood trickled from his lips. Struggling to calm his chest, he continued, "I could not let them kill the white man who first set foot on Mesa Verde, and so I pretended to be a spirit. One of them is dead. The other will never return or mention what he has seen. The fear of death will keep him silent until the end of his days."

Paige kneeled down and took the old man's hand. "Those things you told me—about the desecration of Mesa Verde and my destiny. What should I do?"

"You will find the answer. But know that you were brought here to help me prepare the ground. It was you who provided the way. You have released my spirit and, in so doing, all the spirits of Mesa Verde. One day, we will be together, and you will understand."

Surnia closed his eyes and fought the chill that coursed through his body. "My work is nearly finished. I am ready for my final journey."

Looking up at Paige a final time, Surnia said, "Take the others above. I must be alone with my granddaughter."

Following his wish, they all climbed out of the *kiva* and left him alone with Laurel.

"My child," Surnia began, "I left my people and came to Mesa Verde because the *po-o-kan-te* called me. The power is strong, and it has kept these sacred canyons undefiled for hundreds of years. I thought it was up to me to renew that energy so that Mesa Verde could be protected for another hundred. Now I know the real reason I have come. For six hundred years the souls of the Anasazi have remained here, pulled to the great *po-o-kan-te* they created. But that energy must change—the souls must remain here no more. It is for me to lead the way—in my death, the spirits of Mesa Verde will discover new life. Then Mesa Verde will be free. The whites will come, and though there be desecration of the stones, there will be no desecration of the spirit."

"Must you die?" Laurel asked as a final plea.

Her grandfather laughed lightly. "Would you also try to keep the winter sun from being reborn?"

Laurel leaned over and hugged Surnia. His breathing was more labored, and he pushed his granddaughter away. "Come, there is one more thing I must do. I am the *pwu-au-gut*. I must pass along my gift."

Laurel looked down at him and remembered how he had told her that one day he must initiate another in the secret path—that he must pass along his gift. But as she stared into his eyes, she suddenly knew it was not to be her.

"Bring me the boy," he whispered. "My great-grandson."

Tears filled Laurel's eyes, and she smiled as she rose.

"And there is to be one other," he added, reaching up toward her. "The boy with the third eye. Send them to me, and then take the others down into the canyon."

"I will," Laurel said. "And I will see you again, my grandfather—on the other side."

"The energy must change," Surnia said, his voice weak. "It no longer belongs to the Anasazi. It no longer belongs to the Ute. It must be for all. You are the bridge, Mountain Laurel. The children stand on either shore."

Lucas sat on one side of Surnia, Three Eyes on the other. As the old man spoke, Lucas struggled to read his lips.

"I must speak to you of your father," Surnia told Three Eyes, and the boy moved closer. "He has given you a great gift in his glass eye. It has taught you to look closely at the world and to see it as it really is. He wants you to know that you have another third eye, and it is right here."

The old Indian reached up and touched the boy's forehead. As he did so, the darkened *kiva* seemed to fill with light, and Three Eyes thought he could see the young spirit who lived within this old man's body.

"You must learn to use your third eye, and it will always guide you back to the light."

Surnia turned to his great-grandson. "And now I must speak to you of your mother."

"Laurel?" the boy asked.

"No. The mother of your birth. When she died, you shut out the world with noise. But you have overcome your grief, you no longer need the noise. I have seen your mother. Indeed, I will be with her soon. She wants you to know that you need no longer shut out the world in order to hold onto her memory."

"But how . . . ?"

"You have already learned to see with your inner eye. Now you must listen with your inner ear."

Surnia reached up and closed Lucas's eyelids, then placed his hand over the amulet that rested against the boy's throat—a beaded yellow sunburst in a turquoise sky. The cacophony of noise slowly faded, and as Surnia spoke again, Lucas began to understand the words without looking, almost as if he were reading his mind.

"Speak what is on your mind," Surnia was saying.

Opening his eyes, Lucas slowly and deliberately began to speak, searching for the proper words. "The others didn't see what I saw. I saw you walk to the edge of the cliff and then beyond, like there was a bridge going out over thin air. No one saw that except me and those outlaws. That's why that man rode at you. He—" Lucas struggled for the words, his hand signing his thoughts. Then he continued, "He believed the ground went farther than it did. But his horse knew the truth and stopped at the edge. Why didn't the others see it? Why only me and those two men?"

"Ah, my child, you saw what the others did not because you have learned to see with your inner eye as well as your outer ones. My body did not walk beyond the cliff— but my spirit did. You saw it because you have a gift. Those men saw it because they did not think me a man but a spirit, and so they saw what my spirit showed them. But your friends know me as a man of flesh, and so they saw a man's body standing at the edge of the cliff. We are flesh *and* spirit, and though you may see one, never lose sight of the other."

"Then what am I hearing now?" Lucas asked. "Is it your human voice or your spirit speaking?"

"That is for you to discover. Perhaps it is both, my great-grandson." Surnia closed his eyes and touched the amulet around the boy's neck. "You boys now share a great gift—the gift of seeing from within. Trust that gift, for in it the true teacher may be found." Suddenly the old man was seized by a fit of coughing. When it subsided, he whispered in an exceedingly faint voice, "And now I must go."

"Don't die!" Lucas blurted out.

Opening his eyes, Surnia said, "There is no death, my child. Only the great journey, in which the mountain lion will walk in peace with the rabbit he has devoured." His eyes again closed, and he exhaled a final time.

Lucas felt a cold wave shudder through him, and he shut his own eyes. But even with his eyes closed, he could see Surnia lying on the ground in front of him. The spirit of the old medicine man rose, smiled at Lucas and Three Eyes, and started up the ladder that led out of the *kiva*.

Lucas no longer knew whether his own eyes were open or closed as he turned and looked at his young Indian friend, who stood and joined Lucas at the ladder. Together they followed the old man from the chamber.

Standing above the *kiva*, the boys saw Surnia walking down the steps and out toward the edge of the cliff. Then he walked beyond the edge and continued across the abyss.

The spirit of the *pwu-au-gut* turned and beckoned toward them, and for a moment Lucas thought they were supposed to follow. But then he realized Surnia was looking past them as he chanted:

> *come with me, sacred brothers*
> *our journey has begun*
> *bring us your gift, sacred sisters*
> *our journey has begun*

As Lucas and Three Eyes turned around, they saw hundreds of spirits walking forth from the buildings, all heading to the edge of the cliff and beyond. When the last Indian stepped out across the unseen bridge toward the beckoning Surnia, a final spirit came walking up out of the abyss beyond the ledge—a white man with stringy hair and beard. As Lucas recognized Wade Striker, the man looked up at him with a curiously peaceful smile. Then he turned and fell in step at the rear of the procession. He was followed by the spirit of a large black dog, who turned to Lucas and wagged his tail, then raced off to trot beside the spirit of the man who had killed him.

Surnia turned around and continued his journey, and the procession that followed him slowly transformed into shimmering bands of color. It became a rainbow, which poured upward toward the sun and then was gone. As it disappeared, only Surnia's fading song remained:

> *in the wind a child is born*
> *comes dancing down the mountain*

> *the child bringing the whirlwind*
> *dancing from the mountain*
> *in the whirlwind a child is born*
> *that we may know one another*
> *that we may know one another*

The vision passed, the song was heard no more. Lucas turned to look back inside the *kiva* and was surprised to find that it was empty—the body of Surnia was gone.

"It is finished," a voice spoke behind him, and Lucas spun around to see his Ute friend, Three Eyes.

"What did you say?" he asked, closing his eyes.

"It is finished."

"That's what I thought!" Lucas cried, realizing that he had heard his friend with his outer rather than inner ear. The cacophony had truly stilled, to be replaced forever by the music of the birds and the voices of the ones he loved.

Lucas looked around him at the great cliff house of Mesa Verde. It felt strangely calm, and he knew that it was truly empty now and that there could be no desecration of its spirit. Turning to Three Eyes, he wrapped his arm around his friend's shoulder. Together the boys walked arm in arm toward the trail that led to the canyon below.

One week later, Kate McEwan and Paige rode into the Ute village on a wagon they had rented from the trading post, which the Hallorans had reopened. They had come to say good-bye before departing for Durango, where Kate would complete her magazine articles. Then she would return to Mesa Verde with Paige to explore the ruins further.

"What will you do with your discovery?" Laurel asked.

"I don't know yet," Paige said. "But someday the secret of Mesa Verde will come out, and I'd like to complete as scientific a study as possible before the hordes arrive. But for now we plan to keep the knowledge to ourselves."

"What about you folks?" Kate asked, climbing onto the wagon beside Paige. "You'll stay on at the reservation?"

"That's right," Quint replied, wrapping his arm around Laurel's waist. "We're finally going to have some time together. And we're already making adobe bricks with which to construct a new schoolhouse—but this one will be in the center of the village."

"Paige!" a voice called out, and the Englishman looked up to see Three Eyes running over with Lucas at his side. "Must you really go?" Three Eyes asked.

"Yes, but we'll be back. Until then, I've got something for each of you to remember us by." He turned around and opened a large basket in the back of the wagon. "I had to order it special from Halloran's." He reached inside and lifted up two tiny black puppies, which he held out to them.

Each boy eagerly grabbed one of the dogs and hugged it tight. Lucas's eyes were filled with tears as he turned to Paige and Kate and said, "I'll never forget you both."

"Don't worry about us," Kate said. "Just don't forget to feed that little fellow."

"He won't be little for long!" Lucas declared.

"Three Eyes," Paige said, turning to the Indian boy, "please tell your uncle and mother good-bye for us."

"That must wait," Three Eyes replied. "I am moving in with Lucas for a while. See?" He pointed, and everyone looked to see a rider approaching from the north. As the man drew closer, they recognized him as Painted Wind. Slung across his horse was the body of a deer.

Painted Wind pulled up in front of Singing Water's tipi and tied his horse to a tree. He entered the tipi without even a glance at his sister-in-law, who was seated outside weaving. As soon as he was gone, Singing Water dropped her weaving and rushed over to the horse. Grinning broadly, she untied the deer and began to drag it toward the cook fire.

"What about you?" Quint asked, turning to Paige. "Ever get the urge to go deer hunting?"

"If I ever do," Paige said, "remind me that there's more than one way to skin a deer!"

As everyone began to laugh, Kate playfully cuffed Paige on the cheek. "Come on, *Wellington*, we must be on our way."

Paige turned beet red. "Who told you my name?" he demanded. "It's Paige. Just plain Paige."

"Yes, dear," she replied, giving Three Eyes a furtive wink as she picked up the reins.

"That's what I get for falling in love with a Scot!" he said with a shrug. He leaned over and kissed her cheek.

Kate grabbed Paige and kissed him hard on the lips, then released the brakes and slapped the reins. As the wagon rode away, the young couple could be heard laughing and singing:

> "For auld lang syne, my dear,
>   For auld lang syne;
> We'll tak a cup o' kindness yet,
>   For auld lang syne."

Epilogue

The discovery of the cliff dwellings of Mesa Verde by non-Indians lies shrouded in mystery. A number of explorers traveled through the region in the 1700s and first half of the 1800s, but none reported sighting any cliff dwellings. While rumors of such ruins abounded, the first verifiable sighting was of Two Story Cliff House in Mancos Canyon. William Henry Jackson of the United States Geological and Geographic Survey of the Territories was brought to the canyon in 1874 by miners who had traveled through the area and was shown the ruins, which he photographed.

The Quaker family of Benjamin Wetherill settled near the area in 1881 and spent some of their free time searching for ruins. They became friendly with the Ute, one of whom told them of a cliff house that was far bigger than any yet discovered. He said that his people never went there because it was sacred to the Ancient Ones, as he called the Anasazi Indians, who built the cliff dwellings.

On December 18, 1888, Richard Wetherill, one of Benjamin's five sons, and Charles Mason, Richard's brother-in-law, were searching one of the canyons when a storm forced them to seek shelter among the cliffs. It was there, in the driving snow, that they discovered Cliff House—or Cliff Palace, as it is known today—the largest cliff dwelling of Mesa Verde.

It was a tenacious woman journalist who did the most to ensure that the ruins not be destroyed by amateur archaeologists and eager collectors. Virginia Donaghe McClurg of the *New York Graphic* had long heard rumors of ancient Indian cities, and in 1882 she began searching in earnest but was forced to abandon her efforts by a Ute uprising. She returned in 1885 and 1886, at which time she discovered Three Tiered House, Echo Cliff House, and Balcony House. She was so concerned about the future of the entire Mesa Verde region that she launched a nationwide preservation campaign. That effort culminated in 1906 when Mesa Verde National Park was created.

*   *   *

The story of Mountain Laurel's original stagecoach journey east with her father, Josiah Fox, and young Lucas Burgess aboard Quint's stagecoach is recounted in *Stagecoach Station 17: Durango*. Look for it wherever Bantam paperbacks are sold.

SAN ANTONIO
by Hank Mitchum

In November 1876, Wolf Bixler sits in a prison near Mexico City and waits to die. A white man raised by Comanche Indians, Bixler has always been an outsider. Though he rarely looks for trouble, it has a habit of finding him, and now it comes in the form of a hangman's noose: he is convicted of a murder that was in reality self defense. Bixler has only one chance to cheat death. He has been offered his freedom if he will escort the family of the president of Mexico through the revolution-torn countryside to safety in America. Bixler is not eager to take on such a risky assignment—nor does he want to return to the United States, where he recently escaped from prison—but he sees no other way out.

As Bixler and the small party make their way north, they find themselves up against bandits and armed revolutionaries. Additional trouble comes in the form of U.S. Marshal Stuart Jarrell, who has trailed Bixler to Mexico. The two men realize, however, that they must strike an alliance and work together if any of them are going to make it to Texas alive.

Through their long ordeal, Bixler and Jarrell discover a new bond of friendship. They discover love, as well— one in the arms of a beautiful woman, the other through the love of a small child.

Read SAN ANTONIO, on sale August 1985 wherever Bantam paperbacks are sold.